MW00396951

NEW CITY

NEW CITY

A STORY ABOUT RACE-BAITING AND HOPE ON THE SOUTH SIDE OF CHICAGO

Patrick Girondi

Skyhorse Publishing

Skyhorse Publishing books may be purchased in bulk at special discounts for sales promotion, corporate gifts, fund-raising, or educational purposes. Special editions can also be created to specifications. For details, contact the Special Sales Department, Skyhorse Publishing, 307 West 36th Street, 11th Floor, New York, NY 10018 or info@skyhorsepublishing.com.

Visit our website at www.skyhorsepublishing.com.

10 9 8 7 6 5 4 3 2 1

Library of Congress Cataloging-in-Publication Data is available on file.

Cover design by APOTH Creative + Dan May
Cover art (original painting, *New City*, Acrylic and Mixed Media on Board), 2022 by Megan Euker; Photo of Painting by Luigi Porzia

Print ISBN: 978-1-5107-7684-5
Ebook ISBN: 978-1-5107-7686-9

Printed in the United States of America

Dedications

I dedicate this book to Sister Paulinda, my fourth grade teacher who taught me about love and patience (Lord knows she had a lot of both); Big Mamma, the woman who loved me when I was a fifteen-year-old light brown or beige-skinned string bean; Judge Clarence Bryant, the sage who offered me a choice of jail or the military; Sergeant Smith, the Air Force Master Sergeant who gave me another chance at not being dishonorably discharged and my family members, the patients—many of whom should have already been cured. Had I been shrewder, the project would have never been interrupted in 2010. I apologize and ask for their forgiveness. I will continue to push and ask for your prayers.

To my three sons; the Skyhorse Publishing team; and Megan Euker, my agent; thanks for the confidence and support.

Special Thanks

To the musicians performing the song "Greencastle":
(Song written by Michele Santarcangelo and Patrick Girondi;
Harmonica/Voice: Patrick Girondi)

Bass: Paolo Clemente
Drums: Michele Ciccimarra
Guitar: Michele Santarcangelo
Saxophone: Luigi Lovicario
Trumpet: Giovanni Teot

Advanced Praise for *New City*:

"New City is raw, uncut, and as challenging as my own memories growing up on the South Side of Chicago!"

—Derek Holmes, CEO of TEC-LINK

"New City is a gritty narrative of a forgotten, impoverished part of Chicago. Even though it's economically indigent, Girondi's account of the companionship, loyalty, brotherhood, and community support is impressive. Girondi is a new Saul Bellow or Studs Terkel. It's a must read to understand Chicago."

—Patrick Arbor, former chairman at the Chicago Board of Trade

Contents

Preface

He without sin throw the first stone

By the mid-nineteenth century, Chicago was one of the largest railroad hubs in the world. Trains rattled arrogantly through the city carrying passengers and freight. Sounds of horns, brakes, livestock, and hobos filled the air around the rows of tracks and could be heard for miles at all hours of the day or night.

The railroads hired security to keep the flow of goods unimpeded and their clients' merchandise safe. The power and malice of these sentinels, or dicks, (slang for detectives—in this case, railroad detectives), rose as the value of the transported goods skyrocketed. Life, already low-priced, got even cheaper as the railroad owners drew a zero-tolerance line. Most train yard towers had snipers perched in them, clutching hair-trigger rifles, seemingly willing to slay anyone they believed didn't belong in the fiefdom. Workers wore brightly colored clothing in the hopes of making it back to the slums alive. Mayhem reigned.

Like house paint poured onto a floor, the boundaries spread day by day. Once a zone was covered, the rule of the boss's militiamen became absolute. Workers were warned by family members not to marry pretty women, as a shooting accident often resulted in the commencement of a suspicious courtship of the lovely widow by railroad owners, executives, or even railroad guards themselves.

To satisfy the rapidly growing nation's appetite for meat, the belt developed considerably. Hogs, sheep, cattle, and chicken were hauled to the South Side of the gritty city to be slaughtered, processed, and shipped far and wide. In 1865, the Union Stock Yards was established. The development of the refrigerated boxcar in the 1870s led to an unruly and wild expansion of the bustling, chaotic, and frenzied meatpacking corridor.

In the early 1880s, George Pullman built a factory to make railroad passenger cars, and a "company town" sprang up twelve miles south of the center of Chicago. Pullman strategically erected his factory and accompanying borough on the Lake Calumet port to be close to the steel mills of South Chicago and Gary, Indiana. Soon, the Pullman company town housed almost nine thousand workers and their families. By 1925, Pullman employed twenty-eight thousand conductors and twelve thousand porters to serve customers on their carriages.

Skilled Irish and German butchers, joined by Czechs, Poles, Lithuanians, and Slovaks, were employed in the hundreds of factories and holding stalls of the Union Stock Yards. Most workers took up residence on adjacent tracts of land. In 1889, Chicago annexed the entire area and named it New City. That same year, developer Samuel Gross built a subdivision of cheap workingmen's cottages near the stockyards, attempting to help meet the need for inexpensive shelter. Also in 1889, Chicago annexed the area that included the Pullman factories and the Pullman company town.

By the turn of the century, Catholic parishes served as social, cultural, and spiritual centers for the Slavic enclaves of New City. Dances, horseshoe-throwing tournaments, and boxing contests were organized by church pastors and church nuns.

The boxing competitions were harsh, bare-knuckled, bloody brawls. Father Stanislaus Wasik, a Polish priest, won four consecutive championships in his mostly Polish parish of Saint Augustine. During his fifth run at the now-treasured title, he was challenged by "Bohemian Frank," a novice, who legend has it, had never boxed or fought anyone in his life.

The lot next to the church was jam-packed with anxious bystanders. Children sat on their parents' shoulders and the elderly stood on fruit boxes hoping to get a glimpse of what would surely be

Father Stanislaus's fifth consecutive victory. The timekeeper struck two pieces of steel together and the match began. Swinging like an out-of-control windmill, Bohemian Frank charged the man of God. Initially, Father Stanislaus stood his ground and even landed a few blows, but to everyone's surprise (except Bohemian Frank), the man of the cloth was knocked out cold before the end of the first round.

Spectators rushed the new champ who declined the trophy, a crude steel crucifix embedded in a piece of wood. Out of breath and bleeding from the nose, he puffed, "My mother is the sweetest woman in all of New City." The astonished crowd looked on, wondering what his mother could possibly have to do with him clobbering Father Wasik. They inched closer, vying for spots, near enough to hear him, or at least read his lips. The story would certainly be juicy.

Frank drew a deep breath and continued. "Making my poor mother say five rosaries just because she kicked the neighbor's dog was uncalled for and not fair. That dog has stolen meat, bread . . ." As the spectators looked at each other, whispering to those next to them and shaking their heads in disbelief, Frank squeezed out of the crowd and walked home. Words of his gallantry arrived before he did, and when he walked into his dwelling, he was viciously attacked with a broom by his mother. *No good deed goes unpunished.*

New City's pollution, squalor, and poverty was immortalized in Upton Sinclair's 1906 book *The Jungle*. He spent seven weeks amongst the workers and their families, and his book shed light on a handful of powerful companies that controlled the stockyards, using political influence to repress employees and keep the government far away from their businesses. Workers shoveled carcasses from filthy wooden floors filled with rat droppings onto rotten box carts and pushed them from room to room. They were then piled on murky tables and dissected. For pennies, workers broke their backs, covered in blood, meat scraps, and contaminated fluids, ten hours a day, six days a week.

Sinclair described amputated fingers ground into sausage and laborers falling into vats and turned into lard. Diseased cattle were hit with sledgehammers and processed through the slaughterhouses where meat was stored in great mountains of flesh and bone. Water from leaky roofs dripped over the piles, and thousands of rats gnawed and trampled on the heaps, leaving dung in their tracks.

On a diet of raw meat, the rats grew to be the size of small dogs. Their audacity grew with their bulk. The workers unleashed hundreds of cats and kittens into the fray, but the rats killed and then ate the kittens and only a few gladiator toms stuck around to wage war against the ferocious long-tailed, prowling nightmares. Workers quipped about allowing the felines to carry guns or knives, but the dicks (railroad detectives) would have none of that and the rodent population soared.

The fears of many were realized when rats slew an old-timer, biting off his fingers and wolfing down all of his face and much of the rest of him. When packers arrived at the scene, not all of the predators were willing to leave the dinner table. Men armed with shovels struck to clear the mangled body. As the shovels smacked, rats shrieked and scattered back and forth, trapped under the corpse's clothes. The company doctor said that the man had died of a heart attack before the rats devoured him. A worker quipped after hearing the doctor's verdict, "What else would a company doctor say?"

News of the killer rats circulated. Workers and their families lived in terror. At home, any unrecognizable sound was the dreadful rodents biting through walls, floors, or doors seeking passage to enter and eat the whole family alive. At night, relations squished into single beds so that they would be together if death entered in the form of hundreds or even thousands of long-tailed, red-eyed demons. People were desperate for a solution, and toxin was laid all through the yards. The rats wouldn't touch it. Eventually it was decided to lace fresh bread with poison. The rats must have welcomed a change to their all-meat diet. They died by the thousands and their bodies were found everywhere. Workers routinely scooped the rats and the toxin-laced bread into the giant processing hoppers along with the meat.

Throughout the meatpacking course, products gathered lethal chemicals, dirt, splinters, floor grime, and the mucus of workers who carried tuberculosis and other diseases. To wage revenge for their merciless treatment, disgusted laborers urinated and defecated on the meat. The finished product was then stamped USDA and served on family tables and in fine restaurants all over the land.

Sinclair told the plight of an eleven-year-old boy in the yards who complained of pain. Trying to help, a coworker rubbed the boy's frozen ears, which fell off into the packer's hands.

The sprawling stockyards and adjacent plants, with their unique combination of contamination, erratic work schedules, occupational diseases, and low wages exacted a heavy toll on the New City community in the years leading up to the Great Depression.

During the Great Depression and World War II years, the Union Stockyards workers, mostly New City residents, created a key social movement: The United Packinghouse Workers of America-Congress of Industrial Organizations, or UPWA-CIO. The UPWA-CIO was particularly effective and became a progressive mainstay of the labor movement. While the UPWA-CIO raised wages, stabilized employment, and fought for civil rights in the plants, local organizations in New City, including the Back of the Yards Neighborhood Council, fostered a communal identity among the diverse ethnic groups, addressing an array of concerns.

By 1950, the Union Stockyards was the largest meatpacking plant in the country and populated by some of the most colorful personalities in the world. Workers claimed that the yards were as much a circus as a job. The sprawling chaos offered the perfect backdrop for people who felt the need to leave one life and enter another. Murderers, dancers, doctors, professors, poets, politicians, priests, architects, and acrobats passed through, some hiding, others dodging a past and circumstances that made the choice of becoming a meat packer desirable. A tough Russian Jew, Davey P. Kaye, worked his way up to being the most powerful union steward in Local 714, a Chicago Stockyards affiliated union, only to have it later discovered that he was wanted in Florida for murder. He eventually was convicted on seventy-four racketeering charges and spent eight years of a twenty-year sentence in a Florida prison for shooting a recalcitrant union member seven times and dumping him in a canal while Mr. Kaye was vacationing in Florida.

Some new arrivals claimed that they were on a work sabbatical, others claimed to be dodging a nagging wife and a slew of kids. "I left for cigarettes and never went back," was the line among more than a few of the new people shuffling in. Those who attempted to escape a life of boredom usually succeeded. People in New City lived through some of the most dramatic conflicts of their era or any other. New City received the attention of novelists, activists, and social scientists alike, for most of the remainder of the twentieth century.

The area struggled to retain its Slavic character, but with Chicago's meatpacking industry dribbling to an end in the 1960s and 1970s, New City faced serious economic decline and rapid deterioration. The city attempted to attract new manufacturers to the site of the old and shrinking stockyards, but few companies accepted the invitation to set up among the filth. New City was decimated along with the meatpacking industry. Thousands of families, most of whom could barely afford to, moved away to what they hoped would be greener pastures.

The neighborhood entered a swift, fierce, downward spiral. Those left behind were impoverished and abandoned by city services. Dozens of churches and schools closed, and an estimated 40 percent of the homes were deserted or burned. Destitute folks, mostly Blacks and Mexicans, entered the area to live in the evacuated edifices. New City became one of the most ferocious neighborhoods in Chicago, one of the most vicious cities in the world.

Violence erupted at weddings, graduation parties, baseball games, corner gatherings, and even funerals. New City residents wore the community's incivility like a medal of honor. These were the streets that Danny Nowak and his friend Pat walked in the '70s.

In 2010, the once industrious eighty-eight thousand residents of 1920 were halved to forty-four thousand underprivileged souls.

Introduction

Pat's brother and sisters slept quietly. It was 6 a.m. and he walked down the stairs of the second-floor rear of 1427 West 50th Street. As soon as he hit the screen door, he smelled the roses from old man Vic's garden next door. Pat's frail 4'11", black-haired Italian mother followed him out and into the gangway.

Together they walked to Ashland Avenue and waited for the number 9 bus. When it arrived, they embraced and Pat's mother headed to work. Pat, instead, went searching for adventure. He loved the city at this hour—the streets, barely awake, reminded him of an old man rustled from his sleep. Most foot travelers were under a sort of fairy tale spell. In a sleepy trance, few considered disguising who they were, what they did, or what they thought. It was a magic moment for alert eyes to absorb.

Most called the neighborhood "Back of the Yards." This is because it was just west of the world-famous Chicago Stockyards in the area named New City. Many residents still worked in the packing houses, but most resigned themselves to reality. Meat-packing companies were closing up and disappearing. Many of them had reopened around Omaha, Nebraska. But for the poor workers of the community, it didn't really matter where their jobs went once they were gone. For now, the remaining employed men and women trudged their way to what was left.

Humid air drew scents from the sacred ground, where millions of animals had been housed and slaughtered. Sometimes, just a few drops of dew could cover the whole area in the smell of feces and carcasses. New City dwellers were reminded of a glorious past when jobs were plentiful and life was meaningful. Many of the old-timers got downright teary-eyed when the whole damned neighborhood smelled like cow shit.

As Pat crept around, he thought about the stark difference between the smell of the yards and Vic's roses. He decided that the smell of roses, or any flower for that matter, was overrated. Pat had already lived at a dozen addresses in a half-dozen different neighborhoods. The stockyard smell made him tingle, and at least for the moment, it was home.

"Hot dog!" Pat peered at three Pepsi bottles lying in the grass in front of an abandoned house on Laflin.

Not even to Danny Nowak's house, he thought. He was already up six cents. One by one, he brushed the dirt off them. One bottle had a bit of pop still in it, but Pat wasn't crazy about sweet drinks, and lots of fellows peed before disposing of them to keep the guys getting the two cents from getting anything more than two cents.

Danny Nowak tiptoed down the old wooden steps in front of his house, down the block from Pat on 50th Street. The Nowak home was set back about eighty feet from the sidewalk. The back of the house and one of the sides sat on intersecting alleys. Danny was the eleventh of twelve siblings. There was no sign that anyone else was up yet.

Danny was convinced that his father never slept, and sensed that he was already gone for work or in the basement fixing someone's motorcycle. In fact, Mr. Nowak was known all over the city for the miracles he could do with a Harley in need of fixing. And anyone who knows anything about Harleys knows that more times than not, they're in need of fixing.

In the summer, every morning between 6:15 and 6:30, Danny waited for Pat. Danny disliked precision, and in his mind, 6:15 and 6:30 were the same thing. Danny stood out of view in front of the house next door, not wanting his father to look out and enlist him in any kind of chore.

Pat came into view.

Seeing the Pepsi bottles his friend was toting, Danny smiled. "We got a head start," he said.

Pat nodded. "They were sitting on Laflin in the middle of the block, in the dirt in front of a gray abandoned house."

"Nice," Danny said, "I know that house. It used to be a family with five kids. I think their names were Clancy or Carver, something with a 'C' in it. I could never figure out why anyone would leave that house. It's got that tall elm in front of it. I love elms . . . or any tall tree for that matter. It is the one with the tall tree, ain't it?"

"Yeah, there was a tall tree in front of it, but there's a lot of abandoned homes on Laflin with tall trees in front of 'em," Pat said.

Danny's eyes narrowed as if some sort of tragedy had passed. He smiled. "They're pretty clean. Clyde won't bother us about washing 'em."

Pat nodded. "Looks like it could be a big day. Why walk over to Clyde's now? I want to head south. Let's walk over to D&S Groceries to see if there's any carts outside."

"D&S pulls the carts in," Danny said with a shrug.

"I know, but some customers borrow them to get their groceries home, then to avoid embarrassment they drop them off after dark," Pat replied.

The two headed east on 50th Street, passing Pat's flat, Vic's, the Webers, and the Lahuvagges. The Lahuvagge family inched the Nowaks out with thirteen kids.

When they got to Ranhisbusky's house Danny smiled. "Did Laura let you touch 'em yet?"

Pat smiled. "She lets everyone touch 'em."

"Yeah, you sly dog, you got Nancy Wimoninski's dad to let you clean his garage and tend to his garden. I'll bet he'd tend to you if he knew you were also taking care of his oldest daughter." Danny's smirk was sidelined by his Danny Nowak smile. "Why touch titties when you're getting to hide sausage?" he added.

Pat smiled contritely. "Laura Ranhisbusky's not particular. If a girl's not particular it's always great, but not so special."

Danny nodded. "I take whatever I can get."

"We all do," Pat said. He hesitated. "I just don't get a lot out of touching with my hands." He smiled. "It puts me on a runway too short to take off from."

They walked to Loomis and turned into the alley behind D&S. Sure enough, just like Pat said, there was a shopping cart resting against the phone pole by the store's back door.

Danny slugged Pat in the arm. "You're like one of those psychic dudes."

"Just lucky, Danny, just lucky," Pat smiled.

In the mornings, they hunted bottles. On Friday, Saturday, and Sunday afternoons, you could find them shining shoes on 51st or 47th Streets. Their personalities complemented each other. They never argued and had an inseparable bond. I guess you'd understand if you shined shoes on the street.

Danny and Pat's paradise was interrupted when Pat's family moved out of New City. For his freshman year of high school, Pat went to Saint Joseph's Catholic Seminary, about thirty miles outside of Chicago. He lived there with eighty-two other students and sixty-two Franciscan brothers and priests. Before Easter break of sophomore year, he was asked not to return. Without a lot of options, Pat moved a few miles north of New City to Bridgeport with his father, who had married a woman with six children from a previous marriage. The ol' man and new wife quickly added Georgey, their son together. Pat moved in with his father's new wife and seven other brothers and sisters.

When Pat was sixteen, Clarence Bryant, a kind, dark-skinned judge, suggested that he enlist in the military. Pat accepted the advice, preferring a uniform to jail. Nineteen months later, he was back in Chicago, loading and driving trucks.

In 1973, The Chicago Board Options Exchange was founded. There were no dress codes and the place reeked of pizza, which many employees ate in between making trades. Bobby Hanrahan, a friend of Pat's, had borrowed heavily from Larry the floor manager of

Chicago Corp. Bobby was a gambler but a straight-up guy and when Larry asked him to find a kid from the neighborhood to run orders back and forth between the phone desk and the trading pits, Bobby showed up with Chucky Mack. In the neighborhood he was called "What-the-fuck Chuck." Most said that his bad attitude could only be outdone by his bad temper.

Things didn't go well and Chucky was soon fired. Bobby begged Pat to come to the exchange. Pat accepted. He was hired by a broker after a few months. When his boss forgot to sign Pat's check, Pat signed it himself. When he was questioned, things heated up and Pat socked his direct supervisor. When he went to pick up his last check, Tian Chen, a trader from Singapore, was in the waiting room. Pat told Tian that he had been fired for socking his supervisor and was hired on the spot.

When Tian walked into the pit with Pat, the other traders didn't tease him as they had done in the past. There were no "rots of rucks" or fooling around about Tian's slitted, almond-shaped eyes. Pat, instead, was respectful. Eventually Tian gave Pat a chance to trade, and the deal worked reasonably well for the both of them.

One day at the close, Pat had an altercation with another trader and socked the guy. Pat was fined by the exchange. Tian refused to pay the fine. Pat didn't have the funds and figured that he was done at the Chicago exchange. He went around to the pits to say goodbye to some of the friends he had made. One of them, Billy Byrnes, told Pat to meet him in his office after the close.

Pat met the owners of the clearing firm Securities Option Corp. They gave him a shot at trading for himself and he went on to become one of the exchange's stars. In 1989 Pat was in *Playgirl* (dressed) next to Sylvester Stallone and Magic Johnson as one of America's most eligible bachelors. He was a guest on *The Oprah Winfrey Show* twice.

The shoeshine boys, Danny Nowak and Pat, were reunited in the 1980s when Pat ran in a Cook County election. Later, Pat married an Italian girl and ended up moving to Italy, but whenever he was in town, he got together with Danny, his childhood friend.

Danny, on the other hand, never left New City and bought a house on 50th Street, down the block from where he and his eleven siblings had grown up. New City was a shadow of its bustling past and had been repopulated with impoverished peoples again and again. Danny weathered the storm like an old cargo ship rolling the waves and was one of the last remaining members of the original New City tribe.

Through the years Danny toughed out knife fights and shootings, which came to be commonplace in his beloved community. During an argument about a patch for a bicycle tire, Danny himself was actually shot; the bullet entered and exited his stomach, leaving a clean hole that miraculously healed in just weeks.

Moses Moore

Moses bounced home from school. For as long as he could remember, he bounced. There was some sort of accidental spring in his step and his untidy Afro made all sorts of movements on what Aunt Bee called his nappy head.

Of course Aunt Bee didn't mean anything bad by saying that Moses had a nappy head. He had nappy hair and it was on his head.

Moses remembered his mother, Marla. She was the prettiest thing that he had ever laid his eyes on. Marla hung in Englewood, the sprawling South Side ghetto just south of New City. Unfortunately, in Englewood or New City, Marla was the prettiest thing that many had ever laid their eyes on. She wasn't a bad girl, but she made the rounds between gangsters, detectives, preachers, and politicians.

There was lots of crying when Marla died of a hot dose, but a proper analysis would have disclosed that many of the tears were tinged with relief. The contents of Marla's mental hard drive could have tarnished if not melted a lot of the badges in the area and could have ruined a lot of careers and marriages. Her demise brought peace of mind to more than a few, and her knowledge was laid to rest with what was left of her.

Buried within her recollections was the inside scoop on what could have filled the blogs and tabloids for months after her demise. She'd have been a poster child for "Me Too," the movement dedicated to abused women which put among others Bill Cosby, the once famed and beloved comedian, behind bars at eighty years of age. Yeah, as I said, there was a lot of relief mixed in with those tears.

Marla was somewhat of a local celebrity, and years later, a Chicago artist (Patrick Girondi) wrote and recorded a song about Moses' mom:

Marla, I think you should know,
been better if you skipped off to Mexico,
to be on your beach getting by
not here ready to meet the guy,

cause there's a needle in the packet
and they'll stick it in your jacket,

you should have known, Marla

Aunt Bee and Uncle Rufus kind of won the draw. They had no children and owned their home on 56th Street. Marla wasn't really Aunt Bee's niece, but then who are we really to anyone?

Uncle Rufus was a quiet man. He worked on the South Side at South Works Steel Mill. He got up at dawn and took two buses to work and two buses back home every day. To Uncle Rufus, an automobile was trouble that he had little use for. The neighbors used his garage as their own. He told them to just take care of it and they did so, keeping it immaculately clean. Uncle Rufus never asked for a nickel in rent. He liked his neighbors and it was one less chore.

Aunt Bee wore the captain's hat, but anyone who knew anything observed that Rufus commanded the ship with his eyes. Just a look from him maintained order in the most turbulent seas. Aunt Bee knew her man and gave him what he wanted, often months before he would have even made the request.

Uncle Rufus was a one-woman man, never dating anyone other than Aunt Bee. There was nothing that made her so proud. She had her very own man. He hadn't been all over with everyone. He was hers alone and she too had only dated him, though she made less fuss about this particular. Together, they were simple and unpretentious.

Unfortunately, children never arrived. Moses became the missing piece to their puzzle.

Growing up, Moses' grades were below average, like him. He did seem almost normal until he was five years old and then he just sort of fell off the chart. Moses never thought much about anything. He never got too close to anyone but Aunt Bee and Uncle Rufus. Knowing what the quiet giant and his bride wanted, he rarely disappointed them.

The school suggested psychiatric counseling for Moses, but Aunt Bee would have no one tinkering inside that dear nappy head. The fact that he was so simple and nice meant that only the meanest boys ever messed with him. Moses mostly cowered, but when managed by the right friend a few times, he turned the tables and made those bad boys regret messing with the gentle titan.

Moses' hands were enormous and had the strength of a vice grip. By the time he was seven, he could squash two walnuts in one hand. Unfortunately, Moses just couldn't gauge his strength. He decimated the nuts, turning them into crumbs, almost dust.

Anyway, Moses belonged with Aunt Bee and Uncle Rufus. From the day that he moved in, there was no doubt to anyone in or outside the family that Moses was their boy.

In and out of jail, Darrell, Moses' supposed daddy, never dared to wander onto the scene. Moses may have been his biologically, but there was no upside in making a claim. The boy wasn't normal, and no one chased him for child support. Others, including Aunt Bee and Uncle Rufus, believed that Moses' father was a soft-spoken fellow who went away for killing a cop. At any rate, Darrell left well enough alone. Sometimes things just work out best for everyone.

New City: 2022

Today, a few miles south of the Loop, one of the most pristine centers in the US, lies New City, a partially wooded area with huge swaths of vacant land running through it. New City is smack in the middle of the Chicago municipality. Not quite as violent as the Austin or Englewood neighborhoods, New City can average ten homicides a month, which pushes it off the charts when calculating murders per capita compared to the rest of the world or even most US cities.

Hundreds of once inhabited buildings are demolished each year to keep out the riffraff. Fewer than 70 percent of them are still standing, and many of them are uninhabited. Consequently, many blocks are sparsely populated. Most of its streets are in dire need of repair, but the city's mayor, Carla Redman, is a bottom line politician. New City generates little tax income and with the cost of schools, police, and fire protection, the area costs her administration huge amounts of resources. New City gets what it deserves . . . nothing more than is required by law.

Pricey condominiums and tourism are where the money's at, and the city concentrates a disproportionate amount of resources on the Loop and an area known as the Magnificent Mile (there's really not much magnificent about it unless you're in bad need of a Gucci purse).

It's America's new capitalism; you can't help the poor and disadvantaged by enabling them. CEOs cut their employees' pay, take away their benefits, ship their jobs overseas, receive shareholder praise and millions in compensation. They then blame the unions.

The revised definition of underprivileged is people who lack ambition, are either too lazy, too stupid, or both, to produce in the world's greatest nation. "If you truly love your fellow man, tell the beggar to get a job and send him on his way," they say (some take it a bit further, berating or even physically abusing them).

New City is filled with American elms, box elders, European buckthorns, green ash, and sycamore trees. With all the vacant property, rabbits and possums had moved in on the expanse which was once exclusively controlled by rats. The rats don't give in without a fight, and can still often be seen going at it in the alleys, yards, and even on the streets with the feisty possums. Rabbits try to stay out of the other animals' way, though they have been seen curiously watching their distant relatives ripping each other to shreds, scrunching their noses nervously every second or so.

Folks trying to make shortcuts have been beating paths through many of the vacant lots. Some of these areas are completely covered with shrubs, weeds, and brush. Garbage has mostly been cleared, sometimes by the landlord and other times by the city. In fact, today, the municipality is the rightful owner of most New City properties. The previous owners could not afford to pay the annual property taxes, some of which were three hundred percent of the property's value.

The CEO and the city leadership, overall, have little pity for these deadbeat proprietors who decide not to contribute their fair share. Instead of paying real estate taxes and maintaining proper grass and fences, these good-for-nothings spend their money on medicine and food. *The audacity.*

The major industry in New City is drugs and to a lesser extent prostitution. Initially it's an ego trip for the pusher—all of these gorgeous women trying to gobble you up with one of their holes. Eventually, though, sex is cheaper than drugs and so the drug pushers demand cash, unless the client is truly a star.

Cops have caught nice suburban girls compensating pushers in their boyfriends' cars, with their boyfriends sitting right next to them. The police aren't sure that anything can ever help the area and primarily have adopted two strategies: put them all in jail, even if it means framing them, or just leave them to kill themselves off.

In many of New City's standing buildings there is no heat, water, or electricity and neighbors borrow, swap, or sell these amenities, including wood, with each other in an effort to keep comfortable.

Chapter 1

Danny is a Real Person and This is a Real Story

Danny Nowak has an extension cord running out of his house, traversing the gangway and running into Napoleon's house next door. Danny jumped the meter so it's no sweat off his back. Napoleon's supposed to pay Danny ten dollars a month, and actually did for the first two months, but his only income is Uber and Lyft. With five young mouths to feed, ten bucks takes on a whole new meaning.

Danny loves Napoleon's kids like his own, though most would realize that they're only loosely related. Danny's blood is Polish. Napoleon's people were African. Most of Danny's wives have also been African American. He's treated them all kindly and remains good to each and every one of them, even after the union is over. Just last week he fixed the roof on Janet's house, which she shares with her new husband, Homer. *Husband* and *wife* are terms used loosely to identify the person you live with. Ceremony and government legitimacy is a bit out of reach for most families.

Some of the police are jealous of Danny, an old, ugly Polack with a defined white marble muscular body and equally carved face, who partners with dozens of the neighborhood's black beauties. Danny prefers describing them as chocolate, not black. After all, he's never seen a black woman, and has been with many, many shades of chocolate.

The police often harass the bride and groom, calling Danny's wives crack whores. Danny doesn't care much; he just calls 'em people.

Danny prefers a monogamous relationship to none at all, but it's hard to focus when many neighborhood girls are serving it up from the time they're thirteen or even twelve. Sex is a commodity in New City, and Danny detests child molesters like most red-blooded Americans do. Having said that, if the girls are being bedded, Danny figures that he has an obligation. Better a nice guy like himself, who is kind and would never harm a hair on their heads, than someone who might beat them, turn them into addicts, prostitutes, or even take their lives.

Danny noticed that things changed somewhat, and that the police harassed him less when the Black Lives Matter movement gained prominence. In fact, many police no longer stopped people at all, fearing that they would eventually be charged for some infraction while arresting someone.

Danny didn't much appreciate police; light or dark skin, he had little use for them. Danny himself thought it odd that Black Lives Matter seemed to ignore the fact that hundreds of times more black lives were taken by other blacks than by the police. Danny was an avid reader. There were 221 blacks killed by the police in 2020 in the whole country. Meanwhile, there were 783 murders in the city of Chicago alone.

Each year, the city of Chicago lost tens of millions settling lawsuits with the families of the deceased shot by police. It amused Danny that according to the press, each victim was an exceptional citizen and former honor student.

Danny's handy with just about anything. He could fix your television, computer, fuse box, or clogged pipes. For this reason and many others, he is viewed as some sort of tribal leader. Over the years, as a result of his respected position, he's had many daughters, mothers, sisters, cousins, aunties, and friends.

It was commonplace in New City to hear about twelve- and thirteen-year-olds getting abortions or having children. For the most part, the gang leaders got the pick of the litter. Some mothers were even proud when one of their daughters gave it up to the thugs. It meant that the family was protected royalty.

Danny loved going to the Rawleys. Datisha, the eldest daughter, had an angelic voice and loved to sing. Loving any kind of audience, whenever Danny was there, she always gave a performance. Danny never heard such a beautiful voice and loved her singing.

One day after Danny fixed Mrs. Rawley's sink, she walked in with Datisha. By now, the girl was a blossoming goddess. Danny couldn't help but stare at her long thin legs, tiny protruding butt, and caramel eyes. He swallowed three times, an involuntary reaction to her beauty.

"Datisha, you take care of Danny, he's our friend. He fixed our sink," Mrs. Rawley said.

Danny stared at the screen on the kitchen window above the sink, not knowing if he was dreaming or in heaven. All of a sudden, his pants felt snug.

"What do you want me to do with Danny, Mama?" Datisha asked in a drawn-out drawl.

"Why, you do whatever he wants you to do. Go home with him and don't come back in less than an hour," Mrs. Rawley replied.

Danny stood and switched his weight back and forth from foot to foot. "I don't need anything . . . Mrs. Rawley. Don't worry . . . It's my pleasure to help out," he said, mentally battling to get the words out of his big stupid mouth.

Mrs. Rawley looked Danny in the eyes. "Danny, you done saved our ass a hundred times. You never say no. Now, I don't have no money, but you deserves something, and you is a man. Besides, it's better that she learns love from a gentleman and not from someone who will bust her up." She smiled at Datisha and then looked back at Danny. "Hopefully, she'll demand and understand what kindness and respect means to a woman. It will be a lesson that could end up saving her life."

Datisha's mother noticed the sizable bulge in Danny's pocket and suspected he wasn't carrying a gun. Toying with the statue of a man, she asked, "You don't think my Datisha is pretty, Danny?"

Danny glanced at Datisha, fearful of remaining in a trance. "She's, oh my God, she's beautiful."

"Then take her, Danny, she's yours for an hour or as long as she wants to stay."

Danny looked into Datisha's eyes. Her stare seemed much older than her biological age, but Danny always thought that women were born older. "Is this what you want, Datisha?" Danny asked sincerely.

Datisha smiled slightly, her eyes fixed on his.

Mrs. Rawley took Datisha's right arm and pushed her gently towards Danny. "Danny, Datisha's a good girl. She won't do you wrong." She paused. "It's the least we can do for all you done for us."

From that day on, white marble and milk chocolate got together often to melt into pure rapture.

It was one of those warm summer evenings that turned New City into a paradise. A lake wind danced through the trees, ruffling millions of leaves, softly tugging a few from the branches in a tell-tale story of how in a few months, winter's fist would be violently thrashing and stripping, leaving nary a one.

Danny sat on the top step of his porch. A strong humped nose centered his face. His eyebrows were salt and pepper, and bushy, but everything else about him was defined. His arms and chest were muscular and taut. There didn't seem to be an ounce of fat on him anywhere. Danny considered himself a Polack. That was how he grew up. Mexican kids were Taco Benders, Irish were Micks . . . Danny's clan was Polish and he was a Polack. He wasn't really sure when the media decided that Polacks were white, but to himself he was no way in the world white. He was just an aging Polack.

The stoop was covered with old television sets, boxes, circuits, and all sorts of electronic gizmos. Danny was taking the plastic off the wires and throwing the copper into a bucket on the second stair. Life just couldn't get better.

Duchess sensed Danny's happiness and barked from the ground floor apartment. A big, fat, light-skinned woman had gifted her to

Danny a few years ago. The old girl was now blind and full of arthritis (Duchess, not the lady). Duchess sat contently in her apartment, waiting for Danny to bring food and cuddles a few times a day. The big, fat, light-skinned woman passed by a few times a month with big bags of dog food, enough for all three of Danny's canine friends, including Dude and Elaine, who slept upstairs with Danny.

The woman had a sweet face and was kind. She waddled out of her car with the bags of dog food and brought them to the door on the ground floor. The door was hidden by the front stairs, which led to Danny's apartment. She insisted on entering to pet Duchess; and though the old girl mostly shit and pissed outside, at her age she did have accidents (again, I'm talking about the dog). Danny cleaned the dwelling in the way that made the most sense, but the apartment did carry the scent. The big, fat, light-skinned woman always wore a half-gallon of cheap perfume. When you put that much on, it must be reasonably priced (at least to you) no matter what you paid for it, Danny thought.

Initially, Danny was confused when the big, fat, light-skinned woman stooped over Duchess and wagged her tail (the woman's tail, not Duchess's). By her third visit, Danny put it together; the perfume, free dog food, and a wagging tail meant that she wanted to be petted (not Duchess, the lady). Danny, a baptized Catholic, was more than happy to comfort a person in need. He tried to get the large, light-skinned woman to bob for the apple but she'd have none of that. She also didn't want to see Danny tagging her. From behind, Danny struggled to get her pants down to her knees. The whole while she talked to Duchess as if there was nothing going on out of the ordinary.

Danny rubbed the target and aimed. As he entered, she quieted and remained silent. Suddenly she'd softly groan and straighten her back. Danny would pull out and clean his rifle. The large woman would begin chanting vivaciously to Duchess as if she were warming up to sing in an opera. Danny would help pull her trousers up. She'd then finish petting her old friend (the dog), smile quaintly at Danny, and leave.

Danny was a freelancer when it came to women, but it wasn't always that way. He once had a Guatemalan wife named Paulinda. They had a son named Danny. He still has his son, who used to come over from time to time. But the last time he visited, he told his father that it was the last time they'd see each other. Danny Jr. was into gangs and said that if he was ever followed or if his enemies knew where Danny Sr. lived, they'd harm him.

Danny knew what his son was talking about. In the city of Chicago, or most US cities for that matter (Chicago is only the twenty-fifth most dangerous per capita), crime and thus security was a major concern. Less than ten percent of murders in the US are ever solved, and folks really can't count on the police. The gangs filled the void and from time to time actually do good for the community.

Danny was in love with Paulinda like he had never been with anyone. She was tall for a Guatemalan girl with a body that begged compliments. Everyone in the neighborhood had an eye for her, but she was Danny's from the time she was just a kid. He spent a lot of time trying to understand what she saw in him.

Danny worked at Sweetheart Cup on Cicero Avenue, near the Ford City Shopping Center. He was making good enough change and bought a few properties in New City for less than five thousand bucks each.

The Sweetheart Cup factory was non-union, and the management wasn't what Danny would have chosen. His immediate boss often attempted to bully and berate him and his fellow workers. Danny wasn't one to be bullied or berated.

Over time, Danny observed that, adhering to the idea of Reagan's trickle-down effect economy, Sweetheart Cup stopped paying time and a half for overtime and began cutting every possible benefit. Danny was tempted to walk out a few times every week, but he had Paulinda and Little Danny to consider.

Almost every day after work Danny went to the gym with Manny, a giant Puerto Rican who lived a few blocks from him in New City. They had been thick for seven or eight years. Beyond being built,

Manny was handsome. He was also married, though most thought he played around on the side. Danny didn't care much about gossip or what others thought. He and Manny were tight.

Little Danny was about eight years old. Paulinda hadn't made dinner and big Danny didn't say a word. The woman cooked and cleaned every day. It was no big deal that she didn't cook tonight.

Danny walked into the kitchen, "Honey, you feel like hot dogs? I'll send Danny to the stand and get us some."

Paulinda didn't answer and Danny didn't get it.

"Something wrong, honey?" Danny asked sweetly.

"Everything's wrong, Danny," Paulinda responded.

"Everything's wrong? What are you talking about honey?" He smiled and took Paulinda by the arms. "Life's good, baby; Danny's healthy, doing good in school. We're caught up on all our bills and have some property."

"If that's what good means to you, Danny, you're blind." Paulinda said lifelessly. "It's not about a house, kids, and security. It's about living. And I don't feel like I live anymore."

Danny was as concerned as he was confused. "You wanna go on a camping trip, honey? Wisconsin, Indiana, Michigan?"

Paulinda wrestled free and broke Danny's grip. She turned away. "I slept with Manny, Danny."

"You what with who?"

Paulinda hesitated. The silence was interrupted by Little Danny's entrance.

"What we eating?" the boy asked.

Neither parent answered. Little Danny looked at his father, and his mother, who had her back turned. He sensed that he had come in at an inopportune time.

Danny winked warmly, reached into his pocket and took out some money. "Get yourself a few dogs, son," Danny said.

"What about you guys?" Danny Jr. asked.

"We're good," his father answered.

Little Danny took the cash and walked out.

Big Danny heard the front door close. He gently turned the body of the only woman that he had ever loved. She was now facing him. Her face was pale and blank. Its void was less than nothing, its expression was sickly and vacant. Danny remembered one of his old man's sayings, "When the face is vacant the mind is full."

"I didn't get what you said, something about Manuel," Danny said softly. He had heard every word but was hoping that she would come up with an alternate version he could believe. He'd then tell her he hadn't heard the first time because of the noise at Sweetheart Cup ruining his ears.

She wouldn't look Danny in the eye. Her gaze was focused on nothing. "I slept with Manuel," she said plainly.

Her words were without flavor. It was as if she had surrendered her life to emptiness, to nothingness. Danny let her hands fall and walked out.

After ten minutes or so, he found himself on Manuel's porch on West 47th Place. He didn't remember how he got there, but he knocked on the screen door anyway.

Within seconds, Manuel was at the door smiling. "Danny, what's up, man?"

Danny remained quiet. Manuel's wife Juanita came up from behind. "Hi Danny," Juanita said.

Juanita could have been Paulinda's sister. They were both beautiful Central American vixens.

Danny would never, ever not answer, but he did not say a word to Juanita. Manny, who had seen a bit of the world, nudged her and she walked away obediently, back to somewhere inside the house.

"You slept with Paulinda," Danny said. At this point he was on autopilot, not sure how he would proceed.

Five seconds passed.

"You want to come in Danny?" Manuel asked.

"No, I prefer that you come out," Danny said coldly.

Manny had watched Danny many times in the gym. Manuel might have been bigger, but Danny was certainly stronger. Manny liked to have muscles for exhibition, while Danny's build was genuine steel.

Manny swiveled his head on his neck. He wasn't used to being frightened and thought about grabbing his pistol. He stared at Danny, not trying to intimidate him. He knew better. Danny didn't scare.

Manuel slowly opened the screen door and stepped out. They stood silently for a lifetime. Manuel figured that the more time that passed, the less likely it was that Danny would hit him, but with Danny, you never knew what to expect.

"Danny, man, what did you say, brother?" Manny asked, smiling just enough not to be mocking.

Danny stared into Manny's eyes. Manny couldn't take the pressure. He looked away.

"You slept with Paulinda," Danny said in a low and firm voice.

"No man, that's bullshit. Who said something like that, man? You know the neighborhood is full of crazy rumors, man. I wouldn't do that." Manny knew that he had to look at Danny or risk not being believed. He looked in the other man's eyes and shook his head. "Bullshit, Danny. Who said that?"

"She did," Danny said, as cool as a car hood on a Chicago winter day.

Manny's mind raced like a mouse being chased with a broom. He couldn't take it anymore. He was cornered. "You wanna sleep with Juanita, Danny? She's inside, I'll tell her to sleep with you," Manny threw this out like a slim rope, hoping that Danny would grab on instead of pounding him.

"No, man, I don't want to sleep with your old lady," Danny smashed his hand down on the porch banister. A few of the wooden stakes waved in and out. Danny smashed his hand down again, this time breaking the banister.

Manny watched in fear, and Juanita came to the door. "What's wrong, Manny?"

Danny turned and walked down the porch and back home. He had no words for Manny or Paulinda, who cried and begged for forgiveness.

The anger was momentary, but he knew now, and there was no changing the past. In place of rage was utter disenchantment, disappointment, and discontent. Danny skated through life, smiling on the curves. He never was really sure about the world, but he felt sure about his Paulinda. She was his world. Her infidelity was his tsunami.

Paulinda slowly shook out of her despair and for months cooked Danny's favorite plates. She cleaned the house extra clean and in bed, she did absolutely everything she could think of to seduce him, but nothing she did worked anymore.

Night after night, she cried, kissed and hugged him, all to no avail. Any man would have fallen, succumbing to her beauty, her prowess. Not Danny. He was despondent. He didn't want her anymore and no sexual maneuver could convince his mind otherwise.

It wasn't a decision that he had consciously made to not forgive her, and his sentiment was crueler than indifference. She didn't even exist anymore. She was just a vague memory of someone whom he had mistakenly loved, but had never really known.

Paulinda couldn't imagine life without Danny. They had been with each other since they were kids. He worked at Sweetheart Cup. It wasn't like he was rich. She wasn't being arrogant about his position in life, and she wasn't upset about it either. He had been the only man she had slept with until Manny. She made a mistake, but read that most women had seven partners in life. She only had two. Didn't that make her better, and for that matter, Danny more fortunate than other husbands?

She had made one mistake, she thought. No one is perfect. She deserved to be forgiven. Danny wasn't perfect either.

But for now, Paulinda tried to clear her mind. She needed to be confident and to convince herself that she could accomplish the one thing that she needed to achieve more than anything that she ever needed or wanted in her life, to be desired by her man again.

She now despised Manny. She wasn't even sure how it all happened. Manny flirted with her the way he flirted with all women.

Danny and Little Danny were gone on a long weekend fishing trip. Manny knew that, which was why he came over, *looking for Danny.*

Paulinda knew that he knew, and he knew that she knew, but it just happened. Paulinda had always been attracted to Manny. He was pushy and more like an old-fashioned man. Danny was polite and courteous.

She invited Manny in and before long they were grunting in Danny's bed. It was over in minutes and Paulinda had not even felt Manny inside of her. It was just one of those crazy experiences that you're not really sure why or how it even happened.

It was only once, and Paulinda knew that it wasn't only about scratching an attraction itch. She thought that maybe she did it to get Danny's attention. Initially, she blamed Danny. Had he been more attentive it wouldn't have happened. That didn't deliver the pizza. Reading magazine articles about so-called liberated women didn't make her feel better about herself, but just part of a disgusting and seemingly growing selfish group.

Danny was a good man, much kinder than most, and she didn't want to lose him. She just couldn't understand why he wouldn't forgive her and was she now falling into a deep bitterness. It was impossible that such a banal act could compromise her whole life; and then there was Little Danny.

Before she told Danny about Manny, they hit it at least ten times a week. Now with their tenth wedding anniversary approaching, Paulinda purposely played it cool. She wanted him to believe that she was respecting his wishes. *If Danny didn't want her. . . .* How long could he hold out? She was sure that Danny wasn't getting any on the side, and he was only human.

Paulinda convinced herself that she could, would, that she had to make it right on their anniversary. She had done her penance. She had been punished enough. She arranged for Danny Junior to sleep at her cousin Rita's house.

Danny walked in at six-thirty.

"Tough day, Danny?" Paulinda asked.

"Just a day," Danny said as he removed his jacket.

The aroma of pozole (stew) and chiles rellenos (stuffed peppers) filled his nostrils. He loved all Central American food, but these were his favorites.

"Dinner's ready, Danny," Paulinda said firmly, not wanting to betray her diabolical plan to save their marriage.

"Where's Danny?" he asked as he pulled out a chair.

"He's sleeping over at Rita's. You know how he loves playing with Carlos and Hector."

"Yeah," Danny smiled.

Paulinda filled Danny's plate and placed it in front of him. She filled her own plate and sat next to him. Danny looked at her inquisitively. "Why are you sitting there? You always sit across from me in that chair." He pointed.

Paulinda ignored the question. "Do you know what day it is, Danny?"

Danny looked at her. His eyes grew red. "How much hot pepper did you put in this pozole?" he asked, trying to deflect her recognition of the sentiment tearing up in his eye.

"It's our tenth anniversary," Paulinda said softly.

Danny remained perfectly still and after a few seconds nodded. "Yeah, I guess that's right."

Paulinda laid her hand on top of his and slid it back, closing it around his wrist. This had worked in the past. He knew what that grip meant and looked down. *If it was only that easy.*

At the end of dinner, Paulinda squeezed Danny's wrist tightly again. After about twenty seconds she opened her hand and traced her fingernails over Danny's hand. She stood, smiled down at him, and began cleaning the dishes. Danny walked into the front room, sat in his favorite chair, and read a Louis L'Amour book.

After an hour or so passed, Paulinda walked in. "Let's go to bed, Danny."

"What time is it?" Danny asked.

"Almost nine," she replied.

"Let me finish this chapter," Danny said.

"I'll be waiting," Paulinda whispered, smiling softly.

Danny laid next to her. When he stopped rustling, she pushed her firm, naked body against his. Danny sighed quietly, not looking forward to the next few minutes.

Paulinda kissed him all over and sucked on his thumb. She began moaning softly. Danny had been the only man she had ever loved. Manny had been a disappointment in every way. But Danny, his body was hard like a marble statue. He had a drive that pushed her past ecstasy, each time bringing her to a new location that she'd never been. It was never the same twice. She still couldn't understand why she had done what she did. But she was sure that she never, ever betrayed Danny. She may have been with Manny, but she was never his.

She slipped her hand into his underwear, pulled him out and put him in her mouth. After a few minutes, she laid her head on his stomach. "You must try, amor," she said softly.

"I never had to try before," he answered.

"Danny, I'm so sorry." She began to sob. "I told you a thousand times. It was one time. It will never happen again."

"It was one time too many, Paulinda." Danny hesitated. "I just can't."

"You just can't what, Danny Nowak? You have been with many women. I know, Danny, and I have never let it get in between us, never." Paulinda sat up next to him.

Danny wanted to satisfy Paulinda. He stared into the dark, envisioning Alice, the bubble-butted girl down the block. If he could just get a hold of her for an hour or two. But he was with Paulinda and it didn't work. It had been months and nothing worked.

"Danny please, I promise," she cried, "please, do it for little Danny." She knew that she was begging but she was willing to do anything to have her man back, her family secure.

She pulled Danny's underwear completely off, licked her fingers and wet herself. She tried to mount him, but it was useless. He had as much interest in Paulinda as he had in a sheet of paper that he'd fed into the cup machine at Sweetheart seven years ago.

After torturing herself for another half hour, Paulinda rolled onto her back. "They make pills, Danny," she said.

"There's nothing wrong with me," he answered coldly.

"Everyone takes them Danny, even twenty-year-olds take 'em."

"Paulinda, I ain't taking any pills."

Danny's mind was blank. Anger and despair assaulted Paulinda until she fell asleep. When she woke, Danny was gone. She knew that he'd return in the evening, but resigned herself to the fact that he would never come back.

One day, a few weeks later, Danny came home and discovered that Paulinda and Little Danny's things were gone. A month after that, he quit his job. He hadn't given up. He was just tired of being an hourly paid slave and wanted to begin living. When he was a kid, he lived every summer day as if it was an adventure. He had always thought about laying back and living. Now was the time. From that day on, every moment was an adventure, different and exciting. He began thinking about things he never fathomed, all sorts of things: politics, art, science.

People walked or drove past his home and saw Danny just sitting on the top step, his mind thousands of miles away from New City.

Those first few days turned into weeks, months, and years. He grew a beard in the winter and the outcome of all of his thinking was that he had become an undocumented sage.

He stopped paying real estate taxes on his property and only picked up rent from his tenants when he needed cash.

Danny realized that with a little thought he could resolve almost any problem, whether it was a leaky foundation, an electrical short, a car, a bicycle, or a broken heart. He kind of decided without deciding that this would be his mission in life. He'd fix things. He had never been so happy. He loved his people and they loved him back. He'd lost his wife and inherited a handful of brides.

Beverly was one of Danny's favorites, short and petite with skin as smooth as the top of a Reese's peanut butter cup, strawberry lips, caramel drop eyes, licorice twist hair, and a behind as cute as two perfectly formed Milk Duds. She was a walking candy store.

Beverly was a nurse's aide at Saint Bernard's on 64th Street. Whenever she visited Danny she became a different character. Sometimes she was a food taster, other times a nurse who put the thermometer in her mouth. She did incredible check-ups and when in bed, Danny felt like he was making love to three women.

Beverly was probably the smartest woman he had ever met. Danny learned a lot from her and though her body was a few decades his junior, her mind towered over his by centuries. They were a couple made in heaven.

He listened and concentrated on her every word. Initially, when she told him about the dunking, he had to connect the dots. "I met big guys that couldn't make a shot, and little guys that could dunk," she said. "The most powerful tool is the mind, Danny."

It took some thinking, but Danny realized that her words had nothing to do with basketball.

Beverly wanted children, but nature had other plans. She was raised by her grandfather, who warned her to never, ever trust the white man. Danny laughed when she told him that the first time. He said, "Grandpa doesn't need to worry. I'm Polish. Crayolas can be white, not people."

Most of her family resented people that were light-skinned. Beverly learned time and time again that the shade of a person's skin had little to do with their trustworthiness, or much of anything else. It was curious to her how the media ignored that reality.

Finally, experience also taught her that most men have a one-track mind. Danny was typical in that regard, but he was also affectionate, at times about as funny as fighting squirrels, and she had been attracted to him for years. He was kind, caring, and had the strength and presence of a tall elm.

It was a typical night. Beverly kissed her grandfather and each went to their bedrooms, but the night proceeded differently than any she could remember. She woke in a sweat. Something wasn't right. She sat up. *Grandpa*, she thought. She called him and rushed to his room. The old man was stiff. Life had been absent for some time.

Pulling herself together she realized that Grandpa needed to be cleaned and shaved. On a nurse's aide's salary, she didn't have much money stashed and Grandpa would never approve of her borrowing money to bury him. She could hear him prodding, "Girl, it just don't make sense." This seemed to be the line he used the most while raising her.

Beverly's heart was smashed to bits. She had lost the man who had nurtured and loved her all the days of her life. Her mind was surrounded by jagged, hurtful, broken glass. There was only one thing to do. Danny would make sure that she wouldn't cut herself.

To keep the price down, she'd deliver Grandpa to the Unity Funeral Home ready to be displayed. Grandpa weighed about 130 pounds. She began planning. Again, she thought that the first thing to do was to clean and shave him.

Danny jumped out of bed and onto his bicycle. He was at Beverly's door within fifteen minutes.

"I could flip him over my shoulder and take him to Tyro's barber shop," he said. "I'll call Tyro, he'll open for me."

"Grandpa would have none of that, Danny. He always said that Tyro's shop was filled with shiftless riffraff who sat there all day playing with their phones and gossiping about decent folk," Beverly replied.

She ran warm water in the tub. Grandpa's body was stiff. Danny held him by his waist and carried him to the bathroom.

"Watch his head, Danny," Beverly said.

Danny leaned Grandpa against the wall in the bathroom and removed his pajama top, then tugged on his pajama bottoms.

"Danny, the man deserves some dignity. He don't want his baby granddaughter to see his privates!" she scolded.

"Sorry, would you leave for a minute? I'll get him in the tub, scrub him down."

"You'll *wash* him. You don't scrub him. You scrub the kitchen floor!" Beverly covered her face with her hands. "I'm sorry, Danny. I'm sorry . . ." She burst into tears and disappeared.

Danny thought for a moment. The best thing he could do for Beverly and her grandfather was to get him tidy and to the funeral home expediently. He shaved and bathed the old man gently, remembering what Beverly had said about the kitchen floor.

Beverly was in the other room ironing her grandfather's favorite white shirt. After she finished, she brought a pair of clean underwear and a T-shirt into the bathroom. She handed them to Danny, without looking towards the tub.

Danny toweled the old fellow off. Looking at his kind face, Danny sincerely regretted not knowing him. He was happy that the old man's eyes were shut tight. He had seen his share of corpses, some of them laid out lifeless except for their eyes. Jaguar, a gang leader that Danny had befriended and seen shot down, had lain on the ground wide-eyed like he was watching the guy chasing people with a knife in the film *Halloween*.

Danny got the underwear on and carried the old man into his bedroom. It took almost thirty minutes to get the suit on over his stiff limbs, but they got it done. Beverly looked at Grandpa lying on the bed, smiled, and then burst into tears again, clinging onto Danny like he was a life vest and she was in the middle of a choppy ocean.

Danny gently carried Grandpa to Beverly's car and laid him down in the back seat. They drove to the Unity Funeral Home on 41st and Michigan. The owner lived above the parlor and was open for business twenty-four hours a day.

Beverly, like 69 percent of American families, had less than two thousand dollars in savings. She'd have to make payments for the cost of the funeral.

Grandpa had taught his favorite granddaughter to be sensible. After dropping him off and organizing the wake and funeral with the undertaker, Beverly went with Danny to the thrift store on Halsted.

For seven dollars, they walked out with a bright red tie, cuff links, and a tie clip.

During the day of the wake, Beverly searched for Danny in the crowd. Seeing him there helped hold her in place. He was like the chair under her feet and she was standing on him with a noose around her neck hanging from a pipe.

Most of the family knew who Danny was and actually respected him. Of course, there are good and bad in all shades.

One of Beverly's ex-boyfriends, Rilla, walked into the funeral home with his troops to pay respects. After leaving the casket, Rilla walked straight over to Danny.

"Whatcha doin' here, white man?"

Danny looked right through him.

"Whatcha' doin' here, white man?"

Danny smiled. "You talking to me, Rilla?"

"I don't see any other white men here," Rilla snarled.

Danny looked to the front and spotted Beverly reverently making the last stand with her grandfather.

Rilla, obviously perturbed that Danny was not giving him the respect he was used to, continued. "You're right. I'm looking at a privileged little white boy, bitch." Rilla looked to the side and then stared across, looking into Danny's eyes.

"You know, Rilla, I never thought of myself as being white, I mean, I'm more peach-colored or maybe beige and your mamma had three kids, there were twelve of us."

Rilla noticeably moved up, onto the balls of his feet and stared down into Danny's eyes. "Whatcha talkin' 'bout, Danny?"

"Rilla, we're all just people." Danny looked to the side and hesitated before continuing. He looked back at Rilla. "And anyone saying that privilege has anything to do with the shade of one's skin is just plain crazy."

Danny had one of those sincere smiles that could con a robin into giving you its worm. The funeral ended without incident.

Napoleon's kids were playing in front of their house, or as Napoleon saw it, mostly running in and out the front door. Lippatu, his eight-year-old daughter, sauntered her pretty little self to the bottom of Danny's porch. She was light milk chocolate with braided hair and had an honest smile that Danny believed could convince even a politician to tell the truth. Danny knew what she wanted and purposely played coy.

"Hi, Danny."

"Hi, Lippatu."

"Whatcha doin', Danny?"

"Oh, a little of this and a little of that. You?"

"Me too, a little of this and a little of that."

Danny concentrated on pulling the plastic off the wire in his hands.

"You don't feel like talkin', Danny?"

Danny adored the way Lippatu said his name. She put an extra "ay" in there and he became Dayaynny.

"No, not really," Danny said, looking at the wire in his hands.

Lippatu was confused. Danny always wanted to talk to her, or anyone else for that matter. He raised his hands and scanned her angelic, scrunched face and puckered lips through his fingers and the wire.

After an uncomfortable silence, Lippatu spoke. "Why Dayaynny, we got to talk about som'in'."

"Oh?"

"Yes, you told me yesterday to speak to you today."

"Did I now?" Danny hesitated. "I don't remember." He cupped his chin in his hand.

"Yes, you do remember, Dayaynny Nowak! You remember ever'ting! You's just tryin' to get me to beg, and I ain't gonna!" Lippatu hesitated, beamed, wound up, and smoothed out her delivery. "Napoleon tol' me dat ladies don't beg, Dayaynny."

He didn't know if it was a knuckleball, slider, or a fastball. At any rate, he swung as it whizzed right by him. Not wanting to be humiliated, he brushed off his knees and stared squarely at her without standing. "I see, and you're a lady?" he asked.

Lippatu glared back menacingly, determined to give it all she had. "Of course I is, Dayaynny and you always tol' me so. You tol' me I was your little lady," she said with a seriousness worthy of Margaret Thatcher.

Duchess entered the conversation, barking happily.

"Shut up, girl, Lippatu don't understand dog talk. She's too young."

"What's she saying, Dayaynny?" Lippatu asked.

"She says your bike is all fixed and in her front room."

Lippatu darted to the door under the porch. Danny smiled.

"Duchess, I ain't here to pet you, girl. I'm here to get my bike." Lippatu paused. "Uh-oh, Dayaynny, Duchess had another accident."

"I know honey, she's old. I'll clean it up."

Lippatu closed the door and zipped down the street on her little pink bike. Danny was happy that in New City you could still give a girl a pink bike without being publicly attacked.

"Thank you Dayaynny!" she yelled from down the block.

Chapter 2

Moses

Danny smiled and watched Lippatu pedaling away. Lippatu had Sickle Cell Disease and every so often had a painful crisis. Napoleon refused to go on state aid, so he had to figure out how to keep the little darling safe in other ways. Old Man Johnson was a retired pharmacist and he made pills that resembled Global Blood Therapeutics Oxbryta for Lippatu to take daily. Napoleon said that the treatment would be about ten thousand dollars a month. Old Man Johnson wouldn't accept a penny in compensation. He was a lifesaver who'd go to prison if he was ever caught.

Thinking about Lippatu, Danny didn't notice the arrival of the tall, nappy-haired giant standing at the bottom of his stairs, waiting patiently as if he needed permission to exist.

Danny, who habitually counted on the eyes in the back of his head, was mildly startled. "Moses. I didn't hear your cart."

Moses always traveled with a laundry cart. That way if he found a bottle, can, or just about anything that caught his fancy, in it would go.

"I ain't got no cart, Danny," the giant mumbled submissively. He continued to stare at Danny with the eyes of a five-year-old angel. "Can I pet Duchess?"

"What do you mean, you ain't got no cart?" Danny didn't give Moses time to respond. "Boy, you've been lugging a cart since I known ya, and I known ya for thirty or better."

Moses shifted his weight from one foot to the other, hoping that the motion would help contain the tears forming in his eyes. "They took my cart, Danny."

"Who took your cart? Was it those Price brothers? If it was, we'll go right to their mamma and get it back," Danny said with the solemnity of a grammar school principal.

A tear slowly traveled down Moses' cheek, rolling a bit and then stopping as if picking flowers. Danny watched the quiet mastiff of a man. Moses gaped back while considering wiping the tear off his cheek, also hoping that Danny hadn't noticed it.

Danny stood up brusquely. "Why, you just wait there, Moses. I'll put on my shirt and we'll go right to their mamma."

Danny grabbed for the rope hanging onto the doorknob. On the other side of the door, Danny's dogs, Dude and Elaine, had already begun barking out their welcoming hymn. He walked in and pushed his fans away. He grabbed a corduroy shirt from the chair and headed back out. He tied the rope hanging off his doorknob to the porch railing. Any of his friends would know he wasn't home if they saw the rope tied in place.

Danny turned his attention back to his big friend. "Let's go, Moses."

"It wasn't the Price brothers, Danny," Moses said soberly. "Can't I just go and pet Duchess?"

Confused, Danny hesitated. He stared at Moses and then turned back towards the door as if he was going to go back into his house. Elaine and Dude sensed his return.

"You two shut up. I'm talking to Moses," Danny said with sufficient firmness and volume to penetrate three of the doors in front of him. "Someone took his cart and we're gonna go get it back for him!" Danny yelled, in an effort to cheer the gentle, repentant giant.

"Can't get it back, Danny . . ." Contritely, Moses looked down at his shoes, the same boots he wore in the snow or at the beach. "I'd like to pet Duchess."

"You don't worry, my brother. We'll get it back. Duchess will be here. How's your aunty?" He pronounced it On-tee.

"She's gone too, Danny."

Something was terribly amiss. Danny stared into space as he grasped at sense, desperately attempting to form the right words. Sometimes, all the wisdom and dictionaries in the world can't produce a suitable response.

"You got any ice cream, Danny?" Moses asked with the temperament of an Evangelical preacher giving a sermon.

"Why sure I do, Moses. I picked some up on Tuesday at the Kitchen. Father gave me a gallon tub."

"You don't mind, do you Danny?"

Another tear tenaciously clung to a crease in the big man's face. Danny couldn't resist. He rubbed the wetness into Moses' cheek softly and beamed one of those unmistakably irreplaceable, impossible-to-imitate Danny smiles.

"Are you kiddin', boy? I was just hopin' that someone would pass by and give me some help eatin' it. A gallon's a whole lot of ice cream."

That night Moses slept downstairs with Duchess.

The following day Napoleon told Danny about Moses' predicament. Uncle Rufus had been dead for years, and old Auntie Elizabeth had been found dead in the front room of their house, several blocks away on 56th and Racine. The police arrested Moses on suspicion of murder, but after a few weeks in the fort, decided that they didn't have enough to hold him.

Anyone with a lick of sense could see that Moses would never harm his Auntie or anyone else. The boy was soft and simple at five years old, and had remained the same forty years later; besides, his aunt Elizabeth was every bit of eighty-five, already six years on the other side of the average. It's just difficult for some to realize that not every black woman found dead on the South Side of Chicago was murdered.

Elizabeth, like most of the families living in the neighborhood, hadn't paid the real estate taxes on her home for years. Fortunately for the city, the house was in her name. This made for a nice, clean transaction for the department of municipal planning. While Moses was in the fort at 26th Street and California Avenue, the city disposed of his home. The old frame was demolished and the lot cleaned in a matter of hours.

When Danny prodded Moses for specifics, the big man's eyes just flooded and he didn't have the heart to proceed. The only other details he uncovered about the situation were that after Moses was released and returned to 56th Street, there was no home and no cart. Danny assumed that after nights of sleeping behind where his house used to be, Moses had figured it would be a good idea to come and see him.

Danny let Moses move in. What else could he do? Moses had nowhere else to go.

Before Danny made it to the bottom of the stairs, he let out a yell. "Moses! Oh, Moses! Stop petting that damn dog. We're gonna go to Sherman Park and chop some firewood, boy! Don't let those warm nights fool you! Soon old man winter will be burning our faces off with his wind and pulling our toes and fingers off with his cold!"

Napoleon opened the front door next door. "What's up, Danny?"

"I'm waking Moses, that nappy-haired giant."

"Him and half the neighborhood," Napoleon said with a smile.

"It's gonna be a nice day, Napoleon."

"Always is when I see you in the morning, Danny."

Danny smiled, looked down, and shook his head. "Oh shucks, Napoleon, you make me blush."

When Moses didn't come out, Danny went downstairs. The front room reeked of Duchess's feces and Moses' unwashed body and clothes. The giant was on the floor sleeping, with the dog in his arms. Danny pinched his nose tight and kicked Moses' feet. "Boy, don't you even take them boots off to sleep?"

Moses opened his eyes wide and stared up at the ceiling, not having any idea where he was.

"Don't you even take your boots off to sleep?" Danny repeated.

Moses looked at Danny. Duchess stirred mildly.

"Danny, you woke up Duchess."

Danny nodded. Moses hugged the old dog and kissed the side of her head.

"Don't be kissing that dog," Danny said.

"Why, Danny?"

"Why? Why? Are you going crazy? Because she's a dog!"

"I love her, Danny." Duchess licked Moses' face. "And I know that she's a dog. She got four legs, a tail, and she barks." Moses hesitated. "So what's wrong with kissing her, Danny?"

Danny grinned and rolled his eyes. "Well, big man, I'm starting to get concerned." Danny pointed at Moses with a serious expression. "I mean, it seems that people don't love people anymore. They love dogs. I mean if they love people and dogs, that's great, but they only love dogs!"

Danny looked to the side and back at Moses. "Do as you please, but get up, because today we're gonna cut some wood and then wash in the park sprinkler. This place stinks. Boy, if your Auntie Elizabeth knew that you were sleeping with your boots on, she'd give you what for."

Moses, momentarily frightened, looked to the side and then back at Danny. "Auntie Bee is dead. She ain't gonna find out 'bout my sleepin' with no boots on." He hesitated. "Is she?"

Danny glared affectionately at his overgrown guest and nodded gently. "Moses, two weeks ago I took the motorcycles out of the kitchen and cleared a path from the front room and another to the bathroom."

Moses scrutinized Danny, fearful that the old Polack was slipping. "Danny, my old Auntie ain't never even been here. She don't even knows where you lives. She ain't gonna see me sleeping with my boots on or that you cleared a path in your house."

"I know that," Danny said firmly. "Moses, you know why I cleaned my house?"

"No."

"Do you remember my poppy?"

"Of course I do, Danny. He lived further up on 50th near Laflin Street. But he's dead."

"That's right. But do you know that he visits me in my dreams, and that the other night he told me to clean my house?"

Moses stared solemnly. People coming in dreams was an interesting thought.

Danny continued. "He told me that I had to clear a way to the kitchen and the bathroom or I'd end up killing myself getting up in the night."

Moses nodded solemnly. "He visits you in your dreams?"

"He sure does, and sooner or later ol' Auntie Bee will be visiting you, if she hasn't already."

Moses looked away from Danny, focusing on a hole where light was penetrating in from the outside.

Danny kicked Moses' feet, breaking his concentration. "Now get up! We got to go to Sherman Park and cut some branches!"

Danny walked out of the house only to find a situation more repugnant than his ground floor apartment. The City Revenue truck was parked down the block. Most of the time the municipal agents came around to put boots on cars. The owners couldn't afford to pay their tickets, which was why the city booted their cars. And once their cars were booted, they wouldn't be able to go to work. It was kind of like the way the banks jack up the interest on people who pay late. If someone can't afford a low interest rate, how will they afford one that's even higher? It's all kind of nonsensical and hypocritical, but the poor have been on the losing side forever.

Revenue agents actually have dozens of tools at their disposal to ruin poor people's lives, and eventually, the only way for many to pay their tickets was to prostitute themselves or sell drugs, lately prescription ones. Of course, the CEO and city administration didn't much care where people got the money. Capitalism focuses on results, and the drug industry is outright euphoric.

This agent was thin and of average height with a reedy mustache. He wore a black sports jacket as he walked towards Danny's house.

Danny's instincts told him that the revenue agent wasn't here to boot no cars. He was here for bigger game.

The agent approached the porch. "Mr. Nowak?"

"Mr. Who?" Danny asked menacingly.

"My name is Revenue Agent Burman." He flipped open a badge and sneered arrogantly. "Do you live here?"

Danny had seen hundreds of badges in his life. He nodded. "Is that the name your people gave you? Revenue Agent?"

Burman smiled slightly and pointed at the three-story shack. His facial expression indicated what he thought about the place or anyone who would live in it; it wasn't real positive. "Do you live here?"

"What's it to you?"

"The taxes have not been paid on this building." He paused, and smirked, raising his eyebrows just to drive his point home. "It's over ten years. The property now belongs to the city. It's been condemned. We're going to tear it down."

"People live in this building," Danny said indignantly.

"That's why I have these letters—to notify the residents that they have ninety days to evacuate." The agent smiled thinly. "It's for their own good. No one should be living in this squalor."

Squalor was not a word that pleased Duchess. She barked like five years had been miraculously given back to her.

The agent looked downstairs, toward where the barking seemed to come from. "It's not even fit for dogs," Burman said.

He removed three letters from his jacket. "There's one for each floor. Would you be so kind as to make sure that the residents get them, Mr. Nowak?"

Danny stared coldly.

"It's unjust to the other citizens who pay their fair share to have freeloaders." The man smiled stingily again.

Danny snapped the letters from the agent's hand. At that moment, Moses walked out of the house and stood next to Danny.

"What's goin' on, Danny? Is this guy trying to bother us?"

The agent looked at Moses. Danny watched the man's eyes widen.

"No Moses, he's just leaving, before I forget that I'm a Catholic and he can still walk."

The man almost slipped, turning and double-timed it back to the city vehicle with his tail between his legs. Danny looked up at the broken window on the second floor and rubbed his chin.

"What's the matter, Danny? Is som'in' wrong?" Danny's stillness stirred Moses. "Danny, do you want me to go and get that man?"

The agent climbed into his van and shut the door, immediately hitting the lock button.

Danny's presence gave Moses a strength of character he'd never felt before.

Moses moved in the direction of the van. "I could pull his door off and bring him back here, Danny," he offered.

"No, no, Moses. We got to get firewood. We got to make some scratch. I'm going to Greencastle."

As the white van rolled past Danny's house, Agent Burman rolled down the window. "You'll be homeless soon, you worthless parasite vagrants! You're a drain on this city!"

The van sped off, almost hitting a little girl crossing the street.

Moses looked at Danny. "What's a vagrant, Danny?"

"Vagrant?" Danny looked down. "A vagrant is someone free from the handcuffs of the so-called 'white society.'"

Moses looked down at the same area Danny was staring at. "But you're white, Danny. It's your society."

Danny looked up. "So-called, so-called. There is no white society or orange society, there are just boxes that the powerful stick us in so they can keep us fighting with each other." Danny raised the back side of the papers he had taken from the city official and pushed them towards Moses' eyes. "These are white."

Moses looked at the documents curiously.

"There's no such thing as a white *person*," Danny said. "The whole idea is a concept made up by people trying to keep us divided. It's called the white man's society, but it's really the rich man's society. It belongs to Oprah as much as it belongs to the Kennedy family."

Moses was trying to get his mental arms around these phrases. He had heard of Oprah. Auntie wasn't a fan. Auntie said that Oprah was an overweight, useless woman who made a fortune kowtowing to other useless women like herself.

"Greed, greed," Danny snapped, "greed is colorblind, brother."

"Why do they want people divided, Danny?"

"They want us divided for the same reason from the beginning of time: so they can rule and steal what we produce," Danny said firmly.

"Oh." Moses looked down at his boots. He gently nodded his head. "What about black, Danny? If there ain't no such thing as white people, is there any such thing as black people?"

Danny pointed up to the busted television on his porch. "You see that screen, Moses?"

"Uh-huh."

"That's black."

"You mean there are no such things as black and white people? Is that what you mean, Danny?"

Danny smiled thinly and nodded resolutely. "There's no yellow, brown, or red, neither."

Moses stared sincerely, "but Danny, our skin color is different."

"It's just shades, man, we're all different shades of the same color." Danny's brain was reaching for a simple example. "And there ain't two men in the world with the same shade," he insisted.

"Not even twins, Danny?"

"Not even twins."

"I'll tell you another thing," Danny said as he stared at the basketball court in the park across the street.

Moses continued to contemplate the words of the man who Moses thought might very well have been the greatest person who ever lived.

"Moses, a great man once said that we are all brothers and that there's no need to do anything but love each other."

"Wow, Danny . . . A man really said that? Auntie Bee always listened to news. I listened, but I never heard any of them say that."

Danny focused on Moses' nappy hair and then his eyes fell onto the big man's face. "Sure enough," Danny said, "He said it, and He gave hope to the masses."

"And what happened to that man, Danny? Where is He?" Moses asked enthusiastically. "I'd like to sure meet Him."

Danny turned his head. When he looked back at big Moses, Danny had tears in his eyes. "They crucified Him," Danny said softly, turning away again. He said it in a way that made you think that Christ had been crucified yesterday and that Danny had been there.

If Danny was going to Greencastle, what would happen to Moses? On the way to the park Moses worked up the courage to ask.

"Where's Greencastle, Danny?"

"In Indiana."

"Where's Indiana, Danny?"

"Why do you need to know?" Danny asked.

"Why Danny, you can't leave old Moses behind, can you?"

Danny paused as Moses caught up to him. He looked in the big man's childlike eyes and ran his gaze down to Moses' boots.

"I won't wear my boots to bed in Greencastle, Indiana, Danny."

Danny's silence concerned Moses. "I promise I won't wear my boots to bed in Greencastle, Indiana."

Danny stared at Moses and then looked away and continued to walk towards the park. Moses lagged behind a bit, thinking. It wasn't easy for him to walk and think at the same time, at least not profoundly. "My Auntie Bee, she visited me in my sleep last night!" he screamed to Danny.

Danny looked back.

"You know what she tole me?"

Danny waited as Moses walked towards him.

"Do you know what she tole me?"

"Nope," Danny said.

Moses caught up with Danny. "She told me to stay with you, Danny. 'Danny's gonna take care of you,' she said. Why, she even told me to tell you to take me wherever you go, even to Greencastle, Indiana, Danny."

"Swear?" Danny asked in an instigating tone.

Moses looked to the right, the left, and then back at Danny. "Swear, and Auntie's your elder, Danny, you got to listen to your elders." Moses nodded solemnly.

The big man felt guilty about lying, but he desperately needed to have somewhere to stay and someone to be his friend. While sleeping in the alley behind his old home, the Price brothers and some of the other neighborhood kids had pelted him with stones, called him names, and hit him with sticks. He knew he could have stopped them, and hurt them if he wanted to. But he didn't want to. In his whole life, he never remembered wanting to hurt anyone.

Danny grabbed the gas saw and climbed a tree. He sat on the angle of a large branch and pulled the cord. The motor started instantly and began eating away at the branch that was at least a foot in diameter. Danny concentrated on the task as the wood began splintering.

Suddenly Danny remembered his assistant. He looked down. Moses was directly in the path of the fall. "Get out the way, you goofy bastard, it's coming down!"

The branch roared, cracked off the tree, and slammed down, landing less than a foot from Moses. Danny made fast time down and began cutting it into pieces.

"Why'd you call me a goofy bastard, Danny?"

"I called you a goofy bastard because I wanted you to get out of the way."

"Would you take a goofy bastard to Greencastle, Indiana, Danny?"

"We'll talk later," Danny said, while he continued to cut the branch into foot-long pieces.

"Would you take a goofy bastard to Greencastle, Danny? Indiana?!" Moses yelled.

Danny stopped cutting. "Hush, you're making more noise than the saw, and we got to finish up before the police spot us."

"Why would the police care, Danny? My Auntie Bee says the park belongs to everyone."

"The park belongs to the government, and so do we." Danny stared at Moses. "But I'm gonna break out and go to Greencastle, Indiana." He looked out into the distance. "I'm gonna raise a pig, maybe two, hang bacon, raise some chickens, make myself a little moonshine."

Danny stared up at Moses. "For medicinal reasons." He smiled, nodded, and continued, "and skunk nickel mushrooms and hog lard."

"Would you take a goofy bastard to Greencastle, Indiana, Danny?" Moses whispered, "to help you skunk nickel mushrooms and hog lard?"

"Only if he promised to feed the chickens, hoe the vegetable patch, husk some corn, and generally do what he's told."

"Oh, I'd love to feed the chickens, Danny, especially the little chicks. I love chicks, Danny. Chicks come from eggs." Moses paused and looked at Danny as if he had just fixed the storage problem for the lithium battery.

"Put your arms out," Danny said.

Moses obeyed with the solemnity of an exemplary marine cadet. Danny began stacking wood in Moses' arms.

"Take these logs and park them over in that front yard." Danny pointed to a house across 52nd Street.

Moses waited for Danny to finish loading and walked towards the house, all the time whispering to himself, "I'm goin' to Greencastle, Indiana, I'm goin' to Greencastle, Indiana . . ."

It was almost noon by the time they finished. They ate bread and drank Country Time lemonade on the front porch.

"When you're done with your lunch, you're going to take a shower in the sprinkler," Danny said.

Moses looked at Danny. "Will you take a shower in the sprinkler too?"

Danny said nothing.

Moses continued. "If I take a shower all by myself, people will say, 'There's that crazy Moses, actin' the fool.' But if you take a shower with me . . ."

"Moses, do you know what the opposite of courage is?"

Moses stared and bit his lip, wanting to convince Danny that he was concentrating. "The opposite of courage, let me think . . ." he said.

"Most say that cowardice is the opposite of courage, but you know what I say?" Danny asked.

Moses raised his hand to his mouth and let it slide down, gripping his chin. Continuing to stare at Danny, he raised his two fingers to his bottom lip and squeezed it. He hoped that Danny would think that he was smart.

"Conformity, Moses. That's the opposite of courage," Danny said.

"Comfornity?"

"Conformity, not comfornity, and conformity is the opposite of courage." Danny nodded.

Moses smiled. "Comfornity . . ."

Brass hoses inside four concrete posts sprayed into the center of the sprinkler. Moses' boots were sitting behind one of them. Danny took off his gym shoes and they looked at each other.

Danny knew the answer but asked anyway. "What are you waiting for, Moses?"

Moses remained still. Danny shook his head gently and walked into the center. It was easily ninety degrees out, and the water felt like little beads of heaven. Danny reached down and took off his socks. Then, with a bit more aggression, he pulled off his dego T-shirt.

Moses stared at Danny, who was standing in his jeans with his mouth open, catching droplets of water. Watching him, Moses thought that Danny may have been the nicest man that ever lived.

Danny pulled a bar of soap out of his pants pocket and tossed it to Moses. He watched as Moses' gigantic hand swallowed the bar like a normal man would catch a bottle cap.

"My Auntie always used bar soap," Moses said. "She said it's thrifty."

"Well then, get in here and use it."

Moses inched toward the circle but stopped and turned, looking across the street to see if anyone was watching. Fortunately, Napoleon's kids were sitting on the porch, paying no attention to them. Moses took a sock off. He dropped it under the water and a river of dirty gray ran to the drain in the middle. He took off his other sock and then his shirts. He stood there, in his jeans, a mountain of a man. He stared at Danny, who appeared to be having the time of his life.

Danny shook his head wildly, his unkempt hair slapping around. When he stopped, he stared at Moses. "Come on, boy," he prodded.

Moses walked towards the center, trying to focus on Danny, but the water drops blurred his vision.

"Use that soap, man. When you're done, give it to me."

Moses scrubbed his hair, then his neck, arms, chest, stomach, and feet. He entertained himself watching the dingy, soapy water slowly turning white, running to the center drain. After a minute or so, he ferociously scrubbed his hair and neck again. He held his hand out and looked at the thick suds coating it.

"You done yet?" Danny yelled.

"Yep, all done, Danny!"

"Then toss me the soap!"

By now, Danny and Moses had attracted the attention of all the kids on Napoleon's porch, the teenagers playing basketball and a dozen other neighbors. Moses' muscles were not quite as toned as Danny's but they were enormous. Several of the spectators began making comments.

Danny scrubbed vigorously and at a certain point, turned towards the railroad tracks and stuck the soap down his pants, scrubbing the back and the front.

Moses knew that he had forgotten something. "Danny, I need the soap back!"

After a few minutes, soaked and clean, they walked across the street. As they hit the sidewalk, the spectators on the other side broke into loud applause. Moses wasn't sure how to handle the situation. He looked at Danny.

Danny smiled at the crowd. "Thank you, thank you," he said as he took a bow. "Take a bow, you mountain of a man."

Moses bowed nervously.

"Now go inside and take off your clothes," Danny said.

"Why, Danny?"

"*Why, Danny?*" Danny said mockingly. "Cause I'm going to the laundromat."

"But what will I do?"

"You'll cover yourself with a towel or a blanket, whatever you find, and pet Duchess."

"OK, Danny." Moses walked towards the house.

"Take another bow!" Danny yelled.

Moses turned, smiled, and bowed. The crowd applauded frantically. Moses walked into the house and was home.

Danny washed and dried the clothes and headed back. As he turned the corner, he spotted Moses sitting on the porch wrapped in an old, ragged tarp.

Moses smiled enthusiastically. "Hi Danny, I, I dint want to get the apartment wet, and old Duchess is sleeping."

"Sleeping?" Danny said curiously.

"Yeah, Danny, she don't even wake when I pet her belly."

Danny hadn't heard her barking all day. He sighed and nodded kindly, waited until evening, and began digging a hole in the empty lot next door.

Lippatu stopped as she drove by on her bicycle. "Whatcha doin', Dayaynny?"

"Preparing Duchess's final home." Danny knew that Lippatu loved petting Duchess.

"You gonna build her a house out here?" Lippatu asked.

Danny wiped a tiny bead of sweat from his brow and mixed it with a tear from his eye. "Sort of," he said.

"I haven't heard her barkin' all day, Dayaynny. Usually she barks when she hears me pass on my bike. But you greased my chain and it don't make noise no more. Is that why she don't bark no more, Dayaynny?"

Danny shook his head. "No, honey, that likely has nothing to do wit it."

"She don't feel good, Dayaynny?"

"Honey, she don't feel anything, she's dead," Danny said with the sadness of a peanut butter sandwich with no jelly.

Lippatu looked down at her bike and then turned back towards Danny. "Do puppies go to heaven, Dayaynny?"

"Sure they do . . . and Duchess was an old sweetheart of a dog. I'm sure she's there already," Danny said.

"She wasn't that old, Dayaynny. I mean, to me, she was a big ol' gray-haired puppy." Lippatu stared as Danny began to dig again. "Can I help dig, Dayaynny?"

"Sure you can, honey."

"Do ya think that Duchess would be happy knowin' I was diggin' for her?"

"You bet, honey."

Moses walked out in his newly cleaned clothes. He looked at Lippatu and Danny curiously.

"What you all doin'?"

Lippatu looked at Danny and shook her head gently. Danny smiled.

"Duchess is still sleepin', Danny. Her belly's hard. Do you think she got a bellyache?" Moses asked.

Lippatu focused on the mountain of a man. "You know Moses, you ain't a bad-lookin' fellow when you clean up."

Moses looked at his clothes. He was a bit unsure how to respond, or if he should. No one ever gave him a compliment, other than Auntie Bee. He decided he liked being complimented.

Moses pushed his chest out gently and turned to the side. "I'm goin' to try to wake her up again, Danny. She dint eat all day and it's a shame, that big fat white woman goes to all the trouble to feed her and all."

Danny looked to Lippatu for approval. She nodded. "Moses, Duchess ain't gonna wake up," he said.

Moses stared, confused. "Huh? What you mean she ain't gonna wake up? You mean til tomorrow morning?"

Lippatu shook her head slightly and looked at Danny. He nodded and she continued, "She ain't never waking up." She hesitated, then said, "She's gone to dog heaven, you big mountain of a man."

Moses reflected. The first part of the sentence stung, but the last part felt kind of good.

"Huh?" Moses repeated.

Danny always knew Lippatu was the sharpest of Napoleon's flock. He remembered her mamma, a pretty, skinny woman from Hyde Park, where the University of Chicago is. She mothered Napoleon's last two children, Darren and Lippatu. A few years later she died of an opioid overdose. Listening to Lippatu now, Danny figured that her mother must have been some sort of brainiac.

"Moses, that's where all dogs want to go. There ain't no more sufferin', ain't no more worries," Lippatu said.

Moses looked to the side and then focused on Danny. He wasn't going to have this conversation with a girl that wasn't even ten years old. "If she don't eat her dog food, she'll starve."

"Listen to Lippatu, Moses," Danny said, nodding solemnly. "She's 'splainin."

Lippatu smiled with enough softness to disarm an irritated yellow jacket. Moses stared at her and looked at Danny one last time. Danny was solemn. Moses looked at Lippatu and returned her smile.

"She won't be hungry in heaven, Moses," Lippatu said. "She's perfectly happy. She's at peace." She hesitated. "We're digging a hole for her body. That's all that's left, her corpse. Duchess is already in dog heaven," she said while observing Moses closely.

Moses stared back and nodded. "Auntie Bee says heaven is paradise." Moses looked at his boots. "You said that Duchess is in dog heaven. My auntie is in people heaven. Danny, are dog heaven and people heaven close by one another?"

The question caught Danny a bit off guard.

Lippatu interceded. "Of course they is, you mountain of a man. Just like we're together on earth, we'll be together in paradise."

Moses was hopeful. He bit his lip and stared at Danny for confirmation.

Danny nodded gently. "The little lady knows what she's talkin' 'bout."

There was a soft silence. Not a car passed, there wasn't even the sound of a distant horn. Suddenly they heard the thunder of rattling leaves and a hard gust of wind whipped around the graveside trio.

Dude and Elaine barked passionately from inside the house. Moses was momentarily shaken. He slowly looked around as if he was afraid of what he might see.

Danny smiled. "That was Duchess telling us goodbye. She was always a spirited one."

Another few seconds passed as they enjoyed the soothing sound of the leaves laying back to rest.

"Guess Duchess is with my Auntie Bee," Moses said, staring into space. "Do you think she'll know that Auntie Bee is my auntie?"

Danny nodded and smiled. "Of course she'll know, and she'll know Uncle Rufus is your uncle too. They're all together now."

Lippatu, Moses, and Danny toiled for almost an hour longer. Danny insisted on the hole being deep enough to keep the rats from getting to Duchess's remains. Finally, he was standing in it up to his shoulders. "Let's carry the old girl out," he said.

They wrapped Duchess up in the tarp Moses had used earlier that day. Just as they laid her in the hole, the City Revenue van pulled up.

Burman lowered the passenger side window. "Hey! What are you doing on that lot? That's not your lot!" he screamed. "That's city property." Burman jumped out of his van and walked to the sidewalk.

Burman stared at the freeloading gravediggers and the trio stared back. Lippatu fixed her gaze on Danny. Moses watched her and instinctively followed in step. Danny rolled his tongue against the inside of his cheek as he felt the warmth of their eyes.

These lowlife squatters disgusted him. Burman stood erect, confident in his authority and righteousness.

Danny grinned and took a step towards Burman. "Sir, I'm a Catholic man," he said kindly.

Burman stared at Danny, determined to stand his ground. He was a bit confused. This must be what bravery felt like.

Danny continued, "As a Catholic man, it's my obligation to tell you that you'd be a lot safer in your vehicle."

Burman looked at Moses, Lippatu, and finally back at Danny. He pressed his thin lips together and looked at them sternly. "You're trespassing." Burman hesitated momentarily and then gaining confidence, looked at them one by one, "Why, you're all trespassing!"

Danny shook his head emphatically from side to side and dropped his shovel. Lippatu bit her lip to fight from grinning. Moses didn't even attempt to hide his smile. A ray of sun sparkled off Moses' teeth, causing Burman to squint.

Danny took another brisk step forward. Burman looked from side to side, determined to hold his ground. This was city property. He was an authorized city agent. This was his turf.

"All right!" Danny took another step. Burman nearly shit himself backing away and almost tripped. He regained his balance, turned, and skipped swiftly to his van without looking back. The three "trespassers" stood silently as the enraged revenue agent drove off.

Later that evening, Danny sat on the porch whittling a cross from a branch. Moses was blowing notes on a harmonica that he'd found in the alley. Lippatu rode her bike up and down, gaping every now and then at the progress Danny was making on Duchess's cross.

Dusk crawled in like a slow-moving freight train. The street light sensor hadn't flipped, but would soon. Danny waited for Lippatu to pass again. "Girl, we're gonna put the cross over Duchess and say some prayers."

"OK, Dayaynny, I'll get Napoleon."

All of Napoleon's children called him by his name. Napoleon once kidded that it was because one never truly knows who their real father is. Danny saw Napoleon in each of his kids, though. He was the father. There was no mistaking it. "OK, honey," Danny said.

Minutes later about twenty people stood around waiting for Father Danny to give the send-off.

Napoleon raised his hand to his mouth and reverently cleared his throat. He lowered his fist gently to his side. "Danny, can I say a few words?" he asked.

"Of course, brother, of course," Danny said and nodded respectfully.

Napoleon again cleared his throat in deep respect. "Duchess was a smelly ol', sometimes cantankerous wretch of a dog."

A few of his kids smiled. Napoleon was who he was. The sermon took off like a Formula One race car after a pit stop.

"She never asked for much. She was just here." Napolean stared intensely, looking down before continuing, "And there wasn't a better friend to any of us."

Napoleon turned to Danny. "Danny, do you remember when Duchess was on the porch waiting for you to come back out of the house and that man tried to grab Darren off the corner?"

"I sure do brother, I sure do," Danny said solemnly.

"Why ol' Duchess chased that bast—" Napoleon covered his mouth. "I mean that bad man, he barely made it back to his car."

"That's right, brother," Danny said.

A few of the kids nodded and repeated, "That's right, that's right."

Napoleon nodded before continuing. "She was a wretch . . ."

Napoleon felt Moses' hard, unfriendly glare. He intentionally softened his voice before continuing. "But she was our wretch, and she made each one of our lives a little bit better."

"She sure did, amen," some of Napoleon's kids and other neighbors in the requiem group chanted.

Napoleon made the sign of the cross. Danny, Lippatu, and the rest of the group followed suit.

Napoleon looked down at the mound of dirt and nodded contritely. "We loved her, and she took a little piece of each one of us to dog heaven with her."

Napoleon looked around at his whole family, made up of his kids and neighbors. They were twenty strong, and their skin was twenty different shades of love. They all looked back at Napoleon approvingly. Some nodded and others said "Amen."

Danny bent his head. "Well said brother, well said."

Suddenly, Datisha Rawley broke into song.

"Amazing Grace, How sweet the sound

That saved a wretch like me!"

Tears began to flow and many were wiping their eyes as Datisha continued.

"I once was lost, but now am found
Was blind but now I see

Twas Grace that taught my heart to fear
And Grace my fears relieved
How precious did that grace appear
The hour I first believed."

Danny smiled tenderly at Datisha. She gazed at him and returned the emotion. Mrs. Rawley, Datisha's mother, caught the energy that flowed between her daughter and Danny. She always knew that Danny was a good man and the right man for her girl. He may have been decades her senior, but Mrs. Rawley was wise enough to know that age was just a number.

Unfortunately, the law of the jungle was supreme and Datisha was being sought by Monster, Ugly Carl's brother. Ugly was Datisha's younger sister Janell's baby daddy and one of the more powerful neighborhood gangsters. Until Ugly Carl and Monster were gunned down or killed by a hot dose, any contact or any act of kindness between Danny and Datisha could cost both of them their lives.

Monster wanted to become Datisha's baby daddy, but would never get from her what Danny got from her . . . never. Danny was a gentleman, hard yet soft, funny yet wise. Something in Datisha was his and always would be.

Slowly, each family member took a handful of dirt and threw it on the mound. Ron Carl, Janell's two-year-old, grabbed some weeds and threw them atop (all of Ugly Carl's sons had Carl for a second name).

Slowly, the family departed from Duchess's gravesite until it was just Napoleon, Danny, Moses, and Lippatu. One by one, they looked at each other.

"Sorry, Danny," Napoleon said.

"Sorry, Danny," Lippatu said.

Danny looked up. Moses stared at the grave.

"Sorry, Moses," Danny said.

Lippatu looked from her mentor to Moses. "Sorry, Moses," she said.

"Sorry, Moses," Napoleon finished.

Danny stared at the mound of dirt with the weeds from Ron Carl scattered over the top and finally at the cross. He stood silently as if he was going to erupt with some sort of earth-changing oration but then he made a final sign of the cross, nodded gently, and turned.

Napoleon made a sign of the cross. Lippatu did the same and then so did Moses. Lippatu noticed that Moses made the sign with his left hand. She was confident that the intention was enough and that sometimes the left is just the same as the right.

Danny walked away from the grave with Moses on his tail. The others filed behind their unappointed leader, each with their insides gripped with sorrow yet filled with joy from the beautiful service and the love that surrounded them. This was what family was.

Napoleon and Lippatu were solemnly walking up the stairs to their house when Lippatu fell to her knees. "Napoloeon," she gasped.

Danny watched and sprinted to the bottom of the stairs, just catching Lippatu's head before it hit the concrete sidewalk. Napoleon turned to see Danny holding his girl's head in his hands.

Lippatu's eyes were open but she was having difficulty breathing. The other siblings piled out of the house and neighbors walked to the scene where Lippatu was having her Sickle Cell Disease crisis.

"Hold on, girl," Danny said, as he gently scooted the bottom of her back up so that she could sit on a stair.

"Where's it got you, honey?" Napoleon asked.

"I ache all over," she responded.

"We'll get you to the hospital," Napoleon said.

"No. We can't afford the hospital. I'll be all right." The little woman paused. "Just give me a minute."

"Did you take your Old Man Johnson pill today?" Napoleon asked.

"We ran out three days ago." Lippatu said softly.

"Why din't you tell me girl?!" Napoleon screamed, feeling more guilty than angry. Napoleon looked at the small crowd. "Robert E.!"

"Yes, sir," Napoleon's eighteen year old son answered.

"Get to Old Man Johnson. Tell him it's urgent," Napoleon said.

Robert E. jumped the banister and ran down the street. Within minutes Robert E. returned with a gray-haired man in horn-rimmed glasses. The crowd had dwindled and Old Man Johnson helped Lippatu into the house.

Napoleon looked down at Danny and nodded. "Thanks, brother."

Danny nodded in return.

Danny and Moses walked into Danny's house. Moses broke the calm. "Danny, when we goin' to Greencastle . . . Indiana?"

Danny paused a few seconds and then looked in Moses' eyes. "As soon as I get the money." He hesitated again. "Ten thousand and change," he said, more to himself than to anyone else.

"Why do we need ten thousand and change, Danny?"

"An old friend of my father's, Ralph Ponzi, lives there in Greencastle. He and my dad were in the Korean War together. He wants to move to California and stay with his nephew. He promised me that as soon as I get the ten thousand, the place is mine. He could get more, but it's a favor to my old man."

"The Korean War?" Moses looked into space for the answer. It wasn't there. "Because of the Korean War, we're going to get to live in Greencastle, Indiana?"

Danny looked at Moses. The big guy was right. If there was no Korean War, they wouldn't have the opportunity to move to Greencastle. Danny nodded solemnly.

"And you're takin' me too, Danny, to feed the chicks," Moses said earnestly.

Danny smiled tightly. "Moses," and he clasped the big man's shoulder, "you don't need to be askin' me every five minutes." Danny's smile widened. "And don't tell no one. This is our business."

Moses was quiet. Danny looked in his eyes again. "Promise?" Danny asked.

Moses looked sincerely at Danny. "I won't tell anyone, Danny. I promise."

Datisha continued school, became an accountant, married, and moved to the suburbs. Datisha's only sister, Janell, lived with another gang leader, baby daddy, who had four other baby mamas. Janell and the other baby mamas lived together as a family for the most part while the parents of the brides raised the offspring.

Always flexible, Mrs. Rawley eventually resigned herself to the situation and happily raised Janell's son Ron Carl. His brothers Mark Carl, Tyrone Carl, and Blake Carl were also welcome and often slept over at her home.

Jannell was just a normal part of life in New City and today, there are millions of baby mamas all over the hundreds of ghettos and even some of the middle- and upper-class communities all over the nation.

Mrs. Rawley was sure that knowing Danny, a true man at a young age, was an important piece of what had made a difference in Datisha's life.

To Mrs. Rawley's disappointment, Datisha didn't seem to appreciate the extended family and rarely visited New City.

Chapter 3

A Boarder

Moses didn't like sleeping by himself. He asked Danny if it would be all right for him to move upstairs with Elaine, Dude, and Danny. Dude was OK with the new arrangement, but Elaine growled and snarled when Moses got too close.

"Oh, Danny!" A yell came in from outside.

"Day-nee!" The voice persisted.

It was seven a.m. That distinctive voice belonged to his childhood friend, Pat Gatti. Danny jolted up, his smile lighting up the room. When they were seven, they shined shoes up and down 51st Street together. Later in life, Pat made it big in commodities or something to do with the stock market. Some years back, when Danny got into financial trouble, Pat paid Danny's taxes so he wouldn't get thrown out of his house. Today, between real estate taxes and fines for various building violations, Danny owed the city $130,000 or better. There wasn't a lot of hope left; he knew his days were numbered.

Danny walked out, rubbing his eyes, and found Pat smiling next to his silver Sebring convertible. As long as Danny could remember, Pat had driven a Sebring convertible; one was red, another was white, and this one, gray. They may have been a bit rusted and old but Pat, who was also a street mechanic as a kid, kept them running smoothly.

Pat had an interesting way of telling you a whole lot and nothing. Years ago, for lots of reasons, he had packed up and moved to Europe. From the way Pat talked, Danny inferred that some of the motives for Pat's departure were government investigations. Pat wasn't one to dwell on the past, and the fact that he was seasoned in government harassment only made him one of the family, and more welcome in Danny's neighborhood. There wasn't a household on Danny's block that wasn't badgered by one of the seemingly hundreds of alphabet arms of the "G" (government).

Pat was in the US to clear up a problem for his sick son, something to do with research. From time to time he stopped by Danny's, accompanied by his buddy Calhoun, and a few times by women.

Danny walked down the stairs with Moses in hot pursuit. He paused on the second-to-last step. "Pat, how's she running?" Danny asked.

"Like a charm; bought her for $1,500 three years ago and other than brakes, no major problems. The trans leaks, but it's less than a quart a month. She loses oil, but since I been putting the fifty weight in, I only go through about a quart a week. Whenever I find a sale I stock up. At least I never have to do an oil change." Pat smiled.

Even when they were kids, Pat always found the silver lining, Danny thought.

Pat looked up at Moses and nodded. Moses nodded back.

"Pat, this is Moses. He's staying with me," Danny chirpily stated.

Pat walked up the stairs and shook Moses' hand. He noticed instantly that Moses' mitt swallowed his own like a bear would a berry. Pat's fingertips barely made it out of Moses' grip into the sunlight. Moses was over forty, but Pat sensed a boyish charm. He smiled as he withdrew his hand. Moses smiled. They would be friends.

"Nice to meet you, Moses. I'm Danny's friend for a long time."

"Me, too," Moses said.

"Then that makes you my friend," Pat responded.

Pat turned to Danny. "Wanna do some work? I got to dig next to my building on 28th. We're getting water in the basement."

"Sure," Danny said, "let me get my boots on."

Moses sat down on the porch, carefully looking Pat over. Pat smiled. Moses got a good feeling. Elaine barked. She often did that when she knew Danny was leaving. The crabby old bitch was warming up to Moses, though. She'd even let him pet her last night. Moses smiled thinking about Elaine and then about Pat, who was wearing sheer blue swim trunks and beach flip-flops.

A short time later, Napoleon walked out of his house and up to his blue Toyota. Both Lyft and Uber decals were affixed to the back window. He noticed Pat and Moses and walked over.

"Hey, big guy, how we holdin' up?" Napoleon asked.

Moses scrutinized Napoleon's face. "I'm sittin', Napoleon."

"I mean, I know you're sitting." Napoleon looked contritely. "I know you miss Duchess."

Moses nodded. "Yep, I sure do. Elaine won't let me near her, only once yesterday, but this morning she growled again."

"It will take time, Moses. She'll get used to you."

Napoleon turned to Pat. "What's up Pat, my man?" Napoleon took Pat's hand and they pressed their chests together.

"All well, Napoleon. How's the tribe behaving?"

Napoleon laughed. "Well, they all think that they're the grand pooba . . . and I'm the grand pooba, but other than that, growing up sassy and smart . . . mostly sassy." Napoleon smiled. "Where's Danny?"

Mountain felt it his place to respond. "He went in to put his boots on to do some diggin'."

"Diggin'?"

"Yeah, Danny's tryin' to do all kind of work, savin' his, our money for Greencastle, Indiana." As soon as Moses let out the town name, he clammed up.

Napoleon thought he knew pretty much everything that went on in Danny's life and Danny's mind. This was a new one. Pat stood back and observed.

"Greencastle, Indiana . . ." Napoleon nodded. "They got some nice little towns in that Indiana. I like the state myself."

"Danny told me not to talk about it to no one," Moses groaned.

"I ain't no one, big man. Why, I's as close a friend as Danny got. We been thick for decades, man. Anyway, don't tell me about what Danny's gonna do in Greencastle. Tell me what *you're* gonna do when Danny goes to Greencastle."

"Why, I'm goin' with him," Moses said indignantly, "to feed the chicks." He ended the sentence as if he was willing to fight if challenged.

Napoleon studied Moses' face. "I bet you are. Danny would never leave you here. That's how that man is. There ain't a finer one in all Illinois, I'll bet in all of Indiana either. They're gonna get them a good citizen, Indiana is."

"Danny said that maybe we'll get a few pigs and grow some corn." Moses paused. "But he told me not to tell anyone."

"Tell anyone? Boy, I don't know what you're talking about," Napoleon laughed. As he turned away, he thought for a moment, looked at his car and then back at Moses and Pat. "I got to be goin', got five kids to feed. See you later, Pat, Moses."

Pat nodded as Napoleon sauntered to his car. Napoleon looked at the ground and thought about Greencastle more than about Lyft and Uber. He got into his car and beeped a farewell as he drove off.

Napoleon beeped once more as he hit the corner, focusing on the sound. The noise the horn made had changed. It hadn't been the same for some time. Napoleon searched for meaning in everything. It was time for change. The horn was telling him so.

Danny opened the door and hopped down the steps. At the sidewalk, he turned and looked at Moses. "Hold down the fort, big man."

Moses looked back solemnly and nodded. He never thought of a house as a fort. He liked playing with soldiers and stuff when he was a kid. It was kind of fun thinking of the house as a fort. It made him feel like he was in the army.

As always, Danny did the work of three men.

When Pat returned to his building a few hours later he found Danny heading out. "You done, Danny?" Pat asked.

"Yep."

"Where you goin'?"

"Leavin', got tired of waiting. I figured I'd walk home."

"It's over three miles."

"I got time."

"Hop in."

For the first two or three minutes the only sound was the Sebring, which seemed to clunk and rattle when it hit a bump, pothole, or a shadow. Pat thought about how Danny would never conform, and Danny about getting back home and taking Elaine and Dude for a run in Sherman Park.

"Tacos from 46th Street?"

"Can I get a few for Moses?"

"If you hadn't asked, I'd have insisted."

"I know you would have, brother." Danny nodded and smiled sincerely.

They stopped at the light on Archer and Lock. The telepathy between the two pals was unusually strong considering that there wasn't even a roof on the car to hold it in. Pat knew that Danny had limited time left in New City. It wasn't long ago that Pat could just write a check to help his pal. That no longer was the case, and Danny knew only too well that his time was up.

"Danny, this is the world."

"Yep," Danny nodded.

"The Mexicans are moving in by you, the hipsters and professionals aren't afraid to live with Mexicans. The neighborhood's gonna go and you'll go with it."

As the silence stretched out, Danny's face hardened, and finally he gushed, "I ain't conforming, man. I ain't livin' in the white man's world. You know, I tried it before. I've been free too long to be imprisoned again. I've got to be free."

"I know brother, I know," Pat nodded solemnly.

Silence and wisdom often travel together. They accompanied Danny and Pat all the way to *La Internacional Supermercado* on 46th and Ashland. Danny swore that they had the best tacos in the city.

The two shoeshine pals walked in and got at the end of the twenty-five-foot line leading to the cash register. Once there, Pat didn't even ask; he ordered three tongue tacos for Danny, two pepper tacos, two steak tacos, and two chicken tacos for Moses and himself.

They pulled up to Danny's house. Pat handed Danny a fifty-dollar bill. Moses was waiting like the loyal trooper he was. Pat gazed at the giant sitting solemnly on the steps.

Moses couldn't stop thinking about Danny telling him not to tell anyone about Greencastle, Indiana. He still wasn't sure how it was that he told Napoleon. It really wasn't his fault. Napoleon had tricked him. Besides that, even though he had told, Napoleon was Danny's best friend and Danny would tell Napoleon anyway, and even if Danny didn't tell, Napoleon would know they went somewhere when they were no longer there.

Pat walked up the stairs and handed Moses his three tacos.

"Thanks." Moses focused on Danny. "I held down the fort and I told Napoleon about Greencastle, Indiana," he said in a rush.

Danny was caught off guard. "You held down the fort and told who about what?"

Moses' face carried the expression of a guilt-ridden five-year-old. "Napoleon said he was your best friend and he kind of tricked me, and he'd know anyway when we are no longer here."

Danny measured the weight Moses was carrying and decided not to break his back. He looked kindly at his big friend. "That's all right, big guy, I was gonna tell him anyway."

Moses smiled like someone who had just been reprieved from a twenty-five-year prison sentence. Liberated, he began eating.

Pat looked at Danny. "I went to Greencastle a few times when I was a kid. Great town. I loved it."

Danny smiled. "I'm goin' there. My father's Korean War buddy is willing to sell me a spread for ten thousand. I'm almost halfway there."

"Whose name you gonna put it in, Danny?" Pat asked.

Wasn't it like Pat to always think of specifics? Some said that the devil was in the details. Danny thought that besides the devil, there was a pitchfork, some rusted scissors, and a broken bottle, all waiting for the working class, in the details. He'd never considered the question. "Mine, of course."

"Danny, the city will hound you for municipal violations, back taxes . . . They might even be able to take it off you."

"They can't do that when I'm out of state." He was momentarily thrown off balance. "Can they?" he asked, more scared than curious.

"Danny, the computer, RICO, and the Patriot Act have blurred the lines of freedom and decency. We're a police state." Pat stared at Danny. "Add to that most US states are insolvent. It's less desirable to be a government debtor than to be a terrorist." Pat shook his head. "Unless you're an authorized government terrorist, then they give you a badge, a uniform, and most times a gun."

Danny gazed towards the park. "Wow," he said softly, "I never thought of that. And you're right, Pat, they get their money. Hell, they got half the South Side selling drugs, all to pay their taxes and city tickets. I know people who get scripts for pain killers just so they can sell 'em. It's gotten so that the doctors are making people take urine tests to see if they're taking 'em or selling 'em. So now the people keep a few spares, in case they're called in."

Moses looked at Danny, petrified that Greencastle, Indiana, was being destroyed or at least moving further away. He was relieved when he heard Danny's voice. Danny had the solution for everything.

"I could put it in your name, Pat, the property taxes are like three hundred dollars a year. I'll scrounge that up, inside jobs and I'm gonna grow my own vegetables . . ."

"I'm going to feed the chicks," Moses interrupted.

"Danny, I'm in a world of shit myself. I almost bankrupted in 2013. Hell, I took my name off my mother's mortgage to protect her. You don't want your property in my name."

Pat's phone rang. He answered it. *Probably another girl,* Danny thought. Pat ended the conversation and smiled. "Got to go. Jesus says to love others . . ." He grinned, got halfway to the car, and turned around. "Oh yeah, Danny, here's that twenty I owe you."

Danny spent the next few days mostly sitting on the stairs, stripping copper-filled wire, removing transistors, resistors, capacitors, and diodes. While his hands operated, his mind was immersed in thoughts of Greencastle. He hadn't paid taxes in seventeen years and there were countless unpaid building code violations accumulating penalties and interest.

While the economy struggled to regain its footing, he lived the life of a free man, of a king. No one wanted the property in New City and the authorities cared little about it. He had no one to answer to. Elaine, Dude, and he had free rein over the streets and Sherman Park.

Moses sensed that it was best to leave Danny be. The big man spent most of the day walking up and down the block, back and forth and back and forth.

Danny was a wizard electrical technician. He was able to fix half the broken stuff he found in the alley. He understood amperage, voltage, and current. He knew more about ohms than most people knew about homes. A problem didn't seem to exist that was too much for him. While at the Gonzalez's house, gifting them a blender he'd found in the alley and repaired, he unclogged the kitchen sink, overhauled the toaster, rehung the shower curtain, and fixed a short in the front room hanging light.

The Gonzalezes loved Danny like he was their own son. The couple had moved from Mexico more than fifty years before and lost all three of their sons in paradise. Two were killed in gang violence and their youngest, Paul, OD'd on heroin.

They had considered returning to Mexico. But like so many who found tragedy at the end of their dream, they would feel foolish going back to a place that would have offered a better ending. Mr. Gonzalez read a *Forbes* story which reported that the US Mexican population was shrinking, and more than a million US citizens lived in Mexico. The air that filled his lungs was made of the American Dream; reality or propaganda, it worked like a drug on him and his wife, and it never stopped working.

Many like himself built emotional castles, taking patriotism to new heights. His children might not have had new shoes, but they had the largest flag on the block and spent hundreds on each year's Fourth of July barbecue and subsequent fireworks display. Some years it took the family until Christmas to repay the debt made celebrating being American.

Danny knew that the white van coming down the street meant trouble. If not for him, for someone else. The government had red light cameras, speed traps, and complex parking all over the city. In the past, they claimed that these things were to protect the public, but not even the most Puritan politicians used that line any longer. Everyone knew they were just more taxes. For the wealthy, a two-hundred-dollar fine was insignificant. For the rest of the population, a speeding ticket could eventually cost someone their license, their home, their job, or even their life.

The rich just paid the insignificant infractions, but the ticket for uncut grass was jacked up from fifty dollars to six hundred dollars. The elite had no trouble paying a service to keep their grass trim, but these penalties were bankrupting many poor families. A few terrorists had the audacity to ask, "If it's a free country and I am free, why can't I keep my grass long if I want to?"

The van pulled over next to Napoleon's house. Danny spotted his pal, the friendly city revenue agent. Danny was happy that Moses was in the house petting Dude and Elaine, the latter finally having consented.

The man approached and smiled a grin as friendly as a shark's. "Mr. Nowak, as you know, I'm Agent Burman. I am an authorized city agent."

Burman paused while looking up and down the rundown three-flat. "The city has empowered me to offer you," the agent raised his voice as if he was playing Santa, "and your tenants these alternative shelters."

Danny looked silently. After the Iraq invasion, nothing the government did surprised him. In fact, that was the single saddest event in his lifetime until August 1 of 2014 when President Obama said, "We tortured some folks." The moment Danny heard those words, a cramp hit his stomach. Danny cried as the president went on to talk about the pressure the torturers were under and then moved on to the economy as if nothing was out of the ordinary. Like the Japanese who tortured American soldiers in World War II weren't under any great pressure . . .

The man put his foot on the first step and presented the white papers to Danny.

"I don't want those, man."

"Mr. Nowak, maybe I have not been clear. You and everyone in this building," he paused, looked up to the broken window on the third floor, and continued to slither sarcastically. "This house has been condemned and for all practical purposes, is already city property."

The man put on a sincere, concerned face as he steadied himself on the banister. "Sir, soon we'll be in the heart of winter. The city has enough shelter beds to legally put you out. If you don't want to live in the shelters, you people will be living on the street."

Danny smiled, "At least winter has a heart."

A long moment passed as Danny stared at Burman. The city man took Danny's silence as an effort to intimidate him. "Mr. Nowak, no one is bigger than the government and I represent the government. We will be returning with sheriffs to put you and your tenants out. We are certainly not playing."

"I'm sure," Danny said, nodding soberly. "Me neither." He grabbed a box cutter. Burman's pupils instantly became as tiny as pinholes. He wasn't sure what to do and instinctively shifted his weight to the ball of his foot, preparing to flee.

Danny, still smiling, grabbed a hunk of wire and began stripping it.

Burman was greatly relieved and so, so, so wanted to be in control. "Mr. Nowak, the city is making every attempt to assist people like yourself. I will leave the letters on the step; there is one for each floor. You can read them at your leisure."

"If the city really cares, why don't they just leave us alone?"

The man was not prepared to talk sense with a tax delinquent perpetrator.

"I'll be offended if they touch *my* property," Danny calmly continued, still smiling and concentrating on stripping the thick wire.

The man looked from Danny to the city van. It was close enough and he had purposely violated a strict city regulation by not locking the doors. "Mr. Nowak, this is not about being offended. This is about respecting the law. Other citizens in this municipality pay their share. It's not fair to them."

Danny silently peeled a long piece of black plastic from the copper wire. It fell on a step and the box cutter was pointed at Agent Burman.

"It's my responsibility to see to it that the people in this building are shown every courtesy, and that they *don't* end up living on the streets," Burman said, pondering flight.

Danny nodded slightly and raised his eyebrows. "And they said chivalry was dead."

Burman stared, unsuccessfully attempting to make sense of the other man's words in this context. But it was insane attempting to reason with an obvious lunatic.

While Burman collected himself, a little girl pulled up on a bike. She was between him and safety. He looked at her. She stared defiantly back at him. Her body was that of an eight-year-old, but her facial expression carried an adult maturity, and a shocking hostility. Burman stared at the woman/girl and was startled by Danny's voice.

"Are you hungry, sir?" Danny volleyed.

Nervous, the fellow surmised that Danny was addressing him but instead looked to the girl, who offered no help whatsoever.

Burman turned to Danny. "Hungry? Me? No, I'm, I ate a donut, two Dunkin' Donuts and coffee."

"So you're not hungry?"

"No."

"Not even a little bit?" Danny, still smiling, hacked off a long piece of blue plastic exposing the shiny orange copper.

The conversation was relaxing the city official in a strange way. "No, not at all."

"Then get on your way, because if you leave those letters on my property, I'm going to make you eat them."

Danny was no longer smiling. Lippatu purposely moved her bike, further obstructing the path between the man and his van. Burman, never figuring that he'd be one to be intimidated by the actions of a little girl, quietly moseyed around her bike towards his vehicle. She blatantly stared at him as he opened his door.

He felt an urge to scream in her face that he wasn't afraid of her but instead, closed the door and smiled thinly. He started the motor and turned the air on full blast. As he pulled away, he glanced at his phone and sighed. Rothstein was pestering him to no end. He pressed the button to call the man he loathed, and pulled away from what he was sure was a soon-to-be construction site.

Danny and Lippatu stared as the strange "city man" drove away.

When Burman felt that he was no longer in view, he jerked the phone to his ear. He was not afraid of Rothstein, or the slumlord with a box cutter, or the little girl.

"Rothstein. I told you to stop badgering me," Burman said with a tone of authority. He had just been bullied by a crazy man and a little girl. Rothstein was definitely not getting away with the same. The van sped up towards a pigeon eating in the middle of the street. "I will get the fifty lots that I promised. I'm just leaving a site. We already have the corner and the lot next to it. You're disturbing my progress," he added curtly.

"I need to break ground next summer," Rothstein grunted.

The van sped forward but the pigeon took off. Burman grimaced. "I am not an idiot. Why do you insist on repeating the same information every time we speak?" He couldn't help but think that missing the pigeon might be a sign of bad luck.

"When you're groveling, you don't speak to me in that tone, Burman."

"Rothstein. We're on a phone and phone calls can be intercepted."

"I ain't breaking no law. I'm just saying that when you're looking for a consulting fee that the tone of your voice is much friendlier."

Burman reached a stoplight. He looked around nervously, assuring that he was completely alone. "I'm not having this conversation,

Rothstein. I will do my best, following the laws and making sure that the people in New City pay their taxes or be removed. This is my sworn duty and if anyone else is listening, I am a public servant following orders, the law, and my conscience."

"Stop being so paranoid, you weasel, and you don't have a conscience," Rothstein snapped. "Do you really think the city, state, or the FBI would be listening to one of their top tax-collecting earners? They all directly or indirectly feed their children with the money you bring in. They don't care if what you do is legal or illegal. All they care about is that you continue booting out non-tax-paying citizens and replacing them with tax-paying ones."

"Rothstein, sometimes we're too smart for our own good."

"Don't ever make the mistake of putting me in with your 'we,' dirtbag. Soon, you'll be back looking for some more of that dough that I generate by being too smart for my own good."

The verbal blows ended, as if there was an undeclared ceasefire. Rothstein continued, "I'd like to continue being generous . . ."

There was another quiet moment and Burman thought of the girl on the bike and Nowak. His thought was interrupted. "Just deliver," Rothstein continued, "and the consulting checks to your friend will continue."

Burman was gravely wounded. His facial expression and tone completely changed. "Look, Elliot," he said, showing his belly. "I will hold up my end." Burman hesitated. "I promise."

Rothstein did not respond, and Burman wasn't sure if he'd been hung up on. He set the phone down on the three undelivered letters and pulled a U-turn. Within minutes he was back in front of Danny's.

Burman rolled his passenger window down. "Hey, dirtbag."

Danny continued to attack the wire.

"Hey dirtbag. I'm talking to you." Burman felt reckless and secure. "You're a fuckin' weasel and you and your neighbors are a bunch of freeloaders! Do you know what this block will look like in two years? You and all you lowlifes will be long gone, living on the streets!" Burman laughed out loud, "Or worse, in shelters!"

Danny grabbed another piece of wire.

"You'll be sleeping under some viaduct! You and that monster living with you!"

Danny ignored him. Burman, incensed by Danny's insolence, raised the volume. "You two will have to get it on, on covers, on concrete! How romantic!"

Lippatu pulled up on her bike. Burman stared at her for a moment before continuing. "The good thing about homo couples is that they can't have offspring. I'll bet you like tryin', though! You perverted freaks!"

Danny stood up and raised his right hand. "Shoo," he said, flicking his fingers towards the street.

The city vehicle was already speeding towards Racine.

Lippatu smiled as she heard the bottom scrape as it sped over the speed bump. "That man's senseless, Dayaynny."

"Takes all kinds, honey, takes all kinds," Danny responded gently while examining her bike. "Honey, you been putting on a lot of miles. Let me tighten that chain before it falls off."

Chapter 4

Greencastle Bound; Moses Is Officially Mountain

Moses wiped the sleep out of his eyes and looked at Danny and Lippatu kneeling on the sidewalk next to the bike.

"What you doin', Danny?"

"Tightening this young lady's chain."

"Can I help?"

Danny smiled at Lippatu. "How you gonna help, big guy?"

"I could hold the bike in the air while you work," Moses said.

Lippatu smiled brightly. "I'll bet you could, with one hand, I'll bet you could."

"Who was yelling, Danny? Did I hear yelling?" Moses asked.

"Yeah, Mountain," Danny said, wondering if he should even bother Moses with such details. "It was our friend in the white van, back to pay us a visit."

"My name is Moses, Danny."

Lippatu looked up at Moses and grinned. "Yes it is," she said firmly, "but you sure is one mountain of a man." Lippatu's smile confirmed the gravity of the statement.

Moses was momentarily muddled. He looked at Lippatu and then at Danny.

"The woman's right, you sure is one mountain of a man," Danny said, laughing softly.

Mountain stared down at them, thoughts clogging up the highways of his mind. Lippatu and Danny fixed their eyes on the big man, who gradually began smiling as well.

"I sure am a big mountain of a man," Moses stated, with a new resolve. It was as if he had never before realized how big and strong he was. He shifted his shoulder blades back and put on one of those all lips, confident smiles. "I like when you call me a mountain of a man, Danny. Could you call me mountain of a man all the time, Danny?"

Danny looked to the side and then back at Moses. He didn't ever remember seeing the guy so content. He smiled. "Mountain of a man is a bit long-winded, big guy."

Moses' smile turned upside down. He began moving his feet to and fro. The thoughts on the highway smashed into each other and it was a pileup. Moses didn't even have time to begin to separate the dented and scratched ideas when he heard Danny again.

"How 'bout if we just call you Mountain for short?" Danny proposed.

Lippatu stood up and looked at the big man. "You sure are a mountain," she smiled. "I'll bet you could lift a house."

Moses peered back. "I ain't never lifted no house. I lifted a few cars." Not wanting to disappoint Lippatu, he smiled back, mustering all his determination. "I could lift a house, if I put my mind to it."

Napoleon parked his shiny blue Toyota and walked up to the mechanics. "Is it critical, doctor?"

"Nah," Danny quipped.

"Nothing serious, just the chain, Napoleon," Lippatu affirmed.

"I see. Did you get to your chores, girl?" Napoleon asked, conjuring up just about as much seriousness as he had in his whole body.

"You know I don't leave the house without doin' my chores, Napoleon. I wish we could say that about the rest of your children."

Napoleon was often lost for words with his daughter. Matching wits would be like going against a sharpshooter unarmed. "Yes, I wish we *could* say that for the rest of your brothers and sisters," he surrendered.

Happy to get onto less challenging terrain, Napoleon turned to the giant. "Hi, Moses," he said as he waved up to the big man.

Moses hesitated and then met Napoleon's gaze. "Danny calls me Mountain," he said proudly.

"He does?" Napoleon scrunched his lips together as if he was being forced to kiss the cheek of a tarantula. "Well, I call people by their baptized name. Your auntie never called you Mountain, did she?"

Moses looked at Danny's back, to Lippatu and back at Napoleon. "No," he said hesitantly, "but maybe if she'd of thought of it, she'd of called me Mountain, too."

"Maybe," Napoleon said, disinterested. He looked at the bicycle. "Danny, wanna have a barbecue tonight? I'll grab the dogs and hamburgers. We'll grill out on the sidewalk."

"Man," Danny said, "you remember what happened the last time we barbecued on the sidewalk?"

"Sure, but there's been a hundred shootings in the last few weeks. The blue boys got other things to do besides aggravating law-biding folks for barbecuin' on sidewalks nobody ever uses."

"I use the sidewalks," Lippatu snapped.

"Yes you do, little girl, and there's a law against riding bikes on the sidewalk," Napoleon said matter-of-factly.

Later that evening, a Young Thug song was playing through the computer's speakers. Robert E., Napoleon's eighteen-year-old son, was bobbing his head. His sixteen-year-old sister Shareece was braiding their fourteen-year-old sister Ray-Ray's hair. Darren, Napoleon's twelve-year-old son, was passing his telephone back and forth to eight-year-old Lippatu; they were playing chess.

The Rodriguez family arrived, bringing a few dozen tacos. Danny and Mountain were in the sprinkler. Napoleon pulled up and got out of the car with more food.

Danny and Mountain were showering under the park sprinkler.

"Hey boy, turn that rap shit off. I mean close it down!" Napolean screamed.

"Come on, Napoleon. It's Young Thug," Robert E. whined.

"All the more reason to shut him off. What the hell kind of a name is that?!" Napoleon looked towards Danny. "Hey Danny, what the hell kind of name is Young Thug for an entertainer?"

Danny stepped out of the rain. "Don't be riding those kids, Napoleon. It's their turn in the sun!" Danny yelled.

"We never had no performers named no Young Thug," Napoleon yelled.

"Yeah, we had the Pips, the Temptations, Rare Earth, Three Dog Night, the Vandellas—hey Napoleon, what's a Vandella?" Danny quipped.

Napoleon knew he shouldn't have involved Danny in the skirmish. Danny always, always aligned with the kids. Vandellas was a great name, Napoleon thought. But he kept quiet and let it go. He had a reason to mosey up to Danny this evening.

Danny approached his big friend. "Hey, big man."

Mountain had his eyes closed and moved his feet to the rapper's beat.

"Call me Mountain, Danny. I like Mountain."

"OK, Mountain, get in the house and sort yourself out. Did you forget already? After the barbecue we're going fishing in the Sherman Park Lagoon."

"No, Danny. I didn't forget. I love fishing. Uncle Rufus took me fishing when I was a boy," Mountain said.

"OK, come on then," Danny said.

Mountain opened his eyes, blinking as the sprinkler droplets entered. "OK, so we're going fishing?"

"Yeah, you said you wanted to go. Get in the house. Get on your dry britches and shirt. We'll eat something, shoot a little shit, and go fishing."

"Shoot a little shit, Danny?" Mountain instigated.

"You know what I mean. Get in the house and put your clean clothes on," Danny said, with the demeanor of a drill sergeant.

"Who's you goin' fishin' wit, Danny?" Mountain asked coyly.

"Why, you," Danny said as he squeegeed the water off his chest with the side of his hand. "You know that you're a crazy man?"

"Me who, Danny?" Mountain asked.

Danny smiled. "You," knowing what the big guy wanted to hear.

"Me who, Danny?" Mountain repeated.

"I'm going with you," Danny said flatly.

"I know that!" Mountain said, losing his patience. "But who is I?"

"Why, you know who you is," Danny volleyed like smashing a mosquito.

Mountain remained frozen, the water beading on his ginormous chest.

Danny stared. The water sprinkled them both like little blessings from the sky. He smiled widely and clasped the big man's shoulder with one hand. "You, Mountain, you're coming with me," Danny said sincerely.

Mountain grinned one of those smiles that could light a solemn night and outshine any fireworks on the Fourth of July. "Me, Mountain." He walked out of the rain and shook his nappy locks; the splattering water slapped Danny's face.

"Mountain, flick that stuff the other way, will ya? You're going to drown me."

"Danny," Moses said.

"Yes?"

"Can you tell everyone to call me Mountain?"

"Why don't you tell them?"

"'Cause if you tell them, they'll listen."

Danny put his arm around Mountain's shoulders. "Do you think your Aunt Beatrice will like us calling you Mountain? I mean you ain't no mountain, I mean not really."

Moses desperately looked around for a solution. He turned back to Danny and smiled broadly. "Well we called my auntie Beatrice Auntie Bee and she wan't no bee."

Danny nodded. They entered the house together. After ten minutes or so they joined Napoleon and his tribe. Mountain watched keenly as Danny prepared a hot dog with mustard, tomatoes, and lots of red onions.

"Don't get better than this, Danny," Napoleon said.

Danny smiled. "I love these red onions, brother, thanks for rememberin' me."

"Remeberin' you? Why, you're my homeboy. I love you. I think my kids loves ya as much as they love me. I always tell them, 'If anything happens to me, you go to Danny, he'll make sure things get right.'"

Danny smiled and looked at Mountain. "Moses, how do you want your dog?"

Moses looked at Danny without saying a word and then turned away. Danny called him Moses, and Mountain always hated onions.

Danny slapped his own forehead. "Shit, I mean Mountain. I have an announcement for everyone! Everyone, I have an announcement to make. Gather around!"

Slowly a small crowd gathered around Danny, the wise minister of New City.

Danny cleared his throat and turned his hand into a foghorn. "Ladies and germs!"

"You ain't funny, Dayaynny," Lippatu said.

"Sorry, honey," Danny looked at her, "I thought it was funny and I ain't heard nothing funnier out of your little jaw in a while."

"Robert E.! Turn that damn box off, man. Danny is got an announcement to make!" Napoleon said in a loud orator's voice.

"Aw, man," Robert E. said.

"Aw man nothing! You remember your manners, boy. You always gonna respect Danny, he, he, he's like another pappy to you all."

The box went off and there was silence, except for a distant police siren. "Ladies," Danny looked at Lippatu, "gentlemen, from now on we're going to call Moses Mountain."

Darren, Napoleon's twelve-year-old son, stared across at Danny—across because he was nearly six feet tall. "Why do we got to call him that?"

Danny rolled his eyes. "Son, it's a long story but that's the way it is. Anyone got a problem with that?"

All photos by Megan Euker

Pat and Danny in New City

Danny's house while growing up with eleven siblings

Danny's house

51st Street, where Danny and Pat shined shoes

Back of the Yards tracks where Danny, Pat, and friends played as kids

Pat's home down the street from Danny

Images of fallen police officers on the viaduct, 49th and Bishop

Images of fallen police officers on the viaduct, 49th and Loomis

Stockyards entrance

Mountain smiled shyly. Lippatu broke ranks. "Well, I been callin' this mountain of a man Moses since I looked up to a fire hydrant. If we make a mistake every now and about, Mountain don't take offense."

Mountain smiled. He was happy, it was official. "No, I won't take offense." Mountain looked at Danny and glanced at each person. "We all know that I'm Mountain, though."

"OK, Mountain," Darren said.

Ray-Ray, Napoleon's fourteen-year-old daughter, raised her hand to Mountain. He looked at her and they high-fived.

"All right! My man Mountain!" said Momo, a foxy milk chocolate friend of one of Danny's ex-wives, Janet.

Mountain smiled down at the crowd. "Danny, I take my dog just like you. I love red onions," he said with authority.

Danny distinctly remembered Mountain saying that he hated any kind of onions, a few weeks earlier. Eating a hot dog with red onions was kind of like Moses' initiation . . . family. Danny stared at Mountain and smiled wide. "Coming up, Mountain, coming up."

Napoleon's kids and their friends/fiends filled the porch (Napoleon thought a few of them were fiends). Janet and Momo went up the stairs and into the house. Danny followed them. After a few minutes, the place smelled like skunk. Danny was hoping to spend some time alone with Momo; she was smoking hot. I mean, Danny imagined that she was one of those rare women that look better without clothes.

After thirty minutes, the three of them walked back out of Danny's house. Beer cans were littering the steps. Plastic bottles of rum were being passed around. Napoleon offered Danny a beer.

"Thanks, brother," he said.

Napoleon smiled, about as wide as the Grand Canyon. "Brother, I spoke to Mountain about Greencastle. What's up with you?"

Danny looked at Napoleon's porch and then back at Napoleon. "You paid your taxes?"

"What do you mean, on Uber? Nope. I can't pay taxes with five mouths to feed, Danny. They got all those fat cats paying fifteen percent and they want me to pay forty."

"Some of them don't pay that," Danny said. "How 'bout on the house?"

"Danny, the taxes on this house are almost four hundred dollars a month. Five grand a year, man. The house ain't worth five grand," Napoleon rebutted.

"It don't matter," Danny shook his head, "the man don't give a damn." He looked across at the sprinkler. Nothing he saw changed the situation. He turned back to Napoleon. "I haven't paid either, brother. I'm being booted." Danny pursed his lips and looked at Napoleon and shook his head. "Man, they'll be coming after you too."

"Bullshit. They ain't gonna throw no family with five kids on the street, Danny," Napoleon rebutted.

"Yeah, you're right." Danny nodded. "First they'll come around with letters and brochures about missions and soup kitchens. Then they'll throw you out and the corporate-owned media will paint you as the bad guy if you do anything stupid, like not doing exactly as they suggest. They got it all locked up, homeboy."

Napoleon stared, thinking, how did things get so crazy? He knew Danny was right.

Danny put his hand on Napoleon's shoulder. "Look, man, the Mexicans are spilling over the 50th Street viaduct," he said calmly.

"I know Danny, but some of them ain't paying their taxes either," Napoleon volleyed.

Danny smiled, with one of those, I know and hate to tell you so Danny smiles. "The hipsters aren't afraid to live with Mexicans. They'll move in and the real estate values will rise. After them come the professionals, IT people, architects, lawyers, you know, and the values will skyrocket. The coffee shops and art galleries will follow and the city will not only have a steady tax income, but double it in quick time."

"Yeah, Danny, I know you know all about that real estate stuff, and then what?"

"Then the values of our houses will rise. There will be buyers at the tax sales for all of these vacant lots and homes like ours." Danny hesitated, wishing there was a way to soften the blow. He looked at the ground and then back at Napoleon. "They'll move you out, just like they're moving me out."

"I don't care, there's always a solution," Napoleon said flippantly.

Danny scanned Napoleon's face. The man seemed awfully confident.

"That's right Danny, I get it. I watched those people run to the suburbs forty years ago and now their kids are running back to get bargains. I'm not an idiot, I got it figured out and I'll land on my feet, with my family."

"That sums it up, brother. What does it have to do with your situation?" Danny asked.

"Nothing, I'm just telling you how this situation happened."

Danny smiled. "I know how it happened." He put his hands on Napoleon's shoulders and looked into his eyes. "What are you gonna do, brother?"

Napoleon hesitated and then mustered one of those faces you make when looking for a bank loan. "I got an idea, Danny."

"Yeah, great, OK," he replied, staring at Napoleon waiting for the big answer.

Napoleon fidgeted a bit, looked down, and spotted a half-eaten hot dog with ketchup and relish. "Ray-Ray! You get over here and eat that hot dog, girl."

"It ain't my hot dog, Napoleon!"

"Ketchup and relish. Don't be telling no lie," Napoleon said as he looked from the hot dog to Danny. "Can't be letting these kids waste, brother."

"What ya gonna do, Napoleon?"

Napoleon shook his head a few times before responding. "I wanna move my family with you and Mo . . ."—he corrected himself—"Mountain, to Greencastle. I'll begin stashing my cash and I'll pitch in. I can Uber in Greencastle or some of the little towns around there."

Napoleon smiled. "And the best thing is that the Hoosier state has something called Indiana Healthwise and I can get all my kids covered for a small monthly payment based on my income. It's far safer for Lippatu than Old Man Johnson, God bless his heart."

Danny thought for a moment, looked at the sprinkler and then back at Napoleon. "There's only three small bedrooms in the house."

"There ain't no back porch, front porch? Me, you, and Mo, hey man, Mo is short for Mountain."

Danny smiled and yelled over to Mountain, who was in the middle of a deep conversation with Lippatu. "Hey Mountain, Mo is short for Mountain, OK?"

"Mo is short for Mountain?" Mountain asked.

Danny waved Mountain over. He arrived and Danny cupped his ear. "Napoleon's clan is coming with us to Greencastle."

Mountain frowned. "They gonna live with us?"

"Yep," Danny nodded.

Mountain hesitated slightly. "Whose gonna feed the chicks?"

"That's your job, brother. No one's gonna take that away from you."

Mountain beamed. "It's not easy feedin' chicks, Danny, you got to remember and then be careful that they all get their share."

Danny nodded. "There's something else."

Mountain frowned.

"Cheer up, big guy," Danny put his arm around Mountain's shoulder. "No need to fret."

Mountain nodded.

"Now, if someone calls you Mo, they're calling you Mountain. I mean Mountain is a long word with eight letters. Certain mountains are over a mile high."

Mountain thought deeply. "But they won't be calling me Mo for Moses, Danny?"

"Hell no, Mountain. You're our mountain of a man. Didn't you hear me?"

"I heard, Danny." One by one, Mountain looked at a few of the family members. "As long as they're callin' me 'Mo' for Mountain, that'll be all right, but not all the time, just when they got to hurry."

Danny smiled and gave Mountain a thumbs up. He nodded to Napoleon. "I guess it could work, but if you ain't paying your taxes and I ain't paying my taxes, whose name we gonna put the house in?"

"We'll put it in Pat's name," Napoleon offered.

"Already asked. He has his own issues with the man."

Napoleon nodded. Suddenly he smiled and turned to the porch. "Robert E., you is eighteen now, ain't ya?"

Robert E. stood up. "Napoleon, don't you remember? You bought me that shirt and tie a few weeks back. That was for my eighteenth birthday party wit my boys. I was styling." He paused and put a concerned look on his face, "Hey ol' boy, memory slippin'?"

"Don't get cute, Robert E., I likes ya just the way you are," Napoleon shot back.

"Ha ha, lots of comics out of work, not a good career choice, Napoleon," Robert E. returned.

Napoleon turned to Danny. "We'll put it in Robert E.'s name."

Danny smiled.

"How much money do we need?" Napoleon asked.

"I think we'll need about thirteen to get clean. I mean, the house is ten, but we got to move and buy furniture," Danny replied.

"Shit man, we can get all the furniture we need used, out of the alleys, bring what we got," Moses tossed back.

"I've thought of that, but we'll still need three hundred for the first year's taxes, deposits for gas, electricity . . ."

"Three hundred? Danny, that's twenty-five dollars a month. I could Uber that in a couple hours. Where's the school at?"

"Not sure, but if they can't walk, the school will send a bus," Danny said.

"How close are we to the next house, partner?" Napoleon asked, trying to hide his excitement.

"I'd say at least a football field away," Danny said.

Napoleon pinched his lips and looked down. "A football field away, that's awesome Danny." Napoleon looked up at Robert E. "That don't give that boy no excuse to blast that box of his!"

"Loosen up, tiger," Robert E. said and smiled.

"What else, Danny?" Napoleon asked enthusiastically.

"What else what?"

"I mean, does it got grass, trees, birds?" Napoleon asked with the inquisitiveness of a five-year-old on Christmas Eve.

"Brother, it's in Indiana, it's on the outskirts of town, we got trees, grass, bushes, birds, deer . . ."

"Oh that venison is good eating, Danny," Napoleon interrupted.

Danny smiled. "Yes, it is, in hunting season."

"Of course, of course brother, all by the book," Napoleon said.

"And Napoleon," Danny said and stalled.

"Yes?" Napoleon blocked as well. "Damn Danny, yes? What, boy?"

"We got a pond with fish in it," Danny said gravely.

"Whoo! A pond with fish in it?" Napoleon looked all around for something big enough to contain his joy, but there was nothing in sight and all New City couldn't contain his elation.

Lippatu and Mountain stared at Napoleon. He stared back. "You two just mind your beeswax, and Ray-Ray, if you don't eat that hot dog tonight, you'll have it for breakfast, lunch, or dinner tomorrow. You ain't getting nothing else till you finish it."

Ray-Ray walked over slowly. "You didn't say nothing to Shareece."

Napoleon looked up at his sixteen-year-old daughter. "Shareece? Why should I say something to Shareece?"

"She didn't finish her hot dog either. I saw her walk into Danny's house with it and walk out without it. She gave it to Elaine or Dude," Ray-Ray pouted.

"No, I din't," Shareece rebutted.

"Yes you did," Ray-Ray sent back.

Napoleon looked at Ray-Ray. "Girl, eat your hot dog and stop your tattling."

Ray-Ray took the plate in her hand. "Ich! There's an ant on my plate."

"Don't worry, he couldn't have consumed too much. Just flick him off and eat."

Ray-Ray flicked the ant towards Shareece. It landed right on her shoulder. "Ahh! Napoleon, that tattle-taling daughter of yours threw an ant at me!"

"Flick it off and leave me alone, I'm talking to Danny about the future," Napoleon said absently.

"Wow," Robert E. said, "let me get my notebook out. The world deserves to know."

Napoleon nodded. "We'll figure things out: schools, beds, taxes." He reached his hand out to Danny. "We in, brother?"

"Yep." Danny offered a Franklin Delano Roosevelt smile. He and Napoleon were in a world of shit, but there was a path out that led to home.

There were only a few kids left on the porch when Mountain and Danny snuck away. As they walked through the grass in Sherman Park, Mountain turned to Danny. "I ain't never gonna forget to feed the chicks, Danny. As soon as I'm done with breakfast I'll be feeding them." Mountain stopped in his tracks. "Do you think they'll mind if I eat before them, Danny?"

Danny smiled and continued walking. The moon grinned brightly down on the friends. They got to the pier and walked to the end. Each of them sat with a spool in their hands.

"The moon sure is big tonight, Danny," Mountain said.

"Sure is, Mountain."

"Danny, you think the moon is this big in Greencastle, Indiana?"

"I imagine it is, Mountain."

A few moments slid by. "Danny, they got lagoons in Greencastle, Indiana?" Mountain queried.

"There's a pond right on our property," Danny said firmly.

"There is?!" Mountain gushed. "Can we go fishin' in it?"

"Hush, man, it'll be our pond. We can do what we want and can't no one stop us."

"Can't no one stop us," Mountain repeated. He turned to the side and spotted a plastic bottle floating on the water. "I'll tell Napoleon's kids not to put plastic floating bottles in the water, Danny."

Danny played a bit with his line. "Even the ones that don't float."

Mountain thought and nodded to himself. "What fish is in our pond, Danny?"

"I don't know," Danny looked down into the water. "Catfish, bullheads, maybe bluegill." He glanced at Mountain's hand. The spool was completely inside it, not a piece protruded.

"Mountain, wrap the line around your trigger finger," Danny said.

Mountain made a pistol out of his hand and looked at it. After a few moments, he wrapped the line around his finger. Before it was secured, the spool jumped out and onto the pier. Danny lurched at it, barely catching it before it would have rolled into the black lagoon.

"What is it, Danny?"

"What is it? You got a fish, that's what it is!"

"It's my fish, Danny, it's my fish. It's on my spool."

"Why, of course it is."

"If it's small, can we take it home and keep it? I can put it in a bowl and feed it."

Danny let out some line. "This ain't no goldfish bowl fish, Mountain. This is an eatin' fish. It's pullin' like a tugboat!"

"It's pulling like a tugboat!" Mountain repeated. "Can I catch it, Danny?"

"Sure, but if you pull the line tight too fast it'll snap," Danny said. "You got to pull it in gently, just like you're a gentle big mountain of a man."

"Gentle, Danny?"

"You got to play her like a lady."

"Like a lady, Danny?"

"Like a puppy."

Mountain smiled, "OK, Danny, give it to me."

Danny continued manipulating the line for a moment. He looked up at the mountain of a man before handing it to him. "Like a puppy," Danny said.

Mountain gently took the tugging spool into his hands. Danny saw the thrill in Mountain's eyes and patted him softly on the shoulder.

"It's a big 'un Danny," Mountain said.

"I'll bet it's over two pounds," Danny responded.

"We gonna eat her, Danny?"

"Let's take a look when we get her in."

Mountain moved to the edge of the pier. Within minutes he was completely at ease, letting out line, and pulling it in.

"That a boy, Mountain, let her tire herself out before pulling her in."

Danny walked off the pier. He found a stick and tied a line around it to use as a stringer. Slowly, Mountain drew the fish in. When it was about twenty feet from the pier it leapt into the air. The moon shone off its wet body as it flew towards the dark sky, a scene as beautiful as any in Wyoming or Idaho in the middle of a Chicago ghetto.

"What kind of fish is that, Danny?"

"It's a carp."

"Are they good eatin', Danny?"

"You bet your britches. You clean 'em, soak 'em in milk, and then fry them in a beer batter. Boy, you ain't eaten anything better than that."

Mountain smiled.

Danny struggled to get the hook free. The fish exploded with panicked energy and slipped through Danny's grip. Danny cornered the orange creature between his feet. "Run and get that plastic shopping bag over there!" Danny screamed.

Mountain looked towards the bag, crouched, put his hands on his knees, and darted. Within moments, he was back with a large beige

Walmart bag. Danny maneuvered the fish inside and Mountain held the plastic sack tightly as the carp wiggled and revolted.

"We're done, Mountain," Danny said.

"We're done?" Mountain asked.

"Yes, we're done fishing, the stringer I made ain't gonna hold that whopper," Danny answered.

"We gonna cook him up?" Mountain asked.

"Sure are," Danny responded. "Uh, Mountain, you mind sleepin' downstairs tonight?"

Mountain stared at Danny, not sure what to think. "Why, Danny?" He asked.

Danny smiled politely. "Momo's gonna stop by."

"Oh." Mountain nodded. The fish slammed against his leg.

"Hold on there, Miss Fish, we're gonna soak you in milk and roll you in beer batter," Danny said.

Mountain looked at Danny. "How did you know the fish was a she, Danny?" he asked innocently.

"I could tell by the way she pulled," Danny shot.

Mountain looked down at Danny, the kindest, wisest man in the whole world. "I don't mind sleeping downstairs, Danny," he said. "You gonna sleep with Momo?"

Danny didn't answer. Instead he began walking. Mountain lagged behind, holding the Walmart bag with his prized carp wiggling around inside.

If Danny had anything to do with it, Momo would spend more than a few nights in the marbled Polack's lair.

"Yep, Danny, you ain't never eaten anything better than that!" Mountain yelled ahead.

"Quiet!" Danny whispered loudly. "We don't want to announce a fish fry. We'll have half the neighborhood to feed."

They walked into the house. The fish was still flipping and flopping. It was the first time that Elaine saw a Walmart bag that moved. Dude barked. Danny went on the porch and returned to the kitchen with a hammer, a piece of wood, and a long, thick nail.

"Take her out, Mountain," Danny said.

Mountain grabbed the orange fish and held it in his hand. The fish tried to squirm, but Mountain's grip was iron. "What do you want me to do with it, Danny?"

"Put it on the board and hold it down," Danny said.

"You gonna nail it to that board, Danny?"

"Yep, that way we can clean and gut it," Danny said.

Mountain held the fish down. "She's kind of pretty, Danny," he said.

She moved one last time and Danny drove the nail right through her head. He cut behind the gills and a line along her stomach. He had cleaned hundreds of fish with his father and his brothers. Danny peeled the skin off expertly, threw the head and the guts to the dogs, poured milk in a tin bowl, and tossed the fish in.

The next morning, Danny beat three eggs and poured them into a flour and beer mix. He put the frying pan on the hot plate and Mountain watched as the hot metal began to turn red. The carp was cleaned to the bone by 10 a.m.

Mountain had the fever and wanted to fish every day. He walked out of the house early in the morning hoping to find nightcrawlers not fortunate enough to make it home. At first the worms were getting torn in half, but after a while he became an expert at coaxing them out of their holes. If Mountain found bait, they usually found an hour or two to go fishing from the Sherman Park pier.

Fall was moving in and Old Man Winter was on his tail. Mountain and Danny needed to get the money for their new home and spent the greatest amount of their time junking. They walked through the alleys with their carts all hours of the day. The house was cluttered with lamps, tables, chairs, and even mattresses—tossed-out treasures. Every few days they visited the metal collection yard on 42nd and Halsted and sold their scrap. Danny hid the stash under the blankets on Elaine's dog bed. Wasn't nobody getting under Elaine's blankets.

At night, the two grown men laid awake dreaming like children. Each had their hands propped under their heads and each stared up at the ceiling, visualizing scenes of the promised land that neither had ever seen.

"Danny, when we going to Greencastle, Indiana?"

"Go to sleep. It's almost midnight."

"C'mon Danny, when we goin' to Greencastle, Indiana?"

"Soon enough, Mountain, soon enough."

"Tell me about Greencastle, Indiana, Danny."

"Mountain, I tell you twenty times a day."

"Please, Danny, I won't ask again 'til tomorrow."

"It'll be tomorrow in twenty minutes, you big goof."

"C'mon, Danny, just tell me a little and I'll go to sleep."

"Promise?"

"Promise."

"You know a Mountain of a man ain't worth a spit unless your word is good."

Mountain stared indignantly, almost crossly. Even Danny couldn't see in the dark. After a moment, his expression changed. He was fairly certain that Danny could see in the dark. "My word is good, Danny."

"I told you not to tell no one about Greencastle and you told Napoleon."

"He tricked me, Danny. That don't count when you get tricked."

Danny stared through the dark. "We got a whole lot of money stashed in the house. You gotta keep your jaws shut about it."

"I will, Danny, I promise I will, Napoleon tricked me. It ain't proper. He said he was your friend and I was your friend . . ."

"Well, Napoleon is family," Danny interrupted, "so I'll let it pass, but when I tell you to do something, and you promise to do it, you got to do it." Danny hesitated. "Your Auntie Bee would want you to keep your promise, and it will make my life easier. You may as well get used to it now, because when we're in Greencastle, you have to listen to me. And I ain't bringing you with unless you promise to listen."

"OK, I will, Danny, I promise, I will do what you say. Please tell me about Greencastle, Indiana, and the chicks."

Danny smiled. How could one not smile at this mountain of a man who was as big as he was gentle? "Oh, all right, I'll tell you 'cause if I don't we ain't gonna get no sleep around here."

Elaine let out a single bark. "See," Danny said, "even Elaine can't sleep with you yapping."

There was a tiny lull.

"Please, Danny," Mountain implored.

Danny gently sighed. "We're going to get up in the morning, make a little coffee. You'll go out to the henhouse to get some eggs. We'll fry 'em up with onions."

"Red onions," Mountain interrupted. "I like red onions."

"We'll fry 'em up with red onions and eat them with brown bread. In those little towns you can still find good brown bread, you can see the seeds in it, not the white, processed, bleached, tasteless garbage they sell at the big supers or give away at the soup kitchens."

Mountain smiled. "I don't like that white, processed, bleached, tasteless garbage Danny. I like the brown bread, the one you can see seeds in." Mountain hesitated before continuing. "Danny, what's processed?"

"What's processed? Everything today. Them big conglomerates are poisoning us all, trying to save the sweat off a nickel."

"What will we do after breakfast, Danny?"

"Chores," Danny said. "As soon as breakfast is done, it's time to do our chores."

Danny enjoyed the anticipation-filled space Mountain made. Danny could just breathe it in and feel it tickle his stomach from the inside.

"What will my chores be, Danny?"

"Your chores, why, as soon as you're done eating, you'll feed the hens."

"And the chicks, Danny? If we don't feed the chicks, they can't become hens."

"And the chicks. When you're done feeding them, you'll hoe the garden and pull the crabgrass away from our tomato plants, zucchinis, onions."

"Red onions, Danny."

"Red onions, cucumbers, salad, green beans, and spinach," Danny bantered back.

"Do you like green beans and spinach, Danny?"

Danny fixed on the barely visible shadow of the big man. "I love green beans and spinach, Mountain."

Mountain turned to the side and frowned a little, "I love green beans and spinach too, Danny."

"Do ya? That's good, Mountain," Danny said.

"We don't have to eat them every single day, do we Danny?"

Danny's belly was tingling; he never did drugs but imagined that the feeling he got when talking to Mountain about Greencastle must have been similar. "Nah," Danny said, "we'll eat them when they're in season, everything in season."

Chapter 5

Dream of Going Home

Napoleon rolled over and looked at his phone. He had to pick up his first ride in Pilsen, a Hispanic area near the Loop which was quickly being gentrified. Gentrification now had New City in its sights. Napoleon wasn't concerned and had a bounce in his step. New City would soon be filled with hipsters and other riffraff, but he had been doing research on Greencastle, Indiana. Everything he read he liked.

Greencastle was a town of 10,500 people, had two elementary, two middle, and two high schools. It was home to DePauw University, which ranked among the top fifty liberal arts colleges in the country. Ivy Tech, also in Greencastle, was the nation's largest statewide community college with single accreditation. He wasn't sure what the term single accreditation meant, but it sounded very promising. Robert E. would find his way into one of those places.

While driving, Napoleon now preferred to daydream about his new home instead of speaking with clients. One passenger he did mingle with was a history buff. He told Napoleon how John Dillinger and his gang had escaped with $74,782.09 from the Central National Bank of Greencastle, on Monday, October 23, 1933. The robbery, a major event in Greencastle history, made Napoleon giddy. Imagine, living in the town where Dillinger made his largest haul. He wondered if he was the only guy who cheered for bank robbers.

Napoleon looked out the window at 1016 West 18th Street. He was right on time. The door opened and a suited middle-aged man with a beard and brief case entered.

"Good morning," the man said.

"Good morning, sir. O'Hare, sir?"

"Yes," the man responded.

"Would you rather I drop you off by the train? It might be quicker," Napoleon offered. He wasn't looking forward to getting stuck in traffic on the way to the airport or getting stuck in a long waiting line at the airport.

"No, that's fine. I have lots of work to do. I'm heading out to an important rally," the man said in a statesman-like way.

"Yes, sir," Napoleon replied. "What airline?"

"United." The man answered. "The rally I'm going to is important for the whole nation."

"Great, sir," Napoleon quipped in a lackluster tone. He was personally tired of rallies and demonstrations. The nation had never seemed more divided or on edge.

"Yes, the rally is particularly important for your people," the man said.

Napoleon thought that the passenger had said that he had lots of work to do. "My people?"

"Yes, your people," he repeated, in an indignant tone.

"I'm an American, sir. What are you?" Napoleon asked.

"I'm an American. I'm talking about the rallies to further remove the symbols of bigotry in the south," the man explained. "We're doing it for you."

Napoleon had driven a few hundred do-gooders who in his mind were destroying the nation. They were so intent on separating people by race, creed, sex, sexuality, opinions on abortion rights, and on and on that in Napoleon's mind they left common sense out of the equation.

As Napoleon got on the Roosevelt ramp toward the takeoff launch of this world saver, he sighed. Most Uber passengers didn't tip, so who cared? "Thank you, sir, but you ain't doing it for me," he said.

"What are you talking about? The white supremacy people are having rallies all over. What a joke, they call it a freedom of speech rally."

"Oh, and what does this have to do with me, sir?"

"Well, you're black. These people want to hold onto the past. They're against removing statues of Confederate generals and slave owners. They're against the renaming of parks, libraries, and centers with true Americans, people of tolerance."

"I see, sir. Sounds to me like they want to protect history," Napoleon jabbed.

"They want to protect history that should not be protected," the man rebuffed.

"Shouldn't all history be protected, sir?" Napoleon asked. He was still angry that they took *The Dukes of Hazzard* off television because the car used in the series had a Confederate flag on its roof.

"That's an odd question," the man said, actually wishing that he had allowed this driver to let him off at the train station.

"Sir, Auschwitz is a museum. If we begin whitewashing the truths of the past, what will be next?"

"You must be pulling my leg," the passenger said, losing his patience.

"Sir, Theodore Roosevelt wrote a letter condoning the torturing of Filipinos. God appeared to President McKinley in a dream and his administration told troops to burn civilians alive. It's estimated that between 250,000 and 1 million men, women, and children died because of the US's involvement in the Philippines. Should we take Theodore's face off Mount Rushmore? What president, even Obama or Washington, did not make mistakes that hurt folks?"

"Sir, where do you get your history from?"

"Books," Napoleon replied nonchalantly.

"So, you're telling me that you do not believe that the Confederate flag is a symbol of slavery?"

"Not to me it ain't. Growing up, one of my favorite shows was *The Dukes of Hazzard*. I never seen them make one episode about slavery and there was a flag right on the roof of their car."

"This is ridiculous. I'm taking my precious time and spending my own money to go to Boston to protect you people," the man said.

"Sir. My nephews were born and raised in Tampa. They often wear the Confederate flag on their belt buckles, hats, and clothes. To them, the Confederate flag is a symbol for the South, not the South of two hundred years ago but the South of today. You ain't protecting me. I don't give a rat's ass about the Confederate flag and do you know who my favorite American is?"

"No, but I'm sure that you'll tell me."

"Sir, Robert E. Lee did more to instill peace in our great land after the worst war in US history than anyone. He was a scholar and a gentleman. He was a family man and a peacemaker."

"If he was so great, why don't you name your son after him?"

"I did, sir."

The man coughed. Saliva went down his windpipe. "This conversation is over," he coughed. "I'm writing a letter to Uber to let them know what kind of drivers they have."

"If you wish, sir," Napoleon said, "but sir, if you really want to protect my people, why don't you protect us from the billions in subsidies going to the oil companies, or the CEOs who rake in billions and pay a lower tax rate than me? How about protecting us from the Bush tax cuts?"

Napoleon gazed into his rearview mirror. The man stared out the window. His face was red and shiny.

"That's what's really killing my people," Napoleon continued. "I don't give a damn about no flag. I need to feed my children and raise them in a safe environment with good health care and schools. They shouldn't have to put themselves into tens of thousands or even hundreds of thousands in debt to get a good education because their daddy is an Uber and Lyft driver. My baby girl has Sickle Cell Disease and I can't even afford to bring her to the hospital. Thank God for a friend who makes bootleg pills, who'd go to jail if he ever got caught."

After a long silent lull, the man spoke, "This traffic is insane. I should have taken a train."

Napoleon did not answer.

After a few minutes the man repeated. "This traffic is insane. I should have taken a train!"

The man attempted to catch Napoleon's eye in the rearview mirror. Napoleon concentrated on the road and wouldn't give the irate passenger that satisfaction. If he was going to complain to Uber about Napoleon's views, what difference did it make anyway?

After a long silence, the man looked to the side and spoke to the window. "If this is the gratitude that you people are going to show us, I want to turn around and go back home."

Napoleon took the following exit and punched the address that he had picked the guy up at back into his phone.

"Hey, what are you doing? I'll miss my flight!" the man shouted.

"I heard you say that you wanted to go back home, sir," Napoleon calmly chided.

"I said no such thing! You're purposely making me miss my flight! You're insane!" The man rebutted.

"Is that what you call anyone who doesn't buy your gospel, sir?" Napoleon asked.

"Turn this car around! I'm calling Uber now!" The man was yelling at the top of his voice.

"Sir, make up your mind: home or the airport?" Napoleon asked calmly.

"Let me out of this car! Right now! Right here! I will have you fired!" the out-of-control man screamed.

"Sir, I have five children. Is that what you'd do for me, go to a silly rally that I could care a rat's ass about and have me fired from a job that keeps my kids fed and clothed?"

"I certainly would! You swore! You said 'rat's ass!' But most critically, your opinion is dangerous for the entire nation! What kind of land would your children grow up in with idiots who think like you?"

"Probably a whole lot better than it would be with idiots that think like you," Napoleon replied patiently and nodded. "You're going to try and have me fired for the nation." Napoleon hesitated and shook his head. "That's a funny notion."

"That's exactly right!" the man screamed. "You probably think that a bakery shouldn't be forced to make a wedding cake for homosexual couples! Opinions like yours are dangerous! They must be silenced! Let me out! I'll call the police!" The man pulled his phone from his pocket and pushed buttons. "I'm calling the police!"

Napoleon pulled the car to the curb and looked at the enraged freedom warrior who glared back at him.

"Sir, I was brought up on Jesus' words. He said to love all my brothers. I think that what you all are doing is fanning the flames of division. I'm an American, but in all my years, I never heard one black person complain about the Confederate flag. I'll bet you that you'll find many who object to it being removed."

The man seemed calmer. "Are you serious?"

Napoleon smiled. "Certainly, sir. We can't selectively rewrite history. Where would it stop? We're all sinners, sir. We wouldn't have one statue, one monument, or one independent thought if every hero had to not have sinned. And who will decide which sins are important and which ones are not?"

The man stared at Napoleon. Napoleon smiled kindly, one of those disarming Danny Nowak smiles.

After more than thirty seconds, the man slowly smiled. "How long would it take us to get to the airport?"

"Forty, maybe fifty minutes," Napoleon responded

The man looked at his watch and nodded. "We have time."

"Airport, sir?" Napoleon asked politely.

The man grinned contritely, "Yes, please . . . sir."

Napoleon pulled into Terminal One. "We're here, sir, United Airlines."

The man opened the door but before stepping out he looked back. "Did you really name your son Robert E.?"

Napoleon nodded, smiled widely, and grabbed his phone, scrolling through his pictures. He turned the phone around and showed it to the reclaimed passenger. "Robert E. is my oldest. I don't appreciate his taste in music, but he's a good man," Napoleon smiled.

"Napoleon, am I pronouncing your name right?" The client asked gently.

"Sure, just like the French liberator," Napoleon nodded. "Sir, my father was a history buff. He read *everything*. I remember him telling me"—he continued, measuring each word—"Papa told us that history is written by the victors but that there is no completely just or innocent side in any war. His eyes filled with tears each time he spoke of Manifest Destiny, the decree which led to, according to my father, the greatest crime in history, against the American Indians."

The man stared in disbelief at the history lesson he was receiving.

Napoleon continued. "He believed that the dropping of the second atomic bomb was the act of savages."

The man's eyes flared but Napoleon continued, "I think Daddy's right, and excuse the expression. There is no conflict which is all black or all white."

The man's gaze remained fixed on Napoleon.

Napoleon bit his lip. "And before you get out, Papa also taught us that there is no such thing as black or white people, just people. Hell, Andrew Jackson was a wealthy slave owner and infamous Indian killer. The Cherokees called him 'Sharp Knife.' Are we going to take down all his monuments as well? Where will it all end?"

The traveler smiled. "I'll think about our conversation while on the flight to Boston."

The man stepped out, but Napoleon continued. The man turned to listen. "Do that, sir," Napoleon said, "and remember, those people protesting, they're not devils. They're just fellow Americans who happen to have a different opinion. And isn't that a pillar of our nation? People being able to express their opinion, whether we agree with it or not?"

"Napoleon, I'm going to add a ten-dollar tip for each kid . . . five is a handful."

"Thank you, sir!" Napoleon felt sure that the man would do just what he said and was anxious to get home and tell everyone about his tip. It was lunch time and there were probably ribs left in the fridge from the barbecue. He loved ribs, even if it might not be politically correct to do so.

Pulling up, Napoleon spotted the white city van. The presence of city vehicles struck terror into the hearts of most neighborhood residents, and Napoleon was no different.

In the past, the city had booted his car for unpaid parking tickets. If he didn't get the boot off, he couldn't drive for Uber. If he couldn't drive for Uber, how could he afford to pay the tickets? The Gestapo charged him for removing the boot, adding on additional fees and interest. He was on a payment plan and had to pay almost three hundred a month for the next ten months.

This was real oppression. The hell with the Confederate flag. It wasn't preventing him from earning a living. He often wondered how a country with 4 percent of the world's population and 22 percent of the world's incarcerated called itself "the land of the free."

He scanned the block and spotted Burman on Danny's porch. He parked hastily and walked over. Lippatu was already at the bottom of Danny's stairs doing what she could to aid a fellow compatriot. She was just a young girl, but she stood by her people, and Danny was just that.

Napoleon walked towards Danny's. He had half an idea to throw the city worker off the porch, but was sure that the government would figure out how to make that a taxable event.

"What are you doing here, man?" Napoleon asked in a quasi-threatening tone.

Burman continued to peer into Danny's window. Napoleon noticed that Elaine and Dude weren't barking and that the rope was tied around the doorknob. This was Danny's sign to the neighbors that he wasn't home.

The man turned in the direction of Napoleon but didn't catch a glimpse of him (it takes practice to do this). "I'm looking for Mister Nowak. This is none of your affair. Go on with your business."

"This is my affair," Napoleon said firmly. "Mr. Nowak is my brother," he added proudly.

Burman looked slightly at Napoleon, then at Lippatu, nodded, and smiled. "Sure he is. Sure he is," he said in his most patronizing tone.

"You a Christian man?" Napoleon shot back.

The man turned back towards the house door.

"If you is a Christian you're supposed to know that! You ever hear of Saint Paul?" Napoleon was pushing the throttle and happy to demonstrate his biblical knowledge in front of his daughter. "You ever hear of Saint Paul? You should have, he was a brutal tax collector, too! He found the Lord on the way to Egypt."

"Damascus," Lippatu quipped.

The man looked around and picked up a wire brush.

Napoleon looked at Lippatu. "Well, Damascus is in Egypt, smarty pants," Napoleon said defiantly.

"Syria," Lippatu said as if she was bored.

Tired of his little girl always getting the upper hand, Napoleon tried to think of something, but he drew a blank. Luckily, the man began nailing a letter to the door. Napoleon, happy to have been saved from Miss Know-It-All, returned his attention to the tax collector. "Man, Danny ain't gonna like you messin' with his stuff."

"It's not his stuff. This is city property." The man paused. "Just like your house will be shortly. Have you people ever heard the phrase 'real estate taxes?'"

"Man, get off that porch before I forget that I'm a Christian. You ever hear of the phrase 'ass whippin'?"

The man turned and smiled. "I'm finished."

"Pa, I told him that Danny and Mountain were at the park with Elaine and Dude," Lippatu said. "He don't care."

Napoleon looked curiously at his daughter then at the nuisance. "If someone bought his taxes, he got two years to redeem, Jack," Napoleon insisted, wanting to impress his young lioness offspring, who he was pretty sure had just called him Pa.

"This is different," the man retorted. He smiled broadly before continuing. "The city now has a new, expedited way of dealing with freeloaders. New City is in a development district." The man came down the stairs, turned, and took a picture of the letter nailed to the door. "Sixty days. He's got sixty days."

Burman hesitated, purposely not getting too close to Napoleon. "Things have changed. Handouts are a thing of the past. Everyone must be self-reliant," he said with an eerie air of ecstasy. "Non-producers will be dealt with. You have your ideas . . . well, I'm part of this new religion," the man said proudly.

"Yeah, what do you call yourself, a born-again atheist?" Napoleon snapped.

"Sixty days," the man repeated, beaming.

"You got about six seconds to get your skinny little ass out of here," Napoleon threatened.

Burman walked away calmly and entered his vehicle. He started the engine and pulled away. Napoleon watched the van, but suddenly his head snapped toward Lippatu. "What is that you called me?" he glared.

"When, Napoleon?"

"You know when. Just now."

"You mean when you told that man to get off Danny's porch or you'd throw him off?"

"Yep, then. What did you call me?"

Lippatu smiled silently.

"Well, I liked it." He nodded strongly.

Mountain and Danny wound their bikes through Sherman Park. Dude and Elaine stayed even with them, running along the lagoon's shoreline. The wind carried the scent of a skunk or marijuana as they approached a group of dark-skinned guys. Danny thought it was probably the latter.

"Ride on, Danny!" one of them screamed as Danny and Mountain approached.

"Clay, Bruce, Tiger, Back-step, Teeter-Totter, what's goin' on, brothers?"

"Same old, same old," Clay responded.

"What's up with you, bro? Those panchos shooting up the block over there?" Bruce asked.

"They movin' in like cockroaches," Back-step added.

"It's been quiet," Danny responded.

"Quiet? Those taco benders shoot more people than the US Marines," Bruce said, "and that's a whole lot of folks."

New City had been predominantly African-American for decades. The Mexicans were the new folks on the block. Danny tried to make it around the slippery curve. "There's some good folks comin' in," he said.

"Yeah, you been smoking, Danny?" Clay squeezed his thumb and finger together, then moved it to his pursed lips.

"Moses, you lookin' good, blood. Sorry 'bout Aunt Bee," Teeter-Totter said.

Mountain looked at Teeter-Totter. "Thanks Teeter-Totter. I think 'bout her all the time."

"I bet those spics won't give no problem to my man Moses," Clay said.

Danny noticed a bit of discomfort in Moses' demeanor. The marble rolled around for a while, then he stopped it cold. "Fellas, we call Moses Mountain now."

"Mountain?" Teeter-Totter asked. He looked Moses up and down. "Why, I say that fits." Teeter-Totter slapped Mountain's open palm and then slammed his knuckles against the big man's arm. Mountain smiled broadly.

"Mountain," the rest of the crew said one by one.

Elaine began barking wildly. Danny looked at the group. "I got to get over there and see what the girl's up to. See you guys."

"Bye, Danny, bye, Mountain," the guys said one by one.

When Mountain and Danny arrived, they found that Elaine had cornered a bullhead and refused to let him get back to the deeper water. He squirmed like Bill Clinton during the impeachment hearings, but unlike Clinton, made little progress. Every time he got close to being free, Elaine blocked him with her paw. He tried again, but she barked at him and kicked him back towards the shore.

"Let him go, girl. He ain't bothering no one," Danny said.

"Yeah, let him go, girl," Mountain said. "He ain't botherin' no one."

Danny picked up a stick and threw it. Dude darted after it, but Elaine knew what Danny was trying to do and she wasn't buying it.

"Let him go, girl," Danny repeated.

"Let him go, girl," Mountain echoed.

Danny grabbed Elaine by her mane and petted her just long enough for the bullhead to wriggle free. Elaine saw her prisoner escape and barked wildly, chasing the freed fish into the lagoon. She splashed in after it a few times before looking to the shore and barking angrily at Danny.

Danny stared back at Elaine. "What were you gonna do? You weren't gonna eat him raw! Now get out of the water and stop making a spectacle of yourself, you foolish girl."

"Maybe she wanted to take him home and put him in a fishbowl, Danny. I would have fed him," Mountain said. "Why else would she have wanted that old bullhead fish for?"

"We all want things that we don't need, and then they end up in life's garbage can," Danny said as he looked at the large tree next to him, tracing the bark all the way up to the crowning branches.

Mountain wanted to know what Danny was looking for. Even he knew that there weren't no garbage cans in trees. Mountain looked up but didn't see the answer to Danny's riddle or anything else but leaves up there.

Danny often spoke in riddles, but it only made Mountain love him more.

Elaine arrived at the shore and just to be disrespectful, shook water off her wet coat towards Danny and Mountain. Dude barked at Elaine for being so obstinate, and Danny and Mountain stepped back and away from the drops.

The four of them walked over and sat next to a large American elm. Danny made a pillow of his hands and lay down, looking up at the leaves. Mountain looked at his hands and tried to also make a pillow. When he had it figured out, he laid on his hands as well. He was proud when he could do something Danny could do.

He looked over at Danny to see if he had noticed that Mountain had figured out how to make a pillow out of his hands.

Danny didn't notice and was staring up at the leaves on the trees. Mountain spotted two squirrels playing and figured it was all right to look at them too.

After a few minutes, the squirrels vanished. Danny seemed like he was concentrating, maybe counting leaves. Mountain concentrated as well. "How many leaves you think are on this tree, Danny?"

"Lots, Mountain."

"Are there trees like this in Greencastle, Danny?"

"Mountain, there's thousands of trees in Greencastle."

"And can we lay down and count the leaves in the trees in Greencastle?"

"Mountain, we can do anything we want in Greencastle."

Mountain sat up. "I like to look at the lagoon when you talk about Greencastle. Tell me again about Greencastle, Danny."

"Why do you like looking at the lagoon, Mountain?"

"Danny, it makes me feel peace flowing all inside. Sometimes I squint a little and I can see Auntie Bee. You know what she tells me?"

The whole park was silent except for the rustling of the leaves.

"Auntie Bee says, 'Moses,'—she still calls me Moses. Do you think there's a way to tell her to call me Mountain?"

"She's an old woman. I think she'll always call you Moses."

"She says, 'Moses, you listen to Danny, he a good man and when you go to Greencastle don't let those chicks starve and you hoe the vegetable patch.'"

"Well, Mountain, if you squint and concentrate, you'll be able to see Greencastle. There's a little white house on a big piece of land. There's trees, towering tall trees for as far as a man can see."

"As far as a man can see, Danny?" Mountain said, almost too excited to speak. "Tell me more, Danny, tell me more."

"Well, Mountain, the place lays on a bed of green grass and there's hills, beautiful rolling hills flowing up and down all over the place." Danny was also excited. His tummy began fluttering. "And best of all, Mountain . . ." Danny hesitated.

Mountain jerked and looked at Danny. "And best of all Danny, and best of all . . . tell me. Tell me Danny, I'm about ready to bust."

The leaves smiled down at Danny. He saw the figure of his father's head and then his father's face smiling down.

"And best of all, there's a pond about a half block behind the house."

This was too much for Mountain to digest. He squirmed and squirted out, "And we can go fishing, Danny!" Mountain squinted at the lagoon but suddenly looked down at Danny. "But first I'll feed the chicks and hoe the vegetable garden. Ain't no weeds destroying our spinach and green beans." Mountain paused. "That we ain't gonna eat all the time."

Danny remained silent, almost afraid that the happiness building up inside would make him explode. He didn't think he'd ever felt happier.

Mountain sat up and gazed over the water, squinting and concentrating like he never had in his life. Danny was right. After almost a minute, there it was: Greencastle, Indiana.

Danny and Mountain were driving with Pat. Napoleon and his kids were following in their blue Toyota. Mountain saw the WELCOME TO GREENCASTLE sign and it was just like Danny said it was. They made their way up a beautiful, hilly, winding, treed path. It reminded Mountain of the Yellow Brick Road from his favorite film, *The Wizard of Oz.*

They arrived at the house, got out of the car, and walked in. Mountain, Danny, and Napoleon planned how they would close off the back porch and make it their bedroom. They walked off the porch towards the pond. It was beautiful. The Sherman Park Lagoon was mostly black, but their fishpond was a marbled dark blue. And other than the small ripples made by Dude and Elaine drinking at the pond edge, the water was perfectly still.

The trees began whispering lullabies and Danny, already on his bike, kicked Mountain to get him to wake out of his trance.

"Come on, man. We can't stay here all day."

Mountain startled. "Where? Greencastle? All day? Danny, the pond is blue. It ain't black like Sherman Park, Danny. It's blue and the drive is like the Yellow Brick Road, Danny. You was right! I seen it. You said 'Mountain, if you concentrate you'll see Greencastle . . . and I seen it, Greencastle, Indiana."

Danny smiled. "Come on, brother; we're still in New City, but it won't be long, brother, it won't be long." Danny shook his head.

"Danny, you call everyone brother. Why do you call me brother, Danny? Am I really your brother?"

Danny smiled broadly. "Why, you certainly are."

"And Clay and Teeter-Totter?"

"They are." Danny nodded. "We're all brothers," he said solemnly.

"But you said that they crucified the man that said we were all brothers, Danny."

Danny's smirk reeked with tenderness, something that most could never even accomplish with a smile.

"Danny, they won't crucify you, will they? I don't want them to crucify you, Danny."

"They won't," Danny said with a smile.

"Are you sure, Danny?"

"Sure I'm sure."

"How do you know, Danny?"

"I know 'cause they only crucify people who could change their world and Mountain, I can hardly change my own."

Mountain stared and Danny knew that to go further would take more time than they had, today or any other day. "Let's go. This is a Greencastle conversation," Danny said.

"A Greencastle conversation?"

"Yep, on those gray days when the chicks are fed, the chores are done, and the kids are at school, we'll have plenty of time for Greencastle conversation."

"Greencastle conversation?" Mountain asked again.

Danny nodded and winked.

Mountain looked at the pond. Greencastle had disappeared. All that was left was a plastic milk bottle floating on the surface of the water. Moses looked back at Danny somberly. "We goin' junkin' Danny? I want to get to Greencastle."

"We'll see," Danny threw back.

Dude and Elaine stood and stretched. Dude, always the lazier of the two, yawned, opening his mouth high enough to swallow a pop bottle standing upright.

Chapter 6

City Hall Clamps Down

Across town, Burman was on the hot seat in the offices of the ICD: Improved City Development Corporation. Elliott Rothstein was ICD's director and a significant shareholder. ICD was a driving force behind Mayor Redman's election. To say that ICD had clout in Chicago would be like saying that Hitler was less than kind.

An eight-by-eight-foot map of the city was at the center of Rothstein's office. When Rothstein entered, Burman was seated back to the door, with an unopened plastic bottle of water in front of him. Rothstein's secretary always brought a bottle of water for everyone. Elliott was thinking of firing her for bringing one for Burman. It was not only a waste of water but set the wrong tone.

In one motion, Rothstein entered, sat behind his desk, pushed his glasses up into position, and slammed his fist on the desk. Burman instinctively grabbed the end of his penis through his pants to prevent himself from peeing.

"You're an idiot, Burman! I'm calling the mayor right this minute! As we speak, those lots are moving up in price. The goddamn Mexicans are swarming all over Sherman Park. The biggest mass at Visitation Church on 55th Street is the Spanish mass. They've been seen shopping on 63rd Street, you idiot!"

Burman stared blankly. He had gotten his masters degree in city planning at Berkeley. Nothing he'd studied had prepared him for reality. Instead of analyzing graphs, charts, and demographics, he could have saved a few hundred thousand for his folks and a lot of time by grinding the lessons of Machiavelli's *The Prince* into his brain. US cities were now being run like corporations. It was all and only about making the fat cats richer at the expense of who cares.

"Do you have anything to say before I cancel our arrangement, call the mayor, and have you fired?" Elliott asked coolly.

Burman's pupils were larger than most eighth-grade students.

Rothstein stared and sensed insolence. "Do you have anything to say?"

"Visitation is on Garfield Boulevard," Burman said meekly.

"You fuckin' moron, Garfield Boulevard is 55th Street!" Rothstein slammed his fist down again, then moving his hand quickly enough to catch Burman's falling water bottle, smashed it against the map of Chicago.

"You said that you'd get me a thousand lots in New City. We don't even have three hundred! And now that the area is moving up, people are beginning to bid against us at the tax sales! Others are finding the resources to save their property! It's a goddamn disaster!"

Burman remained perfectly still. He did not want to end up splattered across the map.

"It cost a lot of money and favors to pass the new ordinance for City Development which pushes out the deadbeats. Now people are competing with us to take advantage of the law that we passed, that we paid for, and that we instituted . . . for us! Who the fuck do they think they are, anyway?"

"Sir . . ." Burman said.

Rothstein slammed his hand on his desk. "Don't sir me! You told me that this was a piece of cake. I told my investors. They have expectations! I gave them a Gantt Chart [a Gantt chart is a type of bar chart that illustrates a project schedule]! The goddamn chart was all based on your guarantee! And if I don't meet the expectations spelled out on the Henry fuckin' Gantt Chart, funding dries up!"

Rothstein turned, and when he faced Burman again, he smiled kindly. He spoke softly. "When funding dries up, the dominoes fall, and I don't get paid."

Rothstein smiled wider before slamming his fist on the desk again. "When I don't get paid, I'm sure as hell not paying you!"

Burman held tightly onto the head of his penis but knew that as soon as he stood up several drops would escape. The man who invented underwear was a genius.

Rothstein smiled again. "You told me that those people had no gas, no water, and no electricity."

"Many don't," Burman whimpered.

"What do you mean, many don't?" Rothstein was on Burman like an eagle on a bunny rabbit.

"Well, they don't pay their bills and the corporations no longer provide . . . but I've been told that many hot-wire the provider and rig the water and gas meters."

Rothstein was stunned. "I didn't think that they could manage that. You mean you can get around the water, gas, and electric companies? With all the computers and surveillance? Are you serious?"

Burman nodded. "Serious, I mean yes they can, seriously, yes they can."

Rothstein looked at the map on the wall. "So tell the negligent provider to get out there and cut the flow. I'd never own shares of a company that didn't protect their profits."

"Sir, many providers are concerned about sending people in those areas to do that, and quite frankly, some of the people are able to circumvent the service provider's actions within hours."

"Lawlessness . . ." Rothstein said. "This is criminal. How can they do this to us? We pay our taxes, generate value . . . Burman, have you ever heard of Machiavelli?"

Burman nodded. "Sir, I was just thinking about him a few minutes ago. I have a copy of his book *The Prince* in my city vehicle."

"Well then, you know why laws exist?" Rothstein asked with the resolve of a university philosophy scholar.

"To control the masses?" Burman offered on a silver platter.

Rothstein nodded and accepted the gift. "Perfectly stated." He gazed out the window and then returned. "Now Burman, these people we're speaking of, robbing resources are thieves, criminals. Do you agree?"

Burman nodded.

"You know how to treat criminals?"

Burman remained silent.

"Trump, our own president, ex, said to not be gentle when arresting criminals . . . Of course, the rest of the other politicians are upset because he's the first one that says what they all know to be reality. God forbid the public should comprehend the truth."

Rothstein gazed out the window and then looked back at Burman. "The solution to the problems of the world can be solved if everything is run like a for-profit corporation."

Burman stared into Rothstein's eyes. There was a meeting of the minds.

"Everything!" Rothstein yelled.

Burman wasn't going to allow his escape route to close. He nodded and smiled. "I understand perfectly."

"Do you?" Rothstein asked with the intent of a university professor teaching a masters program.

To Burman's dismay, Rothstein wasn't finished.

"Burman," Rothstein continued, "cities are just little corporations, divisions of the huge US Corp. Look at the results that centuries of trying to run nations to serve the people have produced. If you travel a few miles outside the centers of our metropolises, you're in the third world."

Burman wasn't always keen about listening to Rothstein's punishing rants but now he just stared at Rothstein; what wisdom. Burman had never met such a virile, wise, and strong person. Rothstein was his absolute idol. Burman dreamed of someday running his own corporation, his own empire, where he could command and if necessary replace non-producing employees, squash competitors, break rules without risk of prison, make huge profits without paying taxes, and become richer than his wildest dreams.

Burman felt that he already had the CEO attitude. And as a future captain of industry, he would be subject to different rules than the rest. He would have the corporate shield. He thought of the Sackler family, who some blamed for thousands of peoples' deaths. In the end, after all the tough talk of prison by the nation's top prosecutors, they paid a fine and are enjoying the profit created by killing their victims.

Rothstein interrupted Burman's pleasant thoughts. "I'm not going to tell you again, Burman. I want results. Get those homes and lots into the city's control. If the mayor doesn't have them, she can't give them to us." Rothstein smiled. "I mean, he-she can't sell them to us," Rothstein smiled even more brightly.

"Carl?" Burman asked sheepishly.

"Carl Redman! Our wires-crossed, rug-munching mayor."

Burman hadn't heard of Carla Redman being referred to as Carl, but he certainly followed the logic. Rothstein was a living god.

Burman jumped and stood at attention. "Yes, sir, I will not disappoint you." He considered saluting, but he'd never been in the military, never saluted, and was concerned that he might flub it.

On the way to the elevator, Burman nodded to himself. The four Blackwater contractors who were convicted of killing seventeen unarmed Iraqi civilians were pardoned by Trump. People like Rothstein—and himself—were just not held to the same rules as common folk. And rightfully so, there'd be little progress if they were.

Back in New City, Danny and Mountain were on their bikes and almost home. Elaine and Dude followed, stopping to sniff or be petted by a neighbor. As the crew got closer, Danny noticed Officer Brown standing on the corner. No one liked Brown, who had already warned Danny a few times about Elaine and Dude being on leashes. Harassment in the name of security.

Danny arrived and halted four or five feet from Brown. Mountain was a few steps behind Danny. "Hello, officer!" Danny smiled.

"Nowak," Brown said, pointing to Elaine and Dude, "I told you about those dogs. And this is the last time I'm telling you."

"Yes, sir," Danny said, "yes, sir."

Brown pointed to the extension cord running to Napoleon's house from Danny's house. "Now I'm also telling you about that cord. You people are going to have to learn to pay your bills like the rest of us."

Danny smiled. "I know, brother, but Napoleon's got five kids."

"Well then, he should be making a better example for them by paying his bills. Scamming the system is no example. It certainly doesn't teach children how to grow up to be productive citizens."

Danny smiled again. "He's an Uber driver, he barely makes enough to pay for his car and gas. The other day I heard his eldest, Robert E., tell his father that he had a hole in his shoes. Napoleon asked him what color they were. He responded black and Napoleon told him to do what he did when he was a kid, 'Put cardboard in 'em and wear black socks.'"

Danny smiled again; Brown did not. Brown looked at Mountain, who was standing quietly. He looked back at Danny. "You two are thick," Brown said.

Danny nodded.

"You support him?" Brown asked.

"He holds his own," Danny said.

Brown asked, "I never heard of two men being thick unless they were getting it on. You flip, Danny?"

Danny stared, desperately hoping that the peace officer could not read minds.

"Danny the king of the crack ho princesses," Brown laughed. "You been takin' a walk on the wild side? I mean, I ain't judging. Today it's easier getting ahead if a man or woman is flexible, but I never figured you . . . "

Danny smiled again. "Man, his Auntie Bee died," he interrupted, "that's all."

Brown raised his hand. "I got it, it's none of our business. In fact, now they force us to go to courses to embrace perversion. They call it diversity." Brown paused. "I preferred simpler times when they just called a cat a cat and let them eat the rats."

"You won't get no arguments out of me, Officer Brown." Danny smiled again.

Officer Brown actually admired Danny, a sly dog who mastered the art of speaking without saying anything. "Get that wire down," Brown said as he pointed to Napoleon's electric service cable (Danny's extension cord).

Danny nodded and dismounted. "Will do, right now."

Brown got into his car and drove off. Danny spent the rest of the afternoon tunneling the extension cord through his yard into Napoleon's yard, behind his gutter, and into Napoleon's home.

Later that evening Brown drove by and noticed that the extension cord was down. He had no real agenda, other than being respected every now and then. He drove to Sherman Park and opened the window. He loved air conditioning, but the breeze was cool. He watched in his rearview mirror as a car pulled up to a dealer. These people would never change, there was no use trying.

As the business transaction concluded, Brown noticed what seemed to be a city van approaching. He first thought that one of the thugs had stolen it and was surprised when it parked behind him. He was even more surprised when a skinny white man in a black sports jacket and thin mustache hopped out and approached his vehicle.

"Officer, those people behind us," the man turned sideways and pointed, "they're selling drugs."

"Really?" Brown asked sarcastically. "How do you know?"

"I saw them. The guy pulled out a packet from his pocket, gave it to the other guy, and took his money."

"Would you testify?"

"Testify?"

"Yes, will you show up in court and tell the judge, district attorney, the jury, and all their friends what you saw?"

"It's your duty, officer," Burman responded.

"Oh?" Brown quipped. "Are you wearing a wire?"

"A wire?" Burman thought for a moment; the cop meant a device to record the conversation. "Absolutely not," he replied indignantly.

"You got a camera crew in that van filming us?"

Burman hesitated and thought again, which made Brown more comfortable. If he responded to the questions too quickly, it was more than likely a setup.

"Absolutely not," Burman said in a lower voice.

"How do I know that?" the suspicious guardian of the public asked.

"Check me, look in my van."

Brown smiled, "Bub, if you're trying to uncover corruption you need to go further up. I'm just a working stiff. I have a duty to my family to stay alive. Besides, without an ironclad eyewitness, they'd be out of lockup in two, maybe three hours and I'd become their enemy. It's just not in the cards, there's no upside for me. Do you know what becoming their enemy means? Do you know that there were hundreds of police shot last year in our great nation?"

"I see," Burman nodded.

"So, what do you care if they're selling drugs and who are you anyway?" Brown asked.

"I'm Marc Burman, City Planning."

"Well, Marc Burman of City Planning. Today, most of the stuff being sold originates in the pharmaceutical companies. They're the drug dealers—pain, diet pills, opioids, anxiety, restless leg syndrome . . . The Sackler family has been blamed for hundreds of thousands of deaths and suicides by hooking people on their pills. They paid $4.5 billion in fines out of the $11 billion they made and are sponsoring art shows and programs for battered women. Don't tell me about two entrepreneurs selling drugs to make ends meet. Are you from outer space?"

Burman smiled and nodded. "I'm on City Planning. It's one thing watching people buy opioids in Walgreens. But it makes people feel unsafe watching transactions on the street without credit card machines. When people feel unsafe, they move, property value goes down. When property value goes down, the city's revenue goes down and we have a tough time meeting payroll and pensions for people like you, Officer Brown."

Burman was proud of himself. His visit with Rothstein had been a huge motivator. Tell it like it is.

Brown seemed to be thinking. He was probably thinking of the city going bankrupt, like Detroit or any of hundreds of cities, and him not receiving his pension check. He looked back at Burman. "City Planning means City Revenue; you're a tax collector! You guys are responsible for more people dealing and taking drugs than anyone. So tell me why you give a rat's ass about drug dealers?"

Burman looked back at the dealer. Another customer had arrived. He looked at Brown. "Interesting reflection. It's a free country, you can have any opinion you'd like."

Brown smiled broadly. "Ha, free, try telling that to the people who don't have the money to remove the boot off their car or enough money to pay your fines and taxes."

Burman nodded. "Again, this is a great nation because you can criticize it."

"Yeah, and as long as there's no danger that your criticism can change it, they'll let you be, otherwise you go the way of the Kennedys, Epstein, and King."

Burman began losing his patience. It was disheartening how many people digested reality and just looked the other way. "Officer Brown, I know who you are and I have a proposition."

Brown stared coldly.

Burman balked and couldn't find the words.

"Spit it out, tax collector," Brown said.

"There, there could be something in it for you."

Brown nodded. "If you want to continue this conversation, you must do something for me."

"And, and . . . what might that be?" Burman asked, interest piqued.

"Go and buy a dose from the dealer. It'll cost you ten."

"Are you insane?" Burman asked louder than he would have liked. He looked at the dealer, making sure that he had not been heard.

"Look, you could be taping me, filming me, setting me up. I'm a cop, I follow the rules and regulations. If you're not trying to entrap me then you should have no problem. If you refuse, I understand."

Burman stared at Brown.

Brown reiterated, "You need to prove that you're not setting me up. After, and only after you do that can we speak about any favor that you might need."

Burman thought of Elliott Rothstein. He turned and walked toward his van. Brown held his cell phone out the window and watched in his rearview mirror as Burman passed his van and approached the merchant. They made a transaction and Burman walked back toward Brown.

While Burman was still approaching, Brown got out of his squad, pulled his gun out, and walked towards Burman. "You're under arrest."

"What?" Burman asked in disbelief. "You told me to do it."

"And what if I told you to shoot somebody?" Brown handcuffed Burman and gently held his head down to keep him from bumping it as he eased him into the back seat.

"This is insane," Burman mumbled.

Brown got into the front of his batmobile and pulled his phone out. "Look at this."

Burman watched the video of him buying drugs. He shook his head. "I did it because you told . . ."

Brown smiled. "Relax, I'm a conservative guy," he nodded, "and eligible for pension in fifty-three and a half months." He put the phone in his shirt pocket and smiled. "The more they cut benefits, the more my colleagues collaborate with these guys. Me? It ain't my style. I got no nest egg to speak of and the crumbs I did have were taken by my divorce."

Burman stared.

"Move to the side," Brown said. Burman scooted forward and pushed his arms close to the front seat. Brown took the cuffs off.

The following day, Danny was sitting alone stripping copper wires on his porch when Officer Brown drove up and exited the police car. Brown pointed to Napoleon's roof. "Danny, I seen you got that cord down."

"My dad always said that cooperating was the best way to survive," Danny smiled.

"We all know that you're a survivor. You've been shot a few times, haven't you?"

"Truth is, the bullet went through my stomach and out the other side. It made two holes, but I was actually only shot once."

"Got it," Brown said, "what I mean to say is, the neighborhood went to the shitheads and you're still alive, now the spics are invading and you're still here."

Danny nodded and raised his hand, cupping his chin as if in deep thought. Finally he nodded. "That's one way of saying it," he replied with a smile.

"Danny, you know me to be a fair guy, right?" Brown asked.

Danny bowed his head.

"Well, my friend," Brown continued, "I know about you helping a lot of these families. You jump water meters, gas meters, hot wire the connections to Edison . . ."

Danny stared.

"Most don't really care about people scamming the cable companies, Danny." Brown smiled widely. "I mean, who cares about cable? I don't have it; they got me brainwashed with the regular channels."

Brown stared at Danny before continuing. "It's got to stop, Danny." The officer then abruptly climbed three stairs. "Did you hear me, Danny? It's got to stop."

Danny was beginning to boil. First the city tax collector, now a member of Chicago's largest gang, the Chicago Police Department, was pestering him. He continued stripping the wire.

Brown grabbed the banister with his left hand. "My old man stripped copper," Brown said, "and one of his best friends killed himself messing with the wrong wire. *Zaaaappppp.*" The whole porch moved with Brown's buzzing imitation of being electrocuted.

Elaine barked. Brown smiled. "The city wants your house, Danny. They want all the houses in New City. I mean, these shacks are worthless, but you know what I mean."

Danny stared at the wire but momentarily imagined slipping with the knife. Killing the messenger would be futile. Danny wasn't a murderer, and Brown wasn't even close to being the rottenest egg in the crate.

"In a few years, Danny," Brown continued, "these lots will be worth hundreds of thousands each."

Elaine barked again.

"You might find it hard to believe, but I seen it happen in the West Loop, in Pilsen, and it's gonna happen here. Just multiply two thousand lots by three or four hundred thousand. I mean, ain't me or you getting any of it, but the rich, the people who own the country, they always let a few crumbs fall our way."

Brown put his hand on Danny's knee. Danny looked down and then back at Brown.

"And guys like me and you, partner," Brown continued, "we live on crumbs." Brown removed his hand and stood up straight. "The area's going, Danny, and billions will be made. Billions."

Danny wouldn't have been impressed if the moron had said septillions.

"Did you see that new art store on 51st Street? It's a sign of the times." Brown put his two hands to his cheeks and moved his fingers, imitating wings. "Won't see no stairs in that store, Danny. Fairies can fly."

Danny smiled, slightly.

"I hope you ain't sore about what I said about you and your boy. I mean, I got a few cousins locked up in the Cook County jail. I mean, 'love the one you're with.' So much for all that born that way bullshit."

Danny continued to watch, his opinion of Chicago's largest gang falling by the second.

"You won't be the only one to go," Brown continued. "The whole neighborhood will be uprooted soon to make room for the hipsters.

All these empty lots will be built on. The city will erase the deficit. The politicians will get more graft from the developers and raise their own salaries and benefits. The developers will make more millions. My pension will be secure. It's called progress, Danny boy."

"Progress." Danny smiled and nodded.

"Sure, look at the area fifty-hundred North and Throop. Homes go for millions there. The city makes twenty, thirty, even fifty thousand a lot. Here we are, fifty-hundred South, the exact same distance from the Loop and the city loses money on each property."

Danny grabbed another wire. Brown continued from the pulpit. "Mayor Enoch began writing tickets for no fences, garbage, no ownership signs, tall grass. The new dyke mayor is continuing, that way he-she, whatever it is in mode to call the perverts, can squeeze the poor out to an area that's more suited for them."

Danny nodded. "Where might that be, sir?"

"Markham, Posen, those suburbs outside of the city. The US and Chicago in particular is the only place where whole areas such as New City, two or three miles from the center of town, are ghettos. The slums will be moving to Oak Brook, Oak Lawn, Elmhurst, all those tree-named, tooty-fruity areas."

"Yeah, progress." Danny smiled tightly.

"I knew you'd understand. No more helping the riffraff, Danny. You got another few months before the sheriff shows up. Don't make no waves. The city's going to get those folks' homes sooner or later. You can't save them, and helping them only prolongs their agony."

Danny nodded. "I think I get what you're saying." Danny stared at Brown with fake sincerity. "By not helping them, I'm helping them."

Brown reflected and decided that Danny was not being less than sincere.

"Danny, I don't like the situation any better than you do, but we all must realize that in our nation, the strong do what they want and the weak suffer what they must."

There was a moment of silence. Mountain pulled up on his bike with plastic bags on both sides of the handlebars.

"The little lady's home," Brown said, looking down at Mountain.

Mountain stopped at the foot of the stairs. He looked at Brown and then at Danny. "Problem, Danny?"

"No. The kind officer brought us a message and I understood loud and clear," Danny answered.

Brown nodded, walked down the stairs, and looked into the plastic bags. He nodded, "The food kitchen takes pretty good care of you guys: shrimp, pasta, coconut milk?"

"Bring the bags into the house, Mountain," Danny said.

"Mountain, is that a pet name?" Brown asked.

"Look, Officer Brown, I heard you." Danny gave the cop one of those threatening grins that only he could pull off without reproach. "Your message is clear. You wouldn't want to wear out your welcome."

"You're right, Danny, please, I don't want no beef with you." Brown's smile told Danny that he could stick his threatening grin up where the sun don't shine.

Brown continued, "As long as the message has gotten through, loud and clear." Brown offered a Snidely Whiplash smile.

"And Danny," he continued, "different strokes for different folks. I myself am waiting for them to add a 'P' onto 'LGBT' for pedophiles. I mean, where does one draw the line? People are all over the net doing dogs, pigs, horses . . . I got no beef with whatever a man does to get off."

There was a long silence. The trio took turns looking at one another in the mounting tension, as if waiting for the first to draw, in Tombstone.

Brown turned and stared at Mountain. Mountain returned the stare. "Well, get out of the way, you imbecile!" Brown yelled.

Mountain jerked the bike sideways and made room. Brown entered his squad car and pulled away.

Mountain came up onto the porch. "What did he want, Danny? What's the loud and clear message?"

"He wants us to get to Greencastle and the loud and clear message is that he and others will make living here unpleasant until we leave," Danny said, staring in the direction of the vanishing messenger.

"Well, that's good, Danny. I want to leave. I want to get to Greencastle and feed the chicks," Mountain said.

"We need more time, Mountain." Danny bit his lip. "We need more time."

"We can go out junkin' today, Danny. We made twelve dollars yesterday. I think we can make more today."

Danny nodded.

Later that day, Danny reeled the cart into the metal recycling center on 42nd and Halsted. Mountain was still outside looking for coins. Danny separated the aluminum, copper, and iron. "Ready, Joe," Danny said.

Joe walked out of the office and weighed the merchandise. "Eleven-eighty-three."

Danny nodded, took the cash, and walked out.

"I found eleven cents, Danny." Mountain had a dime and a penny in his raised hands.

"Nice job, buddy."

They arrived at home to find Bluto waiting for them. Bluto was a truck driver friend of Danny's.

"How's life, Bluto?"

"Fine as Olive Oyl," Bluto smiled. "You got anyone living in the basement flat, Danny?"

"No, why?"

"I got a boarder for you, he can pay two dollars a day."

"Two dollars?"

"Two, three. He's down on his luck. He used to drive for Marina Cartage but he had a stroke. He got no insurance. As soon as they were able, they pushed him out of rehab. He's trying to rehab himself. His kids are broker than he is. You know the story, Danny."

"Yeah, tough times to be poor," Danny said.

"The computer and all these terrorist laws . . . It's real tough. The rich rob the indigent masses all day and call it business. The executives that devise the schemes to rob them get bonuses, but if the poor rob the rich, they call it crime." Bluto focused on Danny. "He's a big boy, Danny."

"How big?"

"He'd break your toilet if he sat on it."

"No need to worry about that. We got no running water."

"Where do you shit, man?"

"I manage."

Bluto thought. Parks, alleys, dirt, bags, cans . . . "I get you, brother."

When Big Clem arrived, it was nearly impossible for him to walk through the door. He paid a twenty-dollar deposit and Danny rarely saw him after that.

A few days later, Danny was out doing a plumbing job.

The kids had returned to school and Mountain was tired of talking to Elaine and Dude. They never talked back. Danny said that eventually Mountain would understand their language, but for now it was just barking.

Mountain decided to go down to the basement and speak with Clem. He could understand Clem. Mountain knocked.

"Come in," Big Clem said.

Mountain opened the door. Big Clem was lying on the floor watching a video on his phone. "Excuse me if I don't get up," Clem said.

"No problem, Clem. No problem." Mountain smiled.

Mountain looked around and sat on the floor next to Clem.

"What brings you down here, big guy?" Clem asked.

"I don't know, I just wanted someone to talk to I guess."

"We all need someone to talk to. I need someone to talk to, but ain't many folks that like talking to fat men, at least not fat men without money."

"Oh," Mountain said gently.

"I guess there ain't many people that like talkin' to retards either."

Mountain looked confused.

"I ain't saying that you're retarded. But you ain't no Rome [I think he meant Rhodes] scholar either. Is ya?" Big Clem smiled, exposing a large space where four large or five small teeth used to reside.

"No, I ain't no Rome Scholar; at least I don't think I am, I don't even know what it is."

"Don't worry, you're not." Big Clem put his phone down and looked at Mountain. "This place is the pits, man. How do you stay here?"

"It's not too bad. I stay upstairs with Danny. We get along fine."

"Yeah, but no water, no air conditioning, no heat."

"Danny's got a big stove he cooks wood in," Mountain said earnestly.

"You burn wood, big guy, you don't cook wood. You cook food."

"Burns wood in," Mountain replied, beginning to regret his choice to visit Clem.

Clem smiled sardonically. "We's just the bottom of the barrel. But today, most people are bottom of the barrel people. Really, few live the good life. Ninety percent of us just struggle to get by, then we die."

"Me and Danny are going to live the good life," Mountain said as his stomach began to fill with butterflies.

"You is?" Big Clem smiled again. "Jus' how you gonna do that?"

"We're goin' to Greencastle, Indiana. We're gonna raise a few hogs, I'm gonna hoe the vegetables and feed the chicks."

Big Clem stared at Mountain. "They call you Mountain, and I can see why," Clem said.

Mountain stared, sensing that there was something left to the Big Clem show.

"I like you, brother," Clem said sincerely, "so I don't want to shit ya."

Mountain glared.

"Everyone says they gonna live the good life. But today, the average man can't make enough scratch to soothe his own back," Clem said. "Thirty years ago, I made fourteen dollars an hour with great benefits driving a truck. Do you know what I make today?"

Mountain shrugged, disappointed that he didn't know the answer.

"Until I got sick and in rehab, I worked for Cartmar and I made twelve dollars an hour with no benefits." Clem shook his head. "In our country, only the rich live a good life and every time that it seems that the masses are fed up and ready to do something about it, the politicians start a war or blow up some buildings to distract us. Do you know that most people still don't know that 9-11 was a hoax?"

Moses stared. He didn't know what Big Clem meant by 9-11.

"Sure, big guy, most of the morons think we killed Saddam Hussein because he orchestrated 9-11. Not Big Clem. They ain't fooling me. The government blew those towers up in New York so they could start a war, give more of the Palestinians' land to Israel and pass the Patriot Act, probably the most unpatriotic legislation ever."

Mountain couldn't wait for Big Clem to shut up. He couldn't understand him anyway. He waited for Big Clem to take a breath.

"We're gonna live the good life. Danny says so," Mountain insisted.

Big Clem smiled menacingly. Bats could have flown in and out of the breach between his lips. "Danny's a dreamer and he's pullin' your leg." Clem raised his hand. "I mean he ain't playin' ya, he probably believes it too, the poor fool."

Anger was building up inside of Mountain. He had never felt such rage.

Clem continued. "Soon the city will tear this house down and you'll be on the street or under some viaduct, or worse, in one of them city shelters where sex from a toothless woman or man costs a quarter and life even less."

Tears formed in Mountain's eyes.

"You know, big guy," Clem said, "the homeless have become so visible that they're invisible. No one's going to help them and no one's going to help you, or Danny, that dreamer friend of yours. You'll walk back and forth till you get to the morgue and then you'll both be buried and forgotten in Potter's Field."

Mountain tried to digest the encrypted sentences but suddenly his eyes turned fiery. "You're lying. My Aunt Bee told me in a dream to stay with Danny. 'He's gonna take care of you,' she said. Danny and me ain't goin to no Potter's Field! We're goin' to Greencastle,

Indiana, and I'm gonna feed the chicks and hoe the vegetable patch and fish in our very own pond where there's bluegill and catfish!"

Clem grinned slyly. "Mountain, my dear man, I dreamed of bein' skinny and havin' a million bucks." Clem waved his hand at his body and then at the squalor piled around him. "But here I is."

Mountain looked at Big Clem's body and the pile of garbage, clothes, and food containers next to Big Clem. A rat scurried from under a large styrofoam container and darted into what used to be a kitchen. Neither of them stirred more than an English gentleman stirs his tea.

Big Clem was actually enjoying himself. Misery loves company. "Dreams don't mean much, boy. They're like drugs. They feels good while it lasts, but then you wake up and it was just a lie."

Mountain looked out the dingy window and back at Clem. "I don't like how you talk, Big Clem. Danny ain't never lied to no one. Even Napoleon says that he's the best man in New City."

Clem smiled, the first pleasure he'd had in weeks. "OK, big fella, believe what you want but when the dreams turn into nightmares, remember that Big Clem was jus' tryin' to open your eyes."

Mountain walked out, regretting that he had ever entered the basement and promising himself that he'd never go there again. He sat on the porch and waited for Danny, deciding it better not to mention anything about his conversation with Big Clem. After all, he wasn't supposed to tell anyone about Greencastle, Indiana.

After a few minutes, Momo stopped by the stairs. "Hey big man," she smiled, "where's the hunter?"

Momo wasn't Mountain's favorite person. When he wasn't home a few times, she was there when he came back. A few more times Danny and her carried on until all hours of the night on Danny's bed. Mountain wasn't jealous, but Mountain got his sense of decency from Uncle Rufus and Aunt Bee and something about Momo and her situation with Danny just didn't seem proper.

"Danny?" Mountain asked, confident that the hunter she meant was Danny. "I imagine that he'll be by shortly."

Danny showed up and he and Momo went into the house together. Mountain's instincts told him to wait outside. After about an hour Momo left.

Chapter 7

The Trip Is Half the Fun

Danny and Mountain were sound asleep when they heard a screech of tires and a crash. They jumped up and threw on their clothes, walked out of the house, and down to the corner. Danny looked south and saw the smashed car sitting against a pole on Throop between 50th Place and 51st Street.

Danny ran towards the car. "Come on, Mountain, maybe someone needs help."

Danny arrived at the scene. Mountain was a few steps behind him. The car was turned on its side and André Baracca was hanging out of the driver's door, bleeding from the head. André was without a doubt the highest-volume drug dealer in New City.

Danny knelt down next to the body. He wasn't quite sure if André was still alive. He solemnly pressed two fingers to Andre's neck to feel for a pulse.

Danny was prodding when André's eyes opened wide. "Danny, Danny, get me out of here," Baracca said.

"Are you hurt?" Danny asked.

"I don't think so. I don't know," André said in a low subhuman voice.

The street was covered in glass. André placed his two hands on the shiny diamond-like speckles, piercing the skin on both of his hands as he tried to push himself upright. He grunted and pushed. Mountain saw red flowing from beneath André's hands.

Danny and Mountain watched. André pushed again with all his might. He looked at Danny. "My leg's stuck. I can't get it out."

Danny reached in and was trying to free André's leg when two young guys approached the car. Mountain watched as one of them pulled a gun from his waist.

"Danny!" Mountain screamed.

Danny turned and looked at the guy holding the gun and his partner. He didn't flinch. "Cesar, Juan," he said, "help me get André's leg free."

"You know who Baracca is, Danny, he's responsible for more dead kids in New City than the police and gangs put together," Juan said.

Danny turned back. "Juan, put the gun away. Your mother has enough heartache."

"Danny, I'm gonna finish this guy off; someone should have done it years ago," Juan responded.

"You're doin' no such thing, little man, now put the gun away. I can understand you not wanting to help him, but killing him's something else."

"Get out of the way, Danny. It's his turn to pay for the tears of my family and the other families who lost cousins, sons, daughters to his greed," Juan said as he raised the gun to fire.

Danny let go of André's leg and stood up. André groaned.

"Cesar, take your cousin home," Danny said.

"Danny, Juan's right," Cesar said. "We can get rid of this shit and begin cleaning the neighborhood up once and for all," he insisted. "Nobody will miss him, and we can save the agony that his kind brings to others."

Now pointing the gun at Danny, Juan spoke somberly. "Get out of the way, Danny."

The blood in Mountain's veins began to curdle. "Juan, don't point no gun at Danny. He didn't do nothing," the big man said.

"Shut up, Moses. You don't have anything to do with this shit here, so just shut up," Cesar said firmly. "You're from the other side of the boulevard."

Mountain studied the situation and looked at Danny when Juan spoke. "Danny, the cops will get here soon. Get out of the way," Juan said.

"Juan, you'll ruin your whole life. Leave well enough alone."

Juan moved around Danny and pointed the gun at André.

"Danny, Danny," André gasped, "save me, Danny."

Cesar moved around Danny's other side and stared down at André. "Shut the fuck up, you punk, before I kick the shit out of you."

Danny stepped aside. Juan now had a clean shot if he chose.

"No, Danny!" André screamed. "You can't let him do this. I'm . . . I'm unarmed. At least give me the gun out of the glove compartment so I have a chance!"

Danny stepped toward Juan. "Give me the gun, little man."

"Danny, I'll shoot, I swear I will," Juan repeated.

"Like hell you will. It'd break your mother's heart. Give me the gun." Danny extended his hand to Juan, palm up.

"Danny, I ain't playin'." Juan's hand was trembling slightly.

Danny saw Mountain's shoe moving in the corner of his eye. "Stand back, Mountain! This is going to be all right. These are good men."

It would be the first time in André's life that he wanted to see a police car.

"Danny," Juan said. "I'm serious."

"I know you are, little man, but let's use our heads here," Danny said.

Cesar bore a quizzical expression, trying to figure out what Danny had on his mind.

Danny continued. "We got to concentrate on gain, not pain."

"Is that some phrase out of some nineteen-something playbook, Danny? It don't work like that today," Juan said.

Juan pointed the gun at André's temple.

Danny's voice distracted him again. "How can we make this situation work to our advantage?" Danny asked himself more than anyone else.

Everyone including André was wondering what the gringo was thinking.

"One less dealer is gain, Danny," Juan said.

Danny nodded. "Yeah, you're right, but there's witnesses. Me, Moses . . ." Danny looked at Mountain. "Sorry, Mountain."

Mountain nodded. "Tell them Danny, I'm Mountain."

Cesar, André, and Juan looked at Danny and then at Mountain.

"I'll explain later," Danny said as if he was addressing a Little League baseball team. He looked at Juan and then at Cesar. "You prepared to kill us, too?" Danny asked.

"I ain't gonna kill you, Danny. You'd never squeal anyway."

"And Mountain?" Danny jerked his head in Mountain's direction.

"Big man ain't gonna squeal."

"What about the neighbors that might be hidden, watching us from behind their curtains, the kids recording this on their phones. You gonna kill them?"

Cesar nodded. "He's right, Juan."

"Give me the gun," Danny said.

Juan backed off.

Danny put his hand out. "Trust me, little man, we're going to turn pain to gain."

While Juan was rethinking the nineteen hundred and something phrase Danny took the gun out of his hand, stepped to André, knelt next to him, cocked the hammer, and pressed the barrel against André's forehead.

Mountain was beaming inside but remained solemn. He'd never seen Danny move so suavely. Danny did it all before Juan realized he didn't have the gun anymore.

"Danny! Danny!" André cried.

"André, I'm an old guy. I don't mind going away." Danny looked at Juan and Cesar, and winked at Mountain. "Juan's right, you cost a lot of lives, anguish, tears, and fears." Danny looked back at André. "It rhymes, but I didn't do it on purpose. Just like if my finger slips, I didn't do that on purpose. I took the gun off of you and was waiting for the police when, pow!"

André flinched and reached for his chest. "Danny, Danny," André gasped. "I'm having a heart attack."

André pulled his hand away from his breast pocket. He was now holding a .22. Danny batted the gun away and slapped Andre with the open palm of his other hand like a porch rocking chair on a Sunday afternoon.

"You're a fool, André," Danny said.

"Do it, Danny. Do it!" Juan shouted. "Before the cops come."

André began to cry. "Danny, I'll do anything. Please don't make my children fatherless."

Danny pressed the gun harder against André's forehead. "I wish I thought you meant that."

"I do. I do mean it!"

"Anything?" Danny queried.

"Anything. I swear on my kids, all my kids' lives!"

Danny removed the gun from André's forehead and looked him in the eyes.

"Will you stop dealing in New City?"

André hesitated. "Danny, it's my living."

Danny put the pistol back to his forehead.

"I swear! I swear!" André cried.

"I don't believe you," Danny said softly.

"I swear on the Madonna, the Pope, all the saints!"

"What guarantee can you give me?" Danny asked calmly.

"Guarantee? What guarantee?" André, happy to be still alive, gave a slight grin. "Danny, you're not buying a fucking car."

André and Danny both knew the longer they stalled the more likely it was that the police would arrive. That would be good for André but no one else. André owned most of the police.

"Ice him and get it over with," Cesar said, "shit like him could never be trusted and don't deserve to live."

"Juan, do you have your phone?" Danny said as he unzipped his pants.

"My phone?" Juan asked, staring and thinking how bizarre it was that Danny was unzipping his pants. "Sure man, I always have my phone."

"OK. Come closer. You're going to take a picture of me and André. Cut the accident and the car out so that you can't tell where we're at."

André looked at Danny, "I'm not going to do that, man," he said.

Danny pointed the gun at Andre.' "You don't have to. You can die." Danny smiled in that profound way that only he could smile. André fell silent.

Danny had his dick in one hand and the gun in the other. He stuck his dick close to André's mouth. "Open up or I swear I'll shoot you right in the melon."

He turned to Juan. "Hurry and take that picture, I'm sure that I'll enjoy this less than he will."

"Open your mouth, André," Danny said calmly, "Open it up or I swear."

André opened his mouth and Danny pushed in. Juan snapped the picture. Cesar snickered.

"Oh my God Danny!" Juan said. "You're a fucking genius."

Danny stood up. "Now, André, if we ever hear of you selling in New City again, this picture's goin' up on the net. Got it?"

André's face hardened and angered as he spit several times onto the street.

"Got it, André?" Danny asked again.

André nodded, his head moving so slightly that if you weren't watching him closely, you might have missed it.

Danny turned. "Juan, give me the phone."

Juan handed him the phone and Danny pressed some numbers and buttons. When he gave it back to Juan the picture was erased.

"What'd you do with the picture Danny?" Juan asked.

"I forwarded it to a friend," Danny said. He then turned to André. "Now, André, if anything should happen to Cesar, Juan, or me—a drive-by shooting, a hit-and-run accident, if we're killed in a tornado, the picture will be published. Do you understand that?"

André, a bit relieved that Juan and Cesar didn't have access to the picture, nodded again.

Danny looked at Cesar, Mountain, and Juan, "Now help me get this guy's leg unstuck."

Danny stuck the gun in his pocket and kneeled next to André.

Juan and Cesar stooped down. "Thanks, Danny," Juan said.

Danny reached towards the bottom of André's leg. It was caught in between the seat and the dashboard. André moaned as Danny pushed the bottom of his foot and pulled his leg at the same time. Then André was free.

"Cesar, go get André's piece," Danny said, pointing to the gun laying on the street.

Cesar handed the small weapon to Danny.

"Thanks," Danny said. "Juan, I'm holding onto these."

Juan remained silent.

"Call 9-1-1," Danny said.

Juan followed instructions. After five minutes the fire truck sirens were heard.

Danny turned to André. "Remember the old saying, my friend, pictures say a thousand words." Danny smiled that sarcastic yet gentle smile that only he could pull off.

"I *promise*," Danny said, "if anything happens to any of us here or if we hear that you're dealing in New City, my friend will blast your coming-out poster all over social media."

The fire truck pulled up and two men lowered a stretcher from the back of the cab.

Danny watched them for a moment and then turned back to André. He looked solemnly into the injured man's eyes. "André, you've lived here a long time." Danny smiled gently before continuing. "Long enough to know that I don't break my promises."

Later that morning, Mountain and Danny laid on their backs in Danny's apartment. Light was sneaking through the small slits left by the newspaper taped to the windows.

Mountain was still trying to understand all of the moving parts to do with André's accident. He wasn't crazy about complexity.

"Danny, are we ever goin' to Greencastle, Indiana?"

"What?"

"Are we going to Greencastle, Indiana?"

"Sure we are," Danny said, slightly irritated.

"Are you a dreamer, Danny?"

Danny hesitated, "I don't know. I guess I am. I guess we all are."

"Why didn't you kill André, Danny?"

Silence gave way to consideration and then Danny sat up. "Because I'm a dreamer." Danny stared at Mountain's large, dark shadow. "Big man," he continued, "there's good in every one of us. The coldest criminal has warm spots."

Mountain loved when Danny conversed with him. It gave him a good feeling, like he was a regular person, worthy of consideration. And Mountain understood Danny, mostly . . . but a lot of the time he had to investigate, like now. "What do you mean warm spots, Danny?"

"Do you remember Hatchet Hank?"

"Sure, Danny. He killed his cousin and two of his cousin's friends with a hatchet."

"Actually, it was an ax, but I guess folks thought that Hatchet Hank sounded better than Ax Hank," Danny said. "But that's beside the point."

"Ax Hank," Mountain mumbled. "Hatchet Hank," he said to himself and nodded.

"Can I continue?" Danny asked.

"Sure." Mountain smiled. He knew that Danny couldn't see it, but he liked smiling anyway, especially at Danny.

"Two years earlier, I helped him put Red down. Do you remember Red?"

"Red was Hatchet's pit bull. I used to see 'em in the park all the time. Auntie Bee said to stay away from pit bulls. They can't be trusted. It's their nature, she said. It ain't their fault but she told me to stay away from them."

"Well, Hank knew that Red was suffering, so he done what was right and when I was giving Red the heroin into his veins, Hank, who hadn't killed his cousin and his cousin's friend yet, cried like a little baby boy. He knew it had to be done but he cried and cried and he didn't speak to no one, no one at all, for four months."

"Auntie Bee said that Hatchet Hank was a murderer," Mountain offered.

"We're all capable of murdering, big man!"

Mountain wasn't sleepy anymore.

"Some murderers are authorized by the government. You know what they're called?"

"No, I mean, the government . . ." Mountain fumbled the thought around in his head.

"Soldiers," Danny said.

"Soldiers?" Mountain queried.

"Soldiers."

Mountain stared at Danny's shadow, floundering. "Danny, I-I remember seeing Hatchet Hank staring at the Sherman Park lagoon. He'd sit there for hours. I hid behind a tree a few times to watch him. I wanted to know what he was staring at," Mountain said. "I looked in the direction he was looking. I thought maybe he spotted a turtle on top of the water. You know, one of those turtles that come up to the top and look at you like they know just what you're thinking."

Mountain looked to the wall, seeing one of those tortoises in the darkness. "I never seen no turtle. I never seen nothing he was staring at. Danny, what do you think he was staring at?"

Mountain stopped speaking and the silent room shook as Danny snapped up and began doing sit-ups.

Mountain recovered from the jolt and watched Danny going up and down, up and down.

"What was he staring at, Danny?" Mountain asked, "In the Sherman Park lagoon?"

"I'm not sure. I know he loved watching Red playing in the pond, chasing ducks and bullheads." Danny shook his head and smiled. "Boy, I never seen a dog with that much puppy in him."

Mountain smiled, remembering Red. He was a pit bull but he was like Danny said, an eternal puppy. Finally, Mountain concentrated, pursing his lips and raising his hand to his mouth like he had discovered the hydrogen bomb or something. "But sometimes I watched for hours," Mountain lobbed, "and I couldn't see Red," he finished emphatically.

"That's because Red was a part of Hank!" Danny said, jumping up. "Red was a piece of him!"

Mountain reflected before speaking. "So if Red was a part of Hatchet Hank, why did he let you kill him?"

Danny stared at Mountain. "That was his warm spot! He loved Red so much that he let me put him down! Because that's what love is, big man—sacrificing yourself, no matter how painful it is so that the other person will be better off. He loved Red so much that he let me put him down. He let me put him down even though it killed a piece of him for me to do so."

Mountain stared at Danny. "But when you put him down, Danny, Red was dead?"

"Mountain, if my life was going to be full of pain and misery, I'd want someone to put me down."

Mountain concentrated. Tears came to the big man's eyes as if he had some sort of mysterious experience, some sort of premonition. "Me too, Danny, me too. I like livin' like we live, Danny. We're free, we work when we want and we eat when we want. We shower when we want and we talk when we want."

Danny stared at Mountain's shadowy bulk. He had never been prouder of his student-teacher.

"Danny, if my life was going to be full of pain and misery, I'd like someone to put me down too."

Danny smiled. "Get up, big man. No one's putting no one down. We're going junkin'."

Mountain turned abruptly. The light shone on his brown face. Stubble had attacked his upper neck and chin, but his cheek and the pasture under his nose were barren.

"Danny, is Momo coming to Greencastle, Indiana?" Mountain asked.

Danny looked at Mountain, fascinated. "What? Momo? Nah, Greencastle ain't for Momo."

"But my Auntie Bee told me that she slept with Uncle Rufus because she loved him." Mountain swiped the reverence from some make-believe snowy, eagle-filled sky. "You sleep with Momo cause you love her, Danny?"

"What?" Danny squirmed. "Cause I love her? What are you all of the sudden, a Cupid copper?"

Danny tried to look angry, but that wasn't an easy feat when he was confused; and it wasn't easy to confuse Danny. Suddenly he heard the room's silence. The silence instigated him and pushed him to the limit of his limitless patience. "Get yourself together! We're going junkin'!" he yelled.

Mountain fed Elaine and Dude and joined Danny outside. The sun was still orange and the air was as crisp as one of those long salted pretzels. The park sprinkler was still on but wouldn't be for much longer. The kids were back at school and the heat was surrendering, day by day, losing its grip on New City.

Napoleon smiled widely at Danny each time they passed or saw one another. Time was moving quickly, and they needed to strategize as the time to Greencastle was shortening.

For now, Danny was going junkin' and junkin' was an art. One had to know what to take and what to leave, the price of each piece of scrap and where to take it. Many people recycled paper and plastic. Danny was a metal man. He collected cast iron, copper, lead, aluminum, and even accessories like VCRs, old smoke detectors, TVs, cameras, and printers which contained gold.

Danny always went to Joe on 42nd to do his business because Joe knew his stuff and was one of the only guys who paid for old appliances. Some places might have him beat by a few cents from time to time, but Joe was on top of things and luckily for Danny, he was close to New City.

Danny and Mountain each pulled a cart. Danny had made them years ago and each one could handle a few hundred pounds. They began on 28th Street in the Bridgeport neighborhood.

"Why don't we go further Danny, like to 18th Street?"

"Cause that's Chinatown."

"So?"

"The Chinese don't throw anything away."

"Oh."

Between 28th and 29th, Mountain looked up and read, No Garbage Picking. He pointed the sign out to Danny.

"Don't worry, we just need to make sure that we don't leave a mess."

Mountain rummaged through a pile of clothes.

"Leave it alone, big man, you ain't gonna find nothing worthwhile in there."

Mountain continued, grabbed a small box and shook it. It rattled. Danny thought that he recognized the sound.

"What you got there, Mountain?"

"Don't know." Mountain shook the box again. "A box."

Danny took the container out of Mountain's hands and opened it. Danny's eyes lit up. "Mountain! Mountain! You hit gold! This is brass! We'll get a buck-fifty a pound!"

Danny held the treasure chest straight out in front of him and raised and lowered it slowly. "This is twelve to fifteen smackers, big guy."

Mountain wasn't going to let this opportunity pass. "You told me to get out of there and that I wasn't goin' to find anything worthwhile. Didn't you, Danny?"

"Well, usually . . ."

Mountain didn't let Danny finish. "But I did, didn't I, Danny?"

"You did."

"Did I do good, Danny?"

"No."

Mountain's glare revealed his concern. "No?"

"No, Mountain, you did great!"

Mountain smiled proudly. "I did great," he mumbled.

By the time they got to 31st Street, their carts were already half full. Danny pulled into the alley between the CVS and the Subway sandwich shop. "Wait here. I'll be right back."

The line in Dunkin' Donuts was no longer than normal but Danny tapped his foot nervously. They had hit the motherlode this morning. Danny wanted to show Mountain his appreciation and reward him, but he also knew that other junkers were out and about and not real scrupulous. Some had no problem robbing other junkers.

While waiting, Danny remembered when five guys had tried to jump Pat and him for their shoeshine money. They gave up the cash, but when the boys wanted to steal their shine boxes, they drew the line. Danny and Pat walloped them and sent them running.

"Sir?"

Danny snapped to, out of his reminiscences. "Sorry, two coffees with two creams, two sugars, and two chocolate long johns."

Danny took the perks and stuffed the change in his pocket. He walked out the door in a Greencastle sort of mind.

Danny got to the alley. There was a crowd and in the middle of it, Mountain was stooped over and a guy was hitting him in the back with one of the aluminum planks from the cart.

"Hey, stop it!" Danny screamed as he grabbed the guy and took the weapon from him. The crowd multiplied.

The guy clutched Danny's collar. "He's killing my friend!" he yelled.

Danny looked at Mountain's back and sure enough, what Danny hadn't noticed was that there was a man under Mountain and Mountain had the guy's face in his hand.

"Mountain! Let him go! Mountain!"

Mountain heard Danny but wasn't sure what to do. Danny tugged hard and looked in the big man's face. "Mountain."

"Danny," Mountain mumbled. "They was tryin' to steal our motherlode. I told them that we needed it for Greencastle . . . Indiana. I yelled, 'Danny!'" Mountain screamed. "Where were you, Danny?"

"OK, calm down. I'm here now. Now, let the guy's face go."

Mountain looked down at his hand. The man's face was completely swallowed within it. Mountain slowly let go. The man gasped, coughed, and spit out two teeth. His nose was badly broken and bent to the right side of his face.

Mountain stood. "I didn't want them to take our motherlode, Danny. We need it for Greencastle . . . Indiana. I told them, Danny. I told them. They didn't listen." Mountain looked through Danny in a trance. "I called you and you didn't answer."

Danny helped the injured man up. He recognized him as one of the guys who slept under the Cermak viaduct. Poverty, the mother of crime.

The spectators moved on, the culprits split, and Danny and Mountain pushed the merchandise to the middle of the block. One of the coffees had spilled. Danny and Mountain split the other one and ate the long johns. When they were finished, Danny squished the cup and put it in the paper bag, opened a garbage can lid, and tossed it in.

Mountain was still not sure if he was in trouble or not. He looked at Danny with cocker spaniel eyes. "I called you and you din't answer, Danny."

"I know, I'm sorry. It's not your fault. The guy had it coming."

"He did have it coming, din't he, Danny?"

"That's what I said. Now let's get going," Danny said.

It was the biggest haul in years. Joey wrote Danny a check for seventy-three dollars and eighty-five cents. Danny walked into the currency exchange on 46th and Halsted, cashed his check, and walked out. He and Mountain pushed the carts back to the house. Pat was sitting on Danny's porch strumming a guitar.

"Pat!" Danny yelled. "How you doin', brother?"

Pat nodded and continued to strum. Pat never played anything that Danny ever heard of. Danny wasn't sure if they were songs or just stuff Pat picked out of his mind. Some of it wasn't half bad.

"I go to New York tomorrow," Pat said.

"How's the basement holding?"

"All well," Pat replied.

"How you doin', buddy?" Pat looked up to Mountain.

"I'm Mountain."

"You ain't kiddin', I remember you," Pat said.

Danny smiled at Mountain. That must have meant that it was good. Mountain smiled at Pat.

"How'd you hit 'em today, Danny?" Pat asked.

"Biggest haul in a long time . . . Seventy, even after the currency exchange."

"Nice, nice. Still going to Greencastle?"

"You bet I am, that's my plan."

Mountain's stare hit Danny right in the chest. "That's *our* plan," Danny continued. "Mountain found a box of brass. Must've been some leftovers from a plumbing job. The owner pitched 'em."

"Nice," Pat said just as his phone rang. He smiled at Danny and Mountain and answered. "Sure, honey, on my way."

Guitar in hand, Pat stood up. He reached into his pocket and pulled a twenty from a small roll of bills. "Here's that twenty I owe you, brother."

Danny smiled. "I was gonna remind you, but you know . . ."

Pat laid the guitar in the back seat, got in, waved, and drove off.

Mountain turned to Danny. "How many times is he going to pay you that twenty he owes you?"

Danny smiled and clasped Mountain's shoulder. "Brother," Danny said, "being brothers is a lifetime commitment. Let's get something to eat and jump in the sprinkler."

Elaine and Dude jumped all over Mountain and Danny as they entered the house. They weren't inside five minutes when Danny heard someone call his name. He opened the door to find Mr. Gonzalez at the foot of the stairs.

"Good evening, Danny," Mr. Gonzalez said in his warm Mexican accent.

"Good evening, Mr. Gonzalez, how are you today, sir?"

"Not good, Danny. Today we got tickets in the mail for grass and garbage and something about not having our names on the house as managers. The grass isn't that tall but they said ten centimeters. How tall is that, Danny?"

Danny shook his head. "I don't know, Mr. Gonzalez, around four inches, I think."

"Some kid must have thrown a bottle on the lawn, Danny. Is a bottle on the lawn considered trash?" the seventy-seven-year-old man asked.

"When they want your property, it is," Danny scoffed.

"When they want my property. Who wants my property, Danny?" The old man sounded panic-stricken.

Danny shook his head, regretting his last statement.

"Danny, they want a sign with my name on the wall! I have my name on the mailbox. My nephew, he take the pictures. My nephew take pictures of the grass, of the clean yard, Danny. You know that my house is always clean."

"I know, Mr. Gonzalez, I know." The Gonzalezes always brought the tenderness out of him. "Is there something that I can do?"

Tears formed in the old man's eyes. "Oh, praise Jesús, Danny, praise Jesús. I tell my wife that Danny help us."

"Of course, sir, if I can," Danny said, not sure what he could possibly do.

"Danny, my cousin Roberto, you know the one who has the daughter Juanita who works in the *abogado* office?"

"Yes," Danny said, knowing that *abogado* meant attorney.

"Her father, he know about these things 'cause his daughter Juanita tells him all about the court," Mr. Gonzalez gushed.

Danny squinted a bit. "I got it, Mr. Gonzalez, but what can I do for you?"

"My cousin, you know, Juanita's father, he called and he can't come with us to court tomorrow. Can you come with us, Danny?"

"You said you took pictures. Did you have them printed? The grass and the clean lawn?" Danny asked.

"We did, Danny, and we printed a picture of the sign I made with my son Rodolfo's burning wood set."

As soon as Danny nodded, Mr. Gonzalez flew up the stairs, hugged him, and cried. "Muchas gracias, hijo mío, muchas gracias."

Danny put his hands on Mr. Gonzalez's shoulders. "Calma, calma. What time is court?"

"Ten o'clock, Danny. We should be there by nine-thirty. I want to show the judge our respect for the law."

Danny smiled. "I'll have to straighten my clothes."

Mr. Gonzalez pulled a rolled-up red tie from his pocket. "I brought a tie for you, Danny. It was my son Pedro's."

Danny raised the tie to his neck. "How do I look, Mountain?"

Mountain scrutinized him carefully. "You look good, Danny, you look good in red."

"Danny," Mr. Gonzalez whispered, "the tickets are almost two thousand dollars. We have only three hundred and eighty dollars in our savings."

Danny smiled and nodded again. "We'll do our best, Mr. Gonzalez, we'll do our best."

Mr. Gonzalez released Danny, but when he walked to the sidewalk, Mr. Gonzalez hugged him around the neck again. "Danny, we're so scared, we don't know what to do. We don't want to lose our house. Where will we go? My wife, Danny, I haven't seen her cry so hard since we lost Rodolfo. She told me to make the sign with Rodolfo's kit, Danny. She says that he will protect us. Danny, you know Rodolfo died of drugs, but my wife say he will help us. I told her, when my cousin, Juanita's father, he can't come, I told her I go and see Danny. He's like a son to us."

Danny felt embarrassed, not 100 percent sure that he deserved such an honor.

"My cousin," Mr. Gonzalez continued, "Juanita's father, he knows about these things. He had a restaurant, many city big shots come in. He has friends but now he can't come. That's why I asked you to come, Danny. You know the way."

By now tears were flowing heavily from the old man's worn eyes. Danny hugged Mr. Gonzalez hard.

"You're like our own son, Danny. Even my wife, she love you like you were her own child. The Lord took our sons, Danny, but you're here, the Lord put you here for us."

The man began blubbering, "My beautiful sons, the Lord he take them but you're still here."

Danny patted his Mexican father's back. "That's right, and we'll do our best tomorrow. Bring the photos."

Danny and the old couple walked into the courtroom at 9:30. Mr. Gonzalez was wearing the same suit he had buried all three of his sons in. Mrs. Gonzalez wore a long gray dress and a burgundy shawl. Danny was wearing a navy blue suit. His pants showed about an inch of white socks as he walked. The suit sleeves fell about three inches from his wrists.

Danny had the tickets and the pictures in his hand. "Sit down and wait here. I'm going into the hall."

The couple quietly obeyed.

Danny walked up to a man in a shabby beige suit speaking on the phone. He smiled.

The man looked at him inquisitively. "Can I help you?"

"Are you an attorney?" Danny whispered.

"Yes. What can I do for you?" The attorney asked.

"I have these tickets and my neighbors are elderly. They add up to almost two grand." Danny hesitated and then looked desperately in the attorney's eyes. "They can't afford to pay them," Danny said.

"Whose tickets are they?"

"They're theirs."

"Where are they?"

"In the courtroom."

"You want it straight?"

"Of course," Danny answered.

"If you give me three hundred, I can have the fines cut in half. If not, they risk paying the full boat."

"But they're old people. They don't have any money."

"Buddy, if any of those people had money, they wouldn't be here." The attorney smiled cynically. "They're being targeted by the new administration. The city's trying to push them out. It's as simple as that."

Danny liked the guy's frankness. The lawyer appreciated Danny's concern for his neighbors. "Look, they ticket people who can't afford to pay, so they lose their homes. The city takes them over. It's called progress, gentrification, urban development."

Danny looked to the side. "I don't know what to tell them. Christ," he sighed, "a few years ago grass was a fifty-dollar fine."

"You're right, all of these tickets were fifty bucks. Enoch came in and now they're all six-hundred to a thousand dollar fines, plus court costs. The new mayor has already spent the fine money. They're part of the budget."

"That's not fair," Danny said, both to the attorney and himself.

"It's worse than that. The guys writing the tickets get promotions for how good a job they do. Some of them drive around with pop bottles and garbage in their trunk to throw on people's lawns."

"I have these pictures of the house with the ownership sign, the clean lawn and cut grass." Danny offered them to the attorney.

"I don't need to see them," the attorney grimaced, "unless you can prove that they are from the day and the time that the tickets were written."

"Why, no," Danny returned, "it takes weeks for the tickets to come in the mail. The pictures are to show the judge that everything is in order now."

"It won't help." The attorney shrugged. "They only prove that things are in order the day you took them. They don't prove that they were in order the day you were ticketed."

"That's insane," Danny said. "I mean, why make them six hundred dollars? If the city needs the money that bad, why not make them six thousand dollars or six million dollars? For poor folks, it's the same. No judge will make a poor old couple pay those outrageous fines."

"Let's hope you're right." The man smiled sardonically. "I need to get to my clients." The attorney took a business card out of his pocket. "Call me if it doesn't work out."

Danny walked back into the courtroom and sat next to the couple.

"Everything good, Danny?" Mrs. Gonzalez asked.

Danny nodded. She squeezed his arm.

"Gonzalez! 4812 South Elizabeth!" the clerk yelled.

Danny walked towards the bench with his Mexican parents. The acting judge was actually an officer of the City Revenue Department. He wore a plain white shirt with a faded orange stain just under the pocket, and a red tie. Danny was hopeful.

The City Revenue Department officer examined papers in his hands. As Danny and the Gonzalezes approached, he looked up harshly.

"Mr. Gonzalez," he said sternly.

"Yes, I am Mr. Gonzalez," the elderly man said in a soft voice.

"The fine is nineteen hundred and seventy dollars. Pay the clerk on the way out," the agent said without moving one facial muscle other than his lips. This reminded Danny of *Clutch Cargo*, a cartoon character whose face or eyes never moved, just his lips.

"But sir," Mr. Gonzalez replied. "I have pictures. The lawn is clean. The grass is cut and I have a sign on the house."

"When did you take the pictures, sir?" the agent asked impatiently.

"Two days ago, sir." Mr. Gonzalez smiled.

The agent was not used to being challenged, and he wanted to make sure that the people behind this deadbeat, in front of his desk would realize this and save him time. "Sir! The tickets are from over a month ago. I also have pictures."

The agent raised black and white computerized images on white paper. "The grass is over ten centimeters, there is no sign, and there is garbage on the lawn." The judge handed the sheets to Mr. Gonzalez.

Mrs. Gonzalez, who had been silent until then, interrupted and pushed the papers back at the agent. "But sir, me and my husband do not work. We are old. We cannot afford to pay these fines."

"Ma'am, do not push my arm again. If you do, I will have the bailiff arrest you for assault. I am trying to help you and demonstrate that the city has every right to fine you."

"But . . ." Mrs. Gonzalez said.

The agent raised his hand. "Is this your house?" He held the papers out to her.

Mrs. Gonzalez looked at the paper. "Yes, sir, that is our house."

The agent quickly wrote something as if noting an issue of national security. "Ma'am, you just admitted guilt. Pay the cashier."

Mrs. Gonzalez glanced at Danny and at Mr. Gonzalez. Her husband always told her that she talked too much. She felt a rush of anguish and guilt. They would lose their house!

"But your honor, we worked hard all these years for this house. My sons . . ." She fell into Danny's chest, sobbing like a red fox who had just lost her pups.

"If you can't afford to live in the house then you should move to somewhere that you can afford," the acting judge said flatly.

"Sir," Danny said.

"Are you an attorney?"

"I'm Danny Nowak. I'm their neighbor."

"I don't care if you're their son. They can only be represented by an attorney."

"Sir, they can't afford an attorney," Danny said mildly.

"They can't afford to keep up their house, they can't afford to pay the fines because they did not keep up their house. They can't afford an attorney . . ."

Danny raised his hand slightly and nodded. "Sir, can we have a continuance until we get an attorney, sir?"

The acting judge nodded. "We are not without compassion, but you must, I mean they must be prepared to settle the infractions." He slammed the gavel and called the next case. Danny escorted the old couple out of the courtroom.

Danny contacted the attorney from the hall. Pat pitched in five hundred and Danny, four hundred and thirty-five dollars. The Gonzalezes put in the rest. Greencastle moved a little further away, but Danny didn't see any other choice.

Big Clem paid one hundred dollars a month and had been in the basement for forty-eight days when Bluto came by to see him. Danny was upstairs with Mountain.

Bluto knocked and expected to hear the big guy say, "Come in." Instead he heard only silence. Bluto banged the door harder. Elaine and Dude began barking. Bluto pushed the door open. The place was full of stink and flies.

"Danny! Danny!" Bluto screamed.

Danny walked out on his porch.

Bluto ran up the first three stairs. "Big Clem is dead!" he screamed. Bluto began crying. "The poor guy, he was so young. He was two years younger than me. We got to move him out."

"I ain't movin' him out," Danny said calmly.

"But he's dead. We got to have a funeral. His family, friends . . ."

"Bluto, if he does have any true family or friends, they couldn't afford no funeral. I mean, if they could, why would he be living here?"

"What do you mean? I'm his friend. I brought him here," Bluto said, offended.

"That's my point. A funeral will cost. If his family or friends could afford to put him up in a decent place, he wouldn't have been here." Danny hesitated. "He's dead now Bluto, call the police. They'll bury him in Potter's Field."

Bluto stared. "What are you talking about, Danny?" he screamed.

"Burying him in the cheapest way will cost twenty-five hundred. You got twenty-five hundred?"

"No. We'll get a Facebook page and raise it. My cousin did that for her husband."

"OK, Bluto, but in the meantime what do you plan on doing?" Danny looked at Bluto sympathetically. "I don't expect he'll be paying rent. Like you said, you brought him here, now you got to get him out."

"But it'll take time to raise the money on Facebook," Bluto said, his pleading and anger quickly turning into reality.

"Bluto, we don't know how long he's been dead. I can't have the maggots and all that down there. You got to get him out."

Bluto looked at Mountain and then at Danny. "You got to help me," he said.

"Bluto, Big Clem weighs four-fifty, five hundred pounds," Danny said and shook his head.

"Four-eighty, he was on a diet," Bluto returned. "Me, you, an' Moses could move him."

"Don't be crazy, man, we ain't doin' it." Danny shook his head and continued, "Call the police."

The paddy wagon arrived after a half hour. It took four policemen and three technicians the better part of an hour to get Big Clem out and into the paddy wagon.

Luck was not rolling Danny's way.

CHAPTER 8

When It Rains, It Pours

Danny and Mountain took the two junk carts and hid them behind bushes at the park. Danny climbed a tall elm and Mountain handed him the gas saw. Within minutes, Danny was cutting and Mountain stacking the wood. On the way home, they met Raul Mendez, who bought all the wood for fourteen dollars. When they returned to the house, Danny counted his stash. The Gonzalez situation had put a dent in the project, but they were coming back.

Across town, in a Loop high rise, Elliott Rothstein was seated behind his desk, speaking to Mayor Carla Redman, who was seated in a small, battered chair in front of him. "Mayor, we're never going to make projections if the city doesn't speed up reclamation. I've upheld my side of the deal."

"Elliott, I'm not going to repeat to you every time we speak about how difficult it is putting people out of their homes." The mayor spoke in earnest.

"You told me that the new ordinances the city council passed would make this task easier," Rothstein underhandedly lobbed.

"The new ordinances just came into effect. In a short period of time we'll begin seeing results, but you need to be patient," Carla struck back.

"Carla, you're slick. You were incredible on the Police Accountability Task Force. I have as much respect for you as I do for the next ten folks, but we need action not words." Rothstein spoke patronizingly.

Carla needed to get out of the office and make it to City Hall for a council meeting. The municipality was still under water from past administrations' spending habits. She was going to introduce another property tax hike. Property hikes were never really popular with the aldermen, because homeowners voted nearly twice as much as renters and the city had already raised property taxes twice in the last three years.

Carla stood, smiled, and stared into Rothstein's eyes. "You are buying those lots for next to nothing! Do I need to remind you about what happened in Pilsen? Your investors made off like outlaws. The same will happen in New City." Carla's face turned serious. "But you must be patient!"

Elliott was not going to back down. He stood up as well and looked coolly at the mayor. "Pilsen was a successful project, but Carla, no two deals are the same and I'm a prudent man."

Carla returned his gaze. "I'll get the city council to open up the New City Development to bidding. Would your investors like that, Mr. Rothstein?"

Rothstein raised his hands, begging for a truce. "Your reelection is coming up, Mayor." He offered a sinister smile. "Do you think that other bidders would be so generous?"

Rothstein picked up a fidget spinner and began twirling it. "Would you really want to risk that they wouldn't be as generous as us, this close to an election?"

He spun the small device and continued. "As you so eloquently noted, your property tax increases aren't the rave, mayor."

Carla felt her face growing hot. She stared at Rothstein's face, fighting the urge to glance at the damn toy he was playing with.

Rothstein continued, speaking softly. "Prudence obligates me to insist on the timeline set. This is not about patience. This is about business."

"Elliott, my reelection committee told me that your donation was less than we had hoped for."

Rothstein smiled widely. "Uh-uh, Mayor," he said and spun the toy again, stopping his finger close to the mayor's face. "Don't put a number on it or it could be construed as a bribe. One never knows who is listening."

Redman wanted to jump over the desk and strangle the arrogant bastard, but Rothstein was right, it would cost a lot to make the public forget about the property tax increases . . . and another was on the horizon.

"Re-spect time-lines," Rothstein said, one syllable at a time.

"Elliott, you're not as smart as you think you are. We could both be prosecuted if a timeline existed." Redman pointed her finger directly at Rothstein's face. "I gave you a commitment to do what was best for the financial stability of Chicago, which is in the best interest of all of its citizens."

Elliott smiled and pushed Redman's hand away from his face. "Mayor, let's not bullshit each other. I also have a commitment to do what is in the best interest of my investors. We wrote a check of mild encouragement because we see no reason to write one indicating euphoric optimism. Deliver, or our support will remain mild."

"Rothstein, I'm not getting in the government's crosshairs on this. A timeline does not exist. There is only a commitment to do what's best for the city and its citizens."

Elliott nodded and put on a wide, fake smile. "Good, we understand each other. This is all about the citizens." Elliott smiled even wider. Redman thought his skin would crack. Elliott laid down the fidget spinner. "My group will evaluate our support for the candidate whom we see fit, for the good of our investors, many of whom are citizens."

The mayor shook her head lightly. Obama told her that Chicago politics was a cesspool. Of course, she already knew that, which was why she was so enthusiastic about becoming the city's mayor.

Elliott continued, "If I gave, say, half a million to your opponent, I think that it'd cost your reelection committee ten times that number to contain the damage."

Elliott was proud of his verbal toss. He looked down, biting his lip, to fight a smile. When he looked up, he caught the back of the slamming door where Redman had just exited. As soon as she got back to her office, she called Burman.

Burman walked out of the city's CEO office. He needed to get tough. The city desperately wanted the Sherman Park area of New City. Sherman Park was a beautiful sixty-one acres square with two gymnasiums, an auditorium, a fitness center, an outdoor swimming pool, three playgrounds, basketball and tennis courts, baseball/softball diamonds, and soccer/football fields, all just five minutes from the Loop.

Early in the twentieth century, the Olmsted Brothers had transformed this wet site into a beautiful landscape with a meandering waterway surrounding an island of ball fields. The classically designed architecture located at the north end of the park included the field house, gym, and locker buildings, linked by trellis-like structures known as pergolas. Sherman Park was three hundred meters from Danny's home, in the heart of where the development would happen.

Danny was riding his bike. Elaine and Dude were close behind. About a block from his house, he heard a siren. He looked back and saw a squad car driven by that reliable civil servant, Officer Brown. Danny stopped and called the dogs to his side.

Brown drove up and got out of the car. "Not a good day for you, Danny. I told you that things were changing. Those dogs must be on a leash; Chicago Municipal Code twelve, dash seven, dash zero-thirty."

Danny stared at Brown, wondering if this might be payback for helping the Gonzalez family. To some, kindness is highly antagonistic.

Brown moved closer and rolled his eyes as far back as they would go while staying in his head. "Did I hear a growl, Danny?"

Danny looked at Elaine. She wasn't charmed by the uniformed doughnut, but she hadn't growled. "No, sir. I didn't hear anything."

"If I feel endangered, I have every right to shoot the animal, I believe you're aware of that," Brown said wickedly.

"Sir," Danny pleaded. "These dogs never hurt anyone, they wouldn't growl at anyone unless they were breaking into the house or if maybe they were a cat." He smiled, trying to bring a bit of levity to the situation.

"You know I'd hate to do it, Danny," Brown said with a chilly smile, "but children need to be safe on the streets and these animals are a threat to their safety. Now, I'm not going to shoot them, but I am going to write you a ticket . . . this time."

"Come on, officer, they always follow me. We've never had an incident and they love kids," Danny insisted.

Brown glared at Danny. "Did I hear a growl? I could swear that I heard a growl."

"Just give me the ticket," Danny surrendered.

"I thought that you'd see it my way, Danny," Brown said kindly. "They're animals and they're volatile. One can never be too cautious. This three-hundred-dollar ticket will serve as a reminder to you. Someday you'll thank me." Brown's smile turned into a cold stare. "Or maybe you won't."

Brown continued writing and took a picture of the dogs with his phone. He handed Danny the ticket. "Danny, I've always liked you, but for everyone's good you must understand."

Danny took the ticket in his hand and folded it. Greencastle was three hundred dollars further away.

Brown resumed his lecture. "Change is coming, Danny, and to be quite honest, I don't like it any better than yourself. I'd rather live with gangbangers than hipsters. Hell, I can understand gangbangers, shooting it out trying to get to the top, but the hipsters, now that's a breed of selfishness that I'll never fathom." Brown touched his chest with his ticket book. "'It's all about me,' that's how they think, and half of 'em are queer. They need their quiet space and pierced foreheads. Hell," Brown smiled, "They ain't got no sense as it is, why not put holes in their heads?"

Danny stared.

"But Danny, the city needs money, and it's easier to fuck the defenseless than the powerful, it's easier to shit on the poor than the rich." Brown nodded and turned for his car. He opened the door and looked back at Danny. "Sorry, Danny, but it's gonna be like this until you leave."

Danny turned to head for home.

"Oh, Danny!" Brown yelled.

Danny kept walking.

"Nice thing ya done for the Gonzalezes! It bought them a bit more time, but like you, their days are numbered in New City!"

Danny walked home, lower than the Dead Sea Depression. He was studying the concrete of the sidewalk as he turned the corner. He didn't even notice Pat and Mountain sitting on the porch.

"Danny," Pat said.

Danny jerked his head up.

Pat had never seen this type of behavior from his friend. He stood, walked towards his comrade, and put his arms around Danny's shoulders. While doing so, he scanned the ticket in Danny's hand.

"Elaine, Duke, get inside," Danny said.

The dogs ran up the stairs. Elaine untied the rope and pushed the door open. They both disappeared into the house.

"Sucks, Danny," Pat said. "It's a sign of the times. The city wants the tax base to go up, so they displace the poor from desirable areas."

"Yeah, friendly Officer Brown explained the process."

"They just harass you until you give up or can't afford to stay. Sorry, Danny, I don't mean to rub it in." Pat forced a grin. "Give me the ticket."

"What can you do?"

"I'll take care of it. I got a friend."

"Really?" Danny asked euphorically. "Dickhead said that it was a three-hundred-dollar fine."

"Maybe I can get it reduced." Pat folded the ticket and stuck it in his pocket. As he did, his phone rang. "Hey little brother . . . I'll call you later . . . me too."

"Was that Jeff?" Danny asked.

"Nah."

"Georgy?"

"It was Derek."

"Derek?

"I told you about him, he's from New City too. His family lived on Garfield. I put him through Catholic High School and helped him along the way. It's quite a story."

"Yeah, I remember something," Danny said.

Pat smiled.

"Tell us the story, Pat," Danny said. "Me and Mountain want to hear it." Danny looked at Mountain. "Don't we, Mountain?"

Mountain nodded. Danny sat on the porch next to the big man.

Pat looked at them with a Hans Christian Andersen sort of look. He took a breath and began.

"I was a busboy at the Club El Bianco restaurant on 63rd. I should have known better." Pat nodded. "Butchy was gunning for me. He was the owner's son and I think he was jealous that his old man liked me better than him, his own kid."

Pat smiled. "Maybe he was envious of me and Marilyn, the cute blonde waitress he always flirted with, but I don't even think he knew." He winked at Danny.

"How old were you, Pat?" Danny asked.

"Fourteen, fifteen," Pat mused.

"And her? How old was Marilyn?" Danny asked, beaming like a streetlight.

"Twenty-five," Pat said proudly.

"You were always a dog, Pat," Danny said.

"Cad, Danny, cad. Today they'd put her in jail. I think they should give her an award . . . the things she taught me about life." Pat smiled and continued, "I was shooting dice with the fruit truck driver and two busboys. The door burst open and the light shined out from the restaurant. There he stood . . . "

"Who, Pat?" Mountain asked.

"Butchy, the owner's son." Pat said. "I looked up from the ground at him, purposely pausing to gaze at his fat stomach."

Mountain laughed. Danny glared at him.

"I smirked and then looked at his face," Pat continued. "The second dice rolled into his foot. It was a four. I had rolled another seven." Pat smiled. "I told the driver, and Johnny and Tony, the other busboys, that it was my pot. Butchy kicked the dice into the street."

Pat smiled before continuing. "As I reached for the three dollars, Butchy, the owner's son . . ." Pat looked at Mountain, making sure he was following. He was.

Pat continued, "He smashed my hand and the three one-dollar bills to the ground. A thousand thoughts went through my mind as his sole smashed further into my wrist. Danny, you remember, at home my income was critical. How would I tell my mother that I'd been fired?"

"He fired ya, huh?" Danny asked.

"On the spot," Pat replied. "A few days later, I walked into the employment office at Northwestern Hospital. The head of personnel was the daughter of one of Butchy's waitresses. I put in an application and was hired as a dishwasher. My new boss's name was Joe Ross. On my first day, I walked into the kitchen. Six dark-skinned people were punching the time clock."

"Dark-skinned like me, Pat?" Mountain asked.

Pat nodded. "More or less, some were lighter and some were darker."

Danny liked when Pat told stories. "Then what?" he asked.

"Well," Pat nodded, "I'll tell ya, I received the welcoming of a bill collector and Kevin Blackburn, a tall lanky guy, three or four years my senior, smirked. 'You lost, cracker?' he asked.

"I stared and grinned. 'I'm looking for Joe Ross,' I replied.

"A few days later, I was buttoning my uniform in the locker room when Kevin Blackburn entered. 'Honky, you gotta stop working so hard. You're making us look bad,' he said.

"I need this job." I replied. "'How old are you, white boy?' he asked.

"I said I was fifteen, but as I moved to exit, he blocked me."

Pat paused before continuing. "Luckily for me, a woman passed as I pulled the door open. I mean Blackburn had me by a few years and several inches." He nodded before continuing.

"'Kevin Blackburn, you leave that skinny little white boy alone. You're four years older and twice his size.' the passing woman, who everyone called Big Mama, said."

Mountain hung onto every word and Danny smiled.

"Big Mama grabbed me by one arm and Blackburn snatched the other. 'Boy,' she said, 'you let him go or I'll give you what for, and a whole lot of it,"

Mountain smiled. "That woman sounds like my Auntie Bee. She dint take kindly to bullies. She stood right up to my cousin Wilky when he picked on me and my cousin. Wilky's mother is my mother's sister Teetee. Teetee could whup any man in my family."

Pat smiled at Mountain and nodded before continuing. "'I'll get you when she's not around to save you, white boy,' Blackburn growled. Big Mama went back to the food line. That's where she worked. As the trays passed, she and the women read the orders and scooped on vegetables, meat, fish, jello, broth, etc., before it reached the end of the conveyor belt. All of the women on the line wore white smocks and white mesh nets that covered all their hair and much of their faces."

"That's to keep their hair out of the food," Mountain said. "Once, I was eating at a grill wit my Auntie Bee. They served her up scrambled eggs. She saw a hair in it and sent it right back."

Danny turned to Mountain. "It's not your story, big man."

"Just sayin'," Mountain rebutted.

"A few weeks later," Pat continued, "Joe Ross, my supervisor, asked me to help him with algebra. He was studying for a promotion. The next day 'HONKEE KISS ASS' was written in white spray paint on my locker door." Pat smiled. "I figured it was Kevin Blackburn, who spelled honky with two 'e's.'"

Pat continued. "I changed and as I scurried into the hall, I ran head-on into Blackburn. He said a few phrases about my algebra lessons that wouldn't be published in *a Christian Journal* and grabbed me by the neck. A coworker passed us by as if we weren't there." Pat looked at Mountain. "I was in a bad way, Mountain."

Mountain's eyes were glued to the other man. "Then what happened?"

Pat continued. "'I told you I'd get you when Big Mama wasn't around to save your skinny ass.' Blackburn was hissing, I mean, it was as if he was a snake talking to me. He took me into a headlock and ran my head into the wall. My heart beat fast as I felt his fist hit my forehead."

Pat raised his fist to his head. "Bang! Right here he got me. I grabbed his arm as he pulled back for another shot, but his other arm was around my neck. As I squirmed, a woman in white ran toward us. I felt it as she caught Kevin Blackburn on the back with a soup ladle. 'Ouch! Big Mama! Ouch, woman! Leave me alone!' he screamed."

Mountain's smile went from ear to ear.

"Kevin released me and I gasped, slipping to the floor. Big Mama took three more good swings. 'I told you to leave that skinny, white boy alone and I meant it!' she screamed."

"I brushed myself off, but Big Mama didn't say a word or hang around for thanks. Later, I walked to the women dressed in white. It was hard to distinguish one from another. I recognized Big Mama by her glasses and I thanked her, but she hardly paid any notice, having done what was right without expectation."

"That's how my Auntie Bee was," Mountain said. "The payment for a good deed is the good deed."

Danny looked sternly at Mountain for his interruption but at the same time marveled at Auntie Bee's wisdom and how it lived on in Mountain. He smiled.

"She always said it, Danny, a good deed is payment for a good deed," Mountain added.

Pat smiled, noticing Danny's impatience laced with admiration, and continued.

"Life was never boring and a few months later I was at court on 61st and Racine."

"What'd you do?" Danny asked.

"The police caught me heisting a battery out of a police car parked at the 35th Street station."

Danny interrupted. "Let me get this straight. You were stealing the battery out of a police car?" He shook his head.

"It's illegal stealing a battery out of a police car," Mountain added.

Pat smiled and bowed his head. "It was my third time in front of Judge Clarence Bryant in as many months. He gave me the choice of juvenile detention or the military. I knew what juvenile detention was like."

Danny nodded. "Amen."

Pat continued, "Frank Murphy, another guy from my neighborhood, had stabbed somebody and Judge Bryant gave him the same ultimatum."

Pat leaned on the banister. "Boy, I'll tell you, I may not have been able to recognize Big Mama or Judge Bryant on a bus, but they literally saved my life. I mean, Big Mama's love opened my heart. Judge Bryant and the military helped save me from myself."

"My Auntie said that was her job, to save me from myself." Mountain looked at Danny. "Danny, is it your job now to save me from myself?"

"Yeah, I guess, big guy, but who's gonna save me?"

"From yourself?" Mountain asked curiously.

"Yeah," Danny said impatiently.

"Danny, will you save me from myself in Greencastle?"

"Will you please let Pat continue?"

"Indiana?" Mountain added.

"Will you please let Pat continue?" Danny repeated a bit more sternly.

Mountain smiled. "OK, Danny."

"Anyway," Pat continued, "I didn't last long in the military. They said I had an attitude problem." He winked at them. "They might've had a point."

Pat smiled and continued. "One good thing though, while I was in the service, I grew five or six inches and began shaving."

Pat paused. Danny and Mountain's attention were riveted. "Years later I was on the Oprah show as a 'rags to riches' story and in *Playgirl* magazine next to Sylvester Stallone and Magic Johnson as one of America's Most Eligible Bachelors."

"You was on *Oprah*?" Mountain blurted.

Danny stared at his big friend.

"Sorry, Danny, but you din't tell me that Pat was on *Oprah*!"

"Listen to the story, big guy."

"Pat, was you really on *Oprah*?" Mountain probed.

Pat raised two fingers. "Twice." He continued. "Father Frawley, a good Catholic priest and friend of mine, knew that I loved to give back. One day he called me about a kid who wanted to become a priest but didn't have any cake for Quigley South, the Catholic high school seminary. So . . ."

"Cake?" Mountain interrupted.

"Cake is money," Danny said impatiently. "Go on, go on, so?"

"So," Pat continued, "I drove to Visitation Catholic Grammar School on Garfield Boulevard and met Derek Holmes, a tall, respectful dark-skinned kid. I paid for his first year; his grades were outstanding, and I gladly paid for the second, third, and fourth. In time, he became as close to me as any of my brothers."

Pat looked down. When he looked up again, his expression was grief-stricken. "In fact, when my best friend Terry went missing and was spotted in Iowa, I called Derek, who lived there at the time. He drove two hours in the pouring rain to the hotel where my friend was last seen."

Danny recalled the event and shook his head sadly.

Pat continued, "It was too late for Terry, but it drew me even closer to my little brother Derek, who cried as I did when my oldest son was diagnosed with thalassemia, a rare blood disease."

Pat nodded. "Derek once told me that I was around for all the important things in his life, including the period when he fell in love with Jessica, his bride."

"His bride?" Mountain asked.

Pat smiled broadly. "Today they have three sons and a wonderful life. In 2001 I threw a research fundraiser at the Chicago Hilton. Derek bought a few tables. All my life I've written poems and turned them into songs. When I produced my first musical CD to raise money for research, Derek bought a few boxes.

"Good man," Danny said.

Mountain turned to Danny. "Danny, let Pat tell the story," he scolded.

"Sorry," Danny said softly, laughing wildly on the inside.

"I moved to Italy and Derek and his family went to Tampa, Florida," Pat continued. "I flew back and forth for the research company founded to cure my son's disease. On one of my trips to the US, I was driving in Chicago when my phone rang. I knew 813 was an area code for Tampa. I smiled, knowing it was my little brother Derek."

"St. Petersburg, too," Danny added.

Pat continued. "Poor Derek told me that his mother had passed. It was a cold sunny morning, I drove to the funeral in a church on 50th and State."

"My auntie went to that church!" Mountain yelled.

Danny stared at his big buddy. "We gonna let him finish?"

"Greater Harvest Baptist Church!" Mountain proclaimed proudly.

"That's right," Pat said. "That's right. Well, I walked into the church. As I removed my hat I spotted my old boss from the hospital kitchen, Joe Ross. The service had not started and I walked to where he was standing with others. He didn't recognize me until I asked him if he needed algebra lessons."

"'Pat, is that you?' he asked.

"'It is, my friend,' I said.

"'Pat, we're all so proud of you. Oprah show and all.' He smiled widely.

"'Joe, I always wanted to make it back after the military and it's my fault . . . ' I fidgeted, feeling genuinely embarrassed that I hadn't done so.

"'You are all a part of my success.' I hesitated. 'I wanted to especially thank Big Mama. She saved me a dozen times,' I said."

Danny and Mountain were captivated.

Pat continued. "'By the way, Joe, what does Kevin Blackburn do these days, do you know?' I asked.

"'He's a Chicago police officer,' he said.

"I nodded my head and paused. 'Big Mama saved me from him, Joe,' I continued. 'I can't wait to thank her.'

"Joe looked at me curiously.

"Knowing that she was probably retired by now, I asked, 'Do you know where she lives? Do you think she may come today?'"

"Joe looked down and smiled tightly. 'She's here.' He nodded as he spoke.

"My wide smile straightened as he indicated the casket at the front of the church.

"'That's her,' he said. 'This is her funeral.'"

"In the hospital kitchen, the women all wore large white smocks and heavy mesh nets over most of their faces and for all those years, I never had the slightest clue that Derek's mom was my Big Mama too."

Danny and Mountain sat silently for a few seconds. Then Danny stood and hugged Pat. "That's awesome, brother, that's awesome."

Pat took a twenty out of his pocket and handed it to Danny. "Here's that twenty I owe you." He turned, got into his car, and left.

Before hitting Racine, less than two blocks from Danny's, Pat was on the phone with Greg. "I got a ticket for a dog with no leash."

"It's tough, Patty. I can see what I can do but . . . is it the first time he was ticketed?"

"Yeah, I think so," Pat replied.

"I'll meet you tomorrow morning for coffee," Greg responded.

Danny laid on the covers with his hands under his head. Mountain looked at Danny and then put his hands under his head. Danny breathed in deep. Mountain followed suit.

Mountain stared at Danny. "Danny, we gonna get to Greencastle, Indiana?"

Danny remained silent.

"Big Clem said that everyone has dreams but that no one ever gets to Greencastle, Indiana."

"Big Clem didn't know what he was talking about."

"Danny, where do the people in Greencastle, Indiana dream about going?"

"Can't sleep?" Danny asked.

"Danny, I'm scared. I mean, sometimes I lay here and it feels like the walls are coming in, like they're going to smash us to death."

"There's always bumps in the road, big man," Danny offered.

"Yeah, like with Dorothy and Toto, but they got there," Mountain replied happily.

"Go to sleep, Mountain, and think about how you better never forget about feeding those chicks."

Mountain smiled. "I won't." Mountain was smiling to himself, but Danny could feel it. "Night, Danny."

"Night," Danny said.

"Danny?"

"What now, Mountain?"

"Thanks for telling me to think about feeding the chicks. It'll help me get to sleep. Auntie Bee told me to count sheep when I couldn't sleep. Tonight, I'm gonna count chicks."

"Good."

Danny laid awake. Mountain was a concern. Danny had already asked around the neighborhood about relatives, but it seems that no one knew of any. His Auntie Teetee was dead and his cousin Wilky was in jail. Danny couldn't see the big guy living with anyone else, and supposed that Mountain would be his responsibility the rest of his life. Danny smiled. That wasn't such a bad thing. He loved the old lovable bear.

As Danny rolled over trying to get into a good position to sleep he heard the big man murmur "Thirteen chicks, fourteen chicks . . ."

★ ★ ★ ★

Greg was overweight and middle-aged. His skin was pale, his glasses were stock, his shirt and the rest of his attire was completely indistinguishable. Starbucks on 47th and Cicero was a convenient place to meet, even though Pat despised all corporate chains. He believed that franchises and behemoths like Starbucks and Walmart dramatically widened the gap between the haves and have-nots.

Pat was heard more than once saying that since Reagan, the American people had been idolizing company leaders, the same guys that screwed them. "The CEOs robbed benefits off the workers, and the shareholders kicked back 10 percent of the savings," he'd growl.

Pat was right, but this didn't bother Greg in the least. He was a student of history. The rich always screw the poor.

Pat sat down with two coffees.

Greg looked up. "OK, Patty, I can appear for your friend. I mean, I'll say I'm him and get it cut in half."

"Done," Pat said. He reached into his pocket and handed Greg the ticket and two hundred dollars.

"Thanks, Patty." Greg grimaced. "You know, the whole South Side is underwater. The city is tossing out tickets to the poor owners like confetti at a parade. Most of those people will lose their homes."

"Yeah, gentrification," Pat scoffed.

"How's Danny?" Greg asked.

"How can he be?" Pat returned.

"I remember, you borrowed," Greg hesitated, "gave him money to pay his taxes about ten years ago."

"He's really behind the eight-ball now. I think that with real estate taxes, tickets, interest, and penalties he owes the city over two hundred G's."

"The city charges some of the owners more taxes in a year than their properties are worth," Greg said soberly.

"Progress," Pat quipped.

"Where's he gonna live?" Greg asked.

"Good question," Pat replied.

"Patty, he had a good run." Greg looked to the side and then back at Pat. "Most people like Danny end up under viaducts or in shelters."

Pat shook his head gently. "He ain't a shelter guy."

Pat's phone rang. He answered and mumbled something unintelligible into the phone. When he finished speaking, he looked at Greg. "Thanks, gotta go. I love you, Greg."

"I love you too, Patty."

Burman now spent his whole day in New City. Most people shunned him or even hid when they saw his van approaching, but he was just one of many. The city had hundreds of agents, many out as early as 5 a.m., ticketing cars too far from the curb, too close to the fire hydrant, too far into the street, too close to the corner; they also ticketed people without city stickers, with expired city stickers, missing license plates, missing license plate decals, or expired decals.

The tiny license decals were about an inch and a half by an inch and cost between seventy and a hundred dollars each. Most people scored them with razor blades once they were stuck on the plate, so thieves would not be able to peel them off in one piece. Sadly for the victims, the agents gave tickets for partially missing license plate stickers too.

It's still called the Denver boot, but it's used in every major city in the US. Each morning hundreds of these bright yellow metal devices are placed on the wheels of vehicles parked on Chicago streets and even in private parking lots. The government says that all of these taxes and penalties are for the citizens' safety, but even their own officials have a hard time explaining this theory in a way that makes any sense at all. It's just another tariff and like everything else, disproportionately compromises the lives of the poor.

For a rich person, to fork out a hundred bucks is not a problem. The poor are reduced to tears when they get to their car and notice a decal has been damaged or stolen. A rich person might shrug off the boot and its often five-hundred-dollar price tag, but poor people have been known to sell drugs or even prostitute themselves to get the funds to get it removed. The Denver boot has been the source of more than a few suicides. The experience can rip one's whole life apart.

Burman shed no tears. In the greatest nation of the world there is no such thing as poverty or poor, just deadbeats, idiots, and the inevitable results of their laziness and stupidity. The city pushed the state to change the laws, making it easier to put people out of their homes.

People claimed that they were put on the street. The caring public servants bark back that it's an outright lie. They claim that there are more and more shelters to house the growing homeless population and that we all have somewhere else we can leave to. The only people who don't have a roof over their head in the US are outdoor adventurists.

Burman hit a few homes, dropping off warnings, citations, letters, and eviction notices. He enjoyed his job, his responsibility, his influence, and the warm feeling he got knowing that he was a productive citizen. The more industrious he and his fellow agents were, the happier their bosses were, making for more upward mobility. Agents that enjoyed ticketing people became the leaders of tomorrow.

Burman walked up 50th Street. School had begun, yet the sprinkler in the park across from Danny was still on. Burman had already called the water commissioner twice about it.

Danny was standing next to his bicycle in front of his house. Burman looked in Danny's direction, giving him the look of a superior to a worthless element and delivered a letter to Napoleon's house. He walked down the stairs, smiled at Danny, and left.

As Burman made his way to his van, Mountain came out and stood on the porch. He and Danny quietly watched Burman get into his city vehicle. *In medieval times, tax collectors for the kings rode horses, today they ride city vans*, Danny thought.

Danny looked up at the big man. Mountain beamed down at the only real brother he had ever had. "Junkin', Danny?" Mountain asked.

Mountain noticed that Danny's nod was not a carefree one. He was correct. Danny's head was filled with reflections about this evening. It would be an important one. He and Napoleon were scheduled to discuss finances and the future.

Danny still wasn't 100 percent sure about Napoleon. The guy had great intentions but didn't always follow through. Danny pondered the monthly ten dollars that Napoleon promised to pay when he'd hooked up electricity for Napoleon's family. Danny bootlegged his, splicing directly into the generator before the meter. Sharing it with Napoleon was no sweat off his back, but Napoleon didn't follow through. He didn't respect the agreement.

Napoleon's five kids were well behaved for the most part, but him and Mountain living with them twenty-four hours a day would be interesting, to put it mildly.

Danny set off with his colleague, partner, friend in need, brother. Danny's eyes were on the alley and the garbage cans, but his mind was on the future. He thought it a bit odd to be thinking about the future. His brother Stefan thought about the future from the time they were kids. Couldn't get a cent out of Stefan. Danny reflected, *Is that what planning ahead does, makes us cheap?*

Mountain had become a good junker. He seemed to know where to look and what to ignore. As Danny reached into a garbage can to grab a wooden box, a raggedy truck passed by. These guys were also junking but they were looking for furniture, mattresses, the big stuff that they pawned off to the used furniture stores and sometimes directly to hotel employees, who then made some money for themselves.

Danny had dated more than his share of women who cleaned the hotels downtown. According to the hotel servants, only if we kidded ourselves would we ever sleep in a hotel room.

The corporate-owned franchises worked the maids harder and harder, giving them more and more rooms to clean. In the end, they don't clean them. Instead they just do enough to fool the guests. They look over the room and straighten the furniture, do a pubic hair check on the sheets, make the bed, wipe off any fluids left on the furniture, pick up litter from the floor, vacuum if they must, put a paper seal on the toilet, spray some chemicals into the air, and put a chocolate on the pillow. And as long as there were no complaints, the hotel managers are happy.

Danny popped his head up and waved. The two truck passengers waved back. The box ended up being filled with metal and plastic jewelry. Danny stuck it on the cart. He'd do a better investigation at home. They pulled into the new Dunkin' Donuts on 47th Street. Mountain was starved and hoping that Danny would get a few donuts with his coffee. Danny rarely let Mountain down, and got each of them a chocolate long john.

"Remember, big guy, we got that roasted chicken that Father Kurt at the kitchen gave us."

"Danny, don't worry 'bout that. I could eat a chicken, rooster, and a whole cow."

As they walked under the viaduct heading home they heard a cry. They both halted silently. The whine came from the direction of an old mattress lying against the viaduct wall.

They took a few more cautious steps.

They heard the cry again and Danny thought it sounded like a human cry. Babies were found in the neighborhood from time to time, but mostly in the Sherman Park lagoon or in the dumpsters.

They walked towards the mattress that was resting between the wall and a wooden crate. The crying continued and seemed to be coming from behind the mattress.

Danny pointed to the mattress. "Grab that end," Danny said.

"I got it, Danny."

"OK, let's slowly lift it up and rest it flat against the wall."

They placed the mattress against the wall and turned back to investigate. The crying had stopped. They moved the box to find three dead kittens and one barely alive.

Danny was relieved that it wasn't a baby but grimaced as the odor of the dead kittens and their feces made its way into his nostrils.

"Can I have it, Danny?" Mountain asked.

Danny shook his head. "It's not going to make it, Mountain."

Mountain was visibly excited. "How do you know? Can I keep it? I'll raise it up and bring it to Greencastle with us!" He was working his way up to a froth as he continued. "They have field mice in Greencastle and a cat will keep 'em away from the chicks' food."

Danny bent down and cupped the tiny creature in his hand. It weighed only a few ounces.

"Can I keep it, Danny?" Mountain insisted.

Danny breathed in. "Well, I guess if we leave it here, soon it will join the others."

"Where's the mother, Danny?" Mountain asked in a concerned tone.

"She must have been hit by a car or something," Danny replied.

"Once behind Auntie Bee's home, in the alley, I seen three giant rats eating a cat. Do you think that the rats killed their mother?"

"Not likely, or at least not here. They'd have eaten the kittens, too," Danny said.

"My uncle Rufus said that the rats in Chicago were so vicious that the cats should be permitted to carry knives."

When they returned home, Danny sent Mountain to buy a carton of milk. Mountain was joyful. He double-stepped to the store and back.

Danny dipped his finger in the milk and raised it to the kitten's mouth. The kitten licked gently.

"Will she be all right, Danny? Will she?" Mountain pleaded.

"Only time will tell. The kitten's in a bad way," Danny said.

Mountain watched Danny as a newly diagnosed cancer patient watches his doctor.

"I got to go by Napoleon's," Danny said, "to talk about things." He handed the kitten to Mountain and looked in the big man's eyes. "Now, dip your finger in the milk and feed it until it doesn't drink anymore."

Mountain's eyes filled with excitement as he took the kitten into his cupped hands. Five kittens could fit into one of Mountain's gloves.

Danny smirked as he watched the big man. "Dip your finger and show me how you're going to feed the kitten, Mountain," he said.

Mountain dipped his finger in the milk and slowly approached the kitten's face.

"That's it, Mountain, gentle. Now keep doing that until it don't lick anymore. I'll be back in an hour or so."

"Can I come over when the cat's done eating, Danny?" Mountain asked as a schoolboy would ask permission to go to the bathroom.

"Suit yourself," Danny said firmly.

Napoleon was on his front porch, waiting impatiently for Danny. Robert E. was with his father at the top of the steps.

Napoleon aimed his words against his oldest son. "Boy," Napoleon said, "get in the house and do your homework."

"I don't got no homework," Robert E. responded lazily.

"Well, you should have homework. You just used a double negative," Napoleon volleyed.

"A what?" Robert E. asked, confused as a blind dog in a meat house.

Napoleon had been waiting for Danny and had his mind on other business. He decided not to cross that road. "If you ain't got no homework, then get in there and do your chores," he snapped.

"What chores?"

"Clean your room, man! I'll look at it when I'm done with Danny."

"Oh, I forgot, I got to read a book for English," Robert E. said.

Napoleon smiled. "You didn't forget, man; you'd just rather read than clean your room."

Robert E. gazed at Napoleon.

"I don't blame ya, man. Get in there and read your book," Napoleon said.

Robert E. entered the house.

"Close that door, Robert E.!"

Robert E. returned and shut the door.

When Napoleon looked back, Danny was heading up the stairs.

Napoleon smiled and bumped his knuckles against Danny's. "I'm just under three thousand, brother," Napoleon smiled.

Danny smiled. "Me, too." Danny nodded and continued. "I saw that our friend, the city taxman, left you another love letter."

"Yeah, man, they want my house too." Napoleon shrugged.

"They want all of the property here. Within ten years, New City will have all professional people living here."

"Yep." Napoleon said. "Probably right." He paused. "You know, I wasn't happy when the Chicanos started invading and I always got along with the few white holdouts, but the hipsters?" Napoleon shook his head. "I can't stomach them, quintessence of selfishness."

Danny smiled. "Wow, quintessence . . ."

"I mean it, man!" Napoleon insisted. "You know why they call them hipsters?"

Danny's expression was blank.

"Cause they think they's hip, and they want to control your life and your thoughts like they're gangsters. They's anti-family, anti-hetero, and anti-American. They want to destroy everything we hold dear . . ." Napoleon paused. "They ain't hip and they cheap. I hate Ubering them. They ought to call 'em gypsters."

Danny exhaled wearily. "Well brother, soon these streets will be theirs."

Napoleon's expression changed from righteousness to concern. It was like a magic trick. He looked somberly at his neighbor, brother, savior. "Danny, what if we don't make it on time? I mean, can we hide out someplace until we raise the rest of the loot?"

Danny shook his head. "Brother, if we start moving around, we'll never have the money. Something will always get in the way. We'll be spending it on moving around and all the things that entails. I mean, that's at least how I think."

Napoleon nodded. "You right. You right."

Inside, the kitten continued to lick Mountain's milk-covered finger. He set the fragile creature on the table. He watched it affectionately and began stroking its fur. Elaine and Dude sat at Mountain's sides, staring at the tiny, ugly infant feline. The small body moved with Mountain's slightest touch.

Elaine barked softly.

"No, Elaine, you can't play with this kitty. She's too young. You'd kill 'er."

Mountain stared into space momentarily and mumbled, "What do you do with babies?"

The visitor began scooting toward the edge of the table. Mountain scooted it back. This happened a few more times and Mountain decided that Kitty wanted to play. That's it, he'd call it "Kitty."

Mountain began to tease his new pet. The kitten's body moved with Mountain's slightest touch. After a few minutes, Kitty tired and stopped responding.

Mountain flicked his finger into Kitty's chest, but after the third poke the kitten laid still.

Mountain's heart dropped into his stomach. He looked down at Elaine and Dude. They looked at Kitty and then at Mountain, both knowing and fearing what Mountain feared.

"Come on, Kitty," Mountain said softly as he scooted the cat toward the center of the table. Futile and desperate, Mountain dipped his finger in milk and pushed it towards the kitten's face. Finally, he shoved his finger into Kitty's mouth as if the milk would have some miraculous effect on the dead animal.

Dude looked away and then back. Elaine looked at the ground. Needless to say, anything else the big man did was useless.

Tears began flowing down Mountain's cheeks. "Come on, you stupid kitten, wake up."

Elaine barked, trying to tell him to leave the situation alone.

Mountain's desperation had an angry edge. He shoved the fur and bones and it glided across the table. "Wake up," he said sternly. "Or Danny won't take me to Greencastle."

Elaine barked again and Dude agreed.

Mountain looked at them and then back at the kitten. "Wake up!" he said in a stern undertone.

Just then Mountain heard Danny coming up the stairs. He panicked and shoved the kitten's body into the pocket of a jacket hanging on the chair. Danny walked in.

"Where's the kitten, Mountain?"

Mountain's frightened stare told all.

"Where's it at?" Danny asked.

"It ran away, Danny. I gave it some milk and turned to get some more, and it ran right off the table and out the back door."

Danny nodded. "Well, wherever it ran to, it will begin rotting and smelling things up so you got to get rid of it."

"But it ran away, Danny," Mountain reiterated.

"I said, it will begin to smell."

"Danny, I named him Kitty, that's what I named him."

Danny watched.

"If I can't find Kitty, will you take me to Greencastle? Indiana?" The dam burst, and Mountain's eyes were flooded instantly. Danny's eyes began to fill up as well.

"I'm sorry, Danny, I was feeding Kitty . . ." Mountain began to blubber. "I put her in this pocket. It wasn't my fault, Danny. You said yourself he was in a bad way."

Mountain took Kitty out and showed the tiny dead body to Danny.

"Should I bury it with Duchess?"

Danny nodded. "That will work."

Mountain stood. "Can I come to Greencastle, Danny? Please tell me I can come. It wasn't my fault . . ."

Danny's smile rescued Mountain's heart. "Mountain, don't worry. You're coming to Greencastle."

Mountain's tears of misery miraculously became tears of ecstasy. But Danny could do that to folks. Mountain grabbed Danny and hugged him.

"Don't hug me with that kitten in your hands. You'll smash him all over me."

Mountain released Danny and walked out to the cemetery. *Duchess will have a kitty to play with*, he thought.

Letters began arriving daily at Danny's, Napoleon's, and hundreds of residences in New City. Most were notices of fines for tickets that revenue agents wrote for garbage, grass, no signs, broken windows, and hanging gutters. Other letters were warnings that taxes were late or had not been paid; still others notified homeowners that the city had not collected taxes for a certain year and that now penalties and interest were owed.

The grief of the community painted every home. Some residents understood but hid their concern. Frankly, most didn't understand the real danger. Things like this didn't happen in America.

The computer and the new idea of capitalism made collection child's play and pitted the poor against the poor. People across the street, who were in no better financial shape, would often peer through their blinds with a slight air of superiority, watching their neighbors ticketed and eventually put out onto the street.

The city could do just about anything it pleased in collecting delinquent taxes and unpaid fines and interest from deadbeats.

Most Americans live paycheck to paycheck. According to government statistics, 63 percent of US children and 55 percent of US adults live in asset poverty. The fact of the matter is that these people couldn't pay their back taxes and/or fines and interest in a million years.

Maybe misery does like company. Anyway, as the once popular phrase said, the writing was on the wall, and on many New City faces. Terror reigned.

Chapter 9

Do or Die

Summer came to an end. The water of the Sherman Park lagoon was still warm, especially compared to the sometimes brisk air above it. Carp and even some catfish glided to the top and threw themselves into the air. Scientists say they do this to eat, relieve themselves of parasites, or free themselves, but Danny knew. They jumped out of the water and into the air to tease the few fishermen and or cats gazing toward the pond from the shore.

Danny and Mountain rode their bikes. Dude and Elaine were loosely connected by large lengths of rope. As soon as they hit the park, Danny let 'em loose. Elaine always beat Dude to the water, and the ducks either took to the air or to the middle of the pond. Danny and Mountain sometimes sat for hours watching the show. Elaine liked to act as a submarine, diving down under the surface and then reappearing closer to the ducks. Once or twice she got close to capturing one.

Danny, lying on his stomach, rested his head in his hands. Five feet away Mountain lay in a twin pose. Danny carefully pulled a long blade of grass from the ground and placed the white bottom into his mouth. Mountain looked over at Danny sucking on the green. He plucked a piece and stuck it in his mouth.

"Mmm, I like this grass, Danny. How long you been eating grass?"

"I don't eat grass, Mountain. I suck the juice out of the root."

Mountain spit the grass that he had grinded up onto the lawn in front of him. "I know that, Danny, I meant, how long you been suckin' the juice out of the roots of the grass?"

"Almost all my life. My dad loved to find long weeds or even sticks and suck on 'em, sometimes for hours. He said that it was a way for him to load up on life."

"Load up on life?" Mountain asked.

Danny sat up, still sucking on the grass. "Don't get any better than this, big man. I'm sure gonna miss this place."

Mountain stared and then gently tilted his head. "Why's the park always empty, Danny? Don't people like fishin', sittin' and suckin' on the roots of the grass?"

Danny stared into the distance. It seemed like he could see all the way to Boston. "They legalized slavery in the US, big man. They keep the ants runnin' so hard to survive that they ain't got no time to rest. Kind of like the antelope running from the tiger. He might be in the most beautiful part of the jungle, but he ain't enjoying it. He's just tryin' to survive."

Mountain crunched his eyes a bit. *Not always real easy to understand Danny*, he thought. *In Greencastle, Danny'll have lots of time to explain.*

Dude and Elaine were splashing around like two school kids. At home Elaine ran the roost, but in the lagoon, they were on equal footing. In the vastness of the park ocean, Dude showed what seemed to be indifference to Elaine. She didn't seem overly concerned. She concentrated on the ducks.

"Danny, I know you're worried about that ticket man from the city."

"Mmm."

"Why does that man want to give us trouble, Danny?"

"I don't know. I guess he's sad," Danny said solemnly.

"Sad?" Mountain asked.

Danny stared at his partner and nodded. "Yep, sad. People like him are just sad," he said.

Mountain, as usual, was enraptured. It seemed that Danny never said anything that wasn't of paramount importance.

Danny continued. "They're sort of like empty pop bottles; they got just a few drops inside and break easily." Danny focused on

Mountain and smiled. "But, I guess if you can make it to the store with 'em, they'll give you a nickel."

"Yep," Mountain said and nodded. "Just like empty pop bottles, those revenue agents are." He looked at Danny. "Just some drops inside, just good for the deposit."

Mountain watched carefully as Danny pulled a blade of grass. Danny coddled it without breaking it until the white slid out from the grip of the rooted stem.

Mountain nodded. He understood. Danny watched out of the corner of his eye. On the third attempt, Mountain pulled the grass out without breaking it.

Danny smiled as Mountain looked at the white root and gleamed. "I like these roots, Danny." He proudly raised the grass blade in the air to show his partner.

Danny smiled. Greencastle would be perfect for Mountain, and Mountain would be perfect for Greencastle. The grip of Sherman Park and New City was loosening, and Danny spent long periods thinking about their new home, far from the violence of the streets and far from the insolence of the city agents.

"Danny, who gets the deposit out of that revenue worker?"

Danny reflected and then spoke. "Well, I guess in this instance, it's the developers. They'll get the nickel out of him."

"The developers want you out of New City, Danny? That's their nickel?"

"The developers want money. They don't even know I exist. They'd move their own mother out of New City into an old folks home to get that nickel." Danny hesitated before continuing. "And say it was for her own good."

"You know, Danny, my auntie told me my mother was a beautiful woman. She had light brown eyes, like mine!" Mountain looked at Danny wide-eyed.

Danny nodded.

"I was just a baby when they locked up my pa, Danny. They said he killed a policeman. But Auntie told me that any person with even a bird-size brain knew that Pa would never shoot anyone. He never even had a gun."

"Happens, big man."

Danny had heard many stories about Marla and Darrell, who many suspected of being her baby daddy. But it didn't much matter now, what was true and what was false. If Mountain's daddy had killed a cop or not, or if he really was the big man's father or someone else's, people pretty much believe what they want anyway.

"Auntie said that when Pa went to jail, my mother just gave up on life. I was just a pup. Danny, why do people call children pups?"

"It's just a metaphor."

Mountain cleared his throat and nodded. "Just what I thought, a metal for." He considered the two words and decided not to ask.

"My mother died on my second birthday, Danny. My cousin Todd Rondell said that the police killed her, but Auntie said that she accidentally took too much medicine. What do you think, Danny?"

Danny stared at the big man and stuck another blade of grass in his mouth. "I know your Aunt Bee. Aunt Bee never lied to me."

Mountain smiled. "I miss my mama, Danny."

"Do you remember her?"

"I'm not sure, I mean I seen pictures of her and my father. Auntie Bee says theirs was a union made outside of heaven." Mountain paused. "Not sure how that works." He fell deep into thought, staring at his shoe and shaking his head gently. "Not sure how that works," he repeated softly.

"Danny, sometimes I want to just pounce that revenue man." The phrase flew out of Mountain's mouth like one of those motorcycles on the highway that zoomed by you before you even knew they were coming.

Danny gently shook his head. "That's not the answer, Mountain. You just leave things to me."

"Does he know about us goin' to Greencastle, Indiana?"

"Nah." Danny watched the dogs slopping around in the lagoon. He turned back to Mountain. "He don't much care where we go, as long as it's out of New City."

"Danny, sometimes I get mad. I mean I get so much mad in me that I don't know how to get it out."

"You just let it go, big man. If you ever get so mad, you just tell me. I'll try to ease it out of you."

"Danny, Big Clem made me mad." Mountain looked to the side and continued.

"Danny, what if you're not around?"

"Big man, if anything ever happens when I'm not around and you can't wait at the house, you just come right here, right here where we are now and wait for me."

"I'll come here and sit right behind this bush, Danny, and you'll know right where I am."

"Sure, big man, if I ever get home and find you're gone, I'll know right where you are. I'll come over and we'll talk over whatever got you riled."

"Thanks, Danny." Mountain stared out at the lagoon. "Sometimes, Danny, when you're not home, I get to thinking, I get to thinking big thoughts, just like you Danny, and sometimes them thoughts get wild. Why, I feel that they so wild that they gonna knock the walls right out of the house." Mountain turned to the side and then back and looked at his friend. "Danny."

"Yes."

"It wasn't my fault that that kitten died. I didn't kill it. It died by itself, all by itself."

"I know, big man."

"I wouldn't hurt no kitten. I wanted it to keep the mice from eating the chicks' food."

"I know, big man."

"Danny."

"Yeah."

"One time in school when I was in eighth grade I beat a boy up. He made me so mad, Danny. I whupped him good. The police wanted to take me away from Auntie Bee."

"Well, I don't want you beating no one up. We're Christians. We don't do that."

"Danny, in the neighborhood they say that you're one tough man. They say that you put down three all by yourself. Why do they say that Danny, you put down three, all by yourself?"

"That was self-defense, big man, we're all tough when we're fighting for our lives. But I ain't so tough."

"Were you a Christian when you were fighting in self-defense?"

"You know, for a mountain of a man you're astute."

Mountain wasn't sure what a stoot was, but he was sure that it had to be good.

Danny continued, "That question has plagued me all my life, big man."

Danny took the blade of grass out of his mouth and waved it, enveloping the world. It was as if he was addressing the US Senate. "Jesus, He said to turn the other cheek." Danny paused solemnly. "And He let them put Him up on the cross."

"My Auntie says that Jesus is her savior." Mountain sat up and raised his voice, gaining confidence from just being labeled a "stoot," which must have meant he was smart, maybe even a little like Danny . . . "She says He was my savior too," he said emphatically.

Mountain's stare was as serious as an ambulance siren breaking the silence of the night. "If He couldn't stop them from putting Him on a cross, how's He gonna save anyone, Danny?"

"I didn't say He couldn't stop them. I said He let them."

"Well, Danny, why wouldn't someone stop you from putting them on the cross if they could?"

Danny was a lazy man by nature. That was partly why he became so effective. He searched out the quickest path. He looked around now, searching all the rooms for the car keys. He wanted to drive away from New City. He also wanted to find the words to suffice Mountain's curiosity about Jesus' crucifixion.

The big man continued. "My auntie said that Jesus said that life is precious. If life is so precious to Him, why did He let them take His?"

Danny stretched and swung his arms in circles like a boxer warming up. "You know what Socrates said, big man?"

"Am I supposed to?"

"Dude! Elaine! Get out of the water. We're goin' home!" Danny smiled.

"Who is Socrates?"

"Some Greek wise guy."

"You mean like Sam, the guy that makes the gyros on Ashland?"

Danny thought to himself and then nodded. "Yeah, kind of like Sam. Well, Socrates was also like Jesus, in that he also could have saved his own skin." Danny looked at Mountain to be sure that the big man was still following. "But he drank the hemlock without asking for pardon."

"Hemlock?"

"Poison."

"If he could ask for pardon and not have to drink the poison, why didn't he?"

"The same reason that Jesus didn't. He died for his principles, that way his principles lived on long after He was gone."

Danny tied Dude and Elaine, loosely dangling the ropes over his handlebars.

Mountain got on his bike.

Danny continued. "Socrates said, 'I am the wisest man alive, for I know one thing.'"

"Doesn't sound too smart, only knowing one thing," Mountain said.

"Are you gonna talk while I'm talkin' when we're in Greencastle, cause if you are, I think we'll build you a room out in the woods."

"No. Sorry, Danny. What was the only thing that Socrates knew?"

Danny got on the bike and began pedaling. Mountain rushed to keep up.

"What was the one thing Danny, Socrates knew?"

"That he knew nothing at all!" Danny yelled and sped up like he was finishing the Tour de France.

Mountain could never keep up with Danny and almost halted to yell. "Then I think that Sam is a lot more a wise guy Greek than Socrates! Sam knows lots of things, Danny! Sam knows how to cook!"

Danny got home and put Elaine and Dude in the house. When he came out, Mountain was still not back. Danny jumped on his bike and pedaled toward the park. As he turned on Throop he saw Mountain standing next to a squad car with Officer Brown. Danny sped forward.

Officer Brown was writing a ticket. Mountain stood with a dumbfounded look on his face.

"Hello, Officer," Danny said, smiling friendly.

"Don't interrupt," the public servant growled.

"Sir, can I at least inquire as to what's going on?"

"None of your business."

"He's writing me a ticket because I didn't stop at the stop sign. I didn't know that a bicycle had to stop at stop signs, did you, Danny?"

Brown stared sternly at Danny, who remained silent. "Bicycles are vehicles. According to the state laws, cyclists must follow the same rules of the road as anyone else."

"He really didn't know." Danny squeezed out a smile. "Can't you just give him a warning, Officer?"

"Mr. Nowak, you don't pay taxes or your bills. You help others break the law. In my book, that makes you a criminal and an accomplice to others' crimes." Brown looked sternly at Mountain and then at Danny. "You're less than an honorable citizen and I'd advise you to mind your own business. You're the last person that should be offering advice to me or anyone else."

Brown finished writing the ticket and handed it to Mountain. "Moses," Brown smiled, "get a light on that bike or don't let me see you on it after dusk."

Brown got in his car and pulled away.

Mountain looked at Danny. "I'm sorry, Danny. I didn't know that I had to stop. There wasn't no moving cars anywhere."

"Let's go home," Danny said. "It's not your fault, let's go home."

Once home, Danny went to Napoleon's house. Robert E. was sitting on the top step.

"Napoleon home?" Danny asked.

"Yeah, but he's sleeping. He had a long night. He come in at about 7 a.m."

Danny nodded. "When he wakes up, tell him to come by me."

"Got it, chief," Robert E. said and shot Danny a thumbs-up.

Danny gave Mountain five dollars and sent him to the store for bread and hot dogs.

Napoleon showed up shortly after. Danny and he sat on the porch.

"I called Ralph Ponzi in Greencastle," Danny said to Napoleon. "He said that we have until Christmas to come up with the money. He apologized but he is eighty-seven and he wants to settle things up for his people."

"Why does he have to settle things now for them? Where are they?"

"I don't know. Like life in so many small communities, the young often find work outside and never come back. My father says that's what happened to Ralph. I guess he wants to leave things neat for them when he goes. We need to hustle," Danny said.

"Brother, I ain't never hustled like I been now. I can't wait to get out of New City. Did you hear that they killed three on 56th and Halsted last night?"

"No," Danny said. "I didn't hear nothing."

"They say that it was all over a pair of sneakers. Three teenagers robbed a pair of Nikes and then shot it out about who was going to wear them. The last survivor died this morning." Napoleon hesitated. "That's what they said."

Danny shook his head. "All for a pair of plastic shoes that cost three dollars to make in China."

"Anyway Danny, I'm kicking ass. Last night I made a hundred and fifty . . . before taxes."

"Yeah, brother, pay those taxes," Danny quipped.

"I think we'll be able to make the move in November." Napoleon nodded. "Where's Mountain?"

"I sent him for some bread and dogs," Danny responded.

"How long ago?"

"I don't know." Danny looked at Napoleon and nodded. "I better get after him."

Danny jumped on his bike and sped towards the Open Pantry grocery. As he turned west on 51st Street he spotted a crowd near Benny's Bar. He edged nearer. Mountain was in the middle of the crowd. Dillah Price had Mountain by the neck, holding him against the wall.

"Please, leave me alone, Dillah," Mountain cried.

Danny parked his bike and edged his way into the circle. Pee Wee and his brother Walter were on either side of Mountain. They were the eldest of the eight Price brothers and they regularly terrorized the neighborhood.

Papa Price was a tough old guy and he did not tolerate drugs. He beat Walter, the oldest son, almost half to death when he heard that he was hanging with a dealer. The Price brothers were into other activities; they were mechanics, sold used auto parts, and trafficked in Link cards.

Half of their gang of hoods were with them on the corner. The rest of the spectators were neighbors. A squad car passed and continued to head east.

Big Guy Smith, a member of the Price Brothers corporation, grabbed Danny. "Where you going, Danny?"

Mountain spotted Danny. "Danny! Help me, Danny! They're hurting me!"

"Let me pass, Big Guy."

Big Guy smiled. "Not this time, Danny, Moses got to learn some respect. Since he been living with you, he thinks who he is. He ain't white, he ain't no one. Where's he come off telling us we got to call him Mountain. He ain't no mountain. He what he always been—Moses—a big, blubbering idiot."

Danny pushed against Big Guy.

"Back off, Danny, or you'll get your ass whipped too."

Dillah slapped Mountain and backed off. "Come on, Moses, you fairy."

Pee Wee punched him in the stomach. Moses bent over, hoping that his feigned pain would bring his ordeal to an end. It didn't work. Walter socked him in his face.

Danny saw drops of blood falling to the ground. He lunged forward. Big Guy shoved him hard. "Back down, Danny. I'm telling you for your own good."

"Well, at least make it a fair fight, not three against one!" Danny gasped.

Big Guy looked at Danny, nodded, and yelled towards the crowd. "Hey! Danny said to make it a fair fight!"

Mountain was still doubled over crying.

Big Guy looked at Danny. "You pick, Danny. Who? Walter, Dillah, or Pee Wee?"

The brothers stared at Danny. Danny stared back. "Pee Wee," Danny said softly.

"Walter!" Big Guy screamed.

"I said Pee Wee!" Danny screamed.

Big Guy smiled. "You did. You eliminated Pee Wee."

"Come on, man!" Danny screamed.

Danny would have never picked Walter, who was known for his nasty mean streak. He nailed cats to trees, coldcocked old men waiting for the bus, and sprayed dogs with gasoline and lit them up.

"Spread out!" Walter said.

The crowd moved back.

"Tell your boy to stand up like a man," Big Guy said.

"Stand up, Mountain," Danny said softly.

Mountain remained bent over.

"Mountain, stand up," Danny said, louder and with a good amount of sternness.

"Maybe he ain't standing up because he don't know who you're talking to. His name is Moses," Big Guy said.

Walter kicked Mountain in the face. Mountain fell to the ground, and the blood really began to flow.

"Get up, Mountain!" Danny yelled.

Walter kicked Mountain again. Mountain blubbered.

"Get up, Mountain. Get up or you won't come with me to Greencastle!"

Mountain stood. The crowd watched. It was a miraculous event. Mountain was converted, transformed, renewed, reborn.

"Greencastle, Indiana?" the big man asked as if he hadn't a care in the world.

The crowd was silent until Walter punched Mountain squarely in the nose.

"Yes! Greencastle, Indiana! Now put your hands up and defend yourself!"

Walter fired off a few rabbit punches.

"Defend yourself! I mean it or you won't come!"

Mountain moved his enormous hands up and covered his face.

Walter punched his stomach.

"Danny!" Mountain screamed.

"Now defend yourself! Punch back!"

The crowd was concentrated on the power that the strange white man held over the neighborhood idiot, they still thought of as Moses. Mountain stood motionless, his hands over his face.

Walter was frustrated that his punches had less effect than he had hoped. He punched again hard, in the groin area. Mountain bent forward slightly.

"Punch back or you won't ever feed the chicks!"

Mountain peered through his blocking hands at Walter's face. Mountain's baseball glove-sized fist shot out and caught Walter squarely on the nose. Walter fell to the ground, out cold.

The whole crowd gasped in awe.

Danny rushed to Mountain. "OK, fellas, it's over." Danny took Mountain by the shoulders. "Let's go, man."

"Danny, can I still feed the chicks?"

"Yeah, you can still feed the chicks."

"Danny, is Walter hurt? I didn't want to hurt him."

Danny looked at Walter, who was slowly coming to. "He'll be fine," Danny said and smiled slightly.

Danny rushed Mountain away from the group, not wanting to give them time to demand a rematch. *Sometimes you can still manage things without guns and knives*, he thought.

The drug trade had brought most of the viciousness and cowardice onto the streets, and Danny wished that the government would just legalize it once and for all. Of course, the corporations would get all the money and then how would the poor live? I mean, you need only so many baggers and delivery men for Walmart and Amazon.

The "war on drugs" had become the war on the poor as far as Danny was concerned. The rich drove into New City to purchase their goods and if they got caught, bought their way out. The poor sellers were the real victims. They got caught and languished in prison, more alone than ever.

The 1994 Biden crime bill really decimated the poor. Not being able to afford justice, people pleaded out to lesser crimes and then found themselves in prison for thirty years or even for life on the "three strikes you're out" portion of the truly racist bill.

But Danny didn't see racism as white against black in America. That was just a camouflage the rich used for the real prejudice, which was rich against poor.

The lists of "strikes" leading to mandatory life imprisonment varied by state—some included nonviolent offenses like treason, drug trafficking, theft, and bribery.

What it meant to Danny was that a whole lot of poor people filled up the penitentiaries, leaving their families broken and dysfunctional, while the real criminals, the folks doing the greatest harm, the corporations, shipped jobs to China and stripped workers of their benefits while the "fat cat" CEOs and politicians played golf.

The corporations pit the blacks against the whites and the homos against the heteros so that no one bothers them. And we're all too damn stupid to see it.

White supremacy? Danny knew a whole lot of folks that used the word *nigger*; most of them were black. And the way the whites or Hispanics used the word had absolutely nothing to do with slavery or supremacy of any kind. Hell, Danny grew up being called a Polack. So, who cares? That's what he is.

Sticks and stones will break my bones but names will never hurt me.

The real racists, he thought, were the quiet, politically correct people. Their sermons mostly masqueraded the greed and "give a shit" attitudes etched into their hearts.

The whole South Side had thousands of people who used derogatory names for folks everyday, but some of them were the salt of the earth and would help anyone. Try asking most any Chicago University professor to give you a few dollars on a cold day. They'd give you a lecture and frosty words that exited their pursed lips after passing over their frigid hearts.

Lippatu was waiting on the porch for Danny and Mountain.

"Don't you boys think you is too old to be fistfighting?" she asked.

The boys remained quiet.

"Well, don't you think that you're too old?" Lippatu insisted.

Mountain turned toward Lippatu as he would his Auntie Bee. "It wasn't my fault. I didn't start nothing and Danny, he said that I couldn't feed the chicks if I didn't hit Walter."

"If you didn't defend yourself," Danny corrected.

"Well, I hope you ruffians won't be bringing any of this behavior to Greencastle."

"No ma'am," Mountain sighed. "I won'." Before he could get the "t" out to make the word won't, he erupted. "I din't want to hurt nobody. I like the Price boys. They used to take my cart but their mama always made them give it back."

Danny looked at Lippatu and shook his head. "It wasn't Mountain's fault. It was a misunderstanding that got out of control. This won't ever happen in Greencastle."

"Indiana," Mountain added.

Officer Brown pulled up. The three future Greencastle residents silently watched him get out of the car.

"My patience is wearing thin with you boys. I heard that Moses beat up Walter Price, not that he didn't have it coming."

"Officer, he was just defending himself. Walter and Pee Wee hit him repeatedly before he reacted," Danny rebutted.

"Well, I think that I should bring him in for questioning," Brown said as he took out a pair of handcuffs.

Mountain jumped. "No, Danny! No! I don't want to go to no jail. It's full of bad men. They'll hurt me. Please, Danny, stop him."

"Look officer, please, it wasn't his fault, really it wasn't. There's tons of witnesses if you ask around," Danny paused. "Please ask around first. I really wish you would."

Officer Brown put his arm on Danny's shoulder and pulled him away from Lippatu and Mountain. Brown whispered in Danny's ear. "You know what I wish you'd do, Danny?" He didn't give any time to respond. "I wish you and your boyfriend over there would get out of Dodge."

Danny shook his head. "Look, Officer Brown, there's nothing we'd like better and we have a plan. We promise to be out by Christmas. Please don't arrest him."

Officer Brown nodded. "Christmas," he repeated.

That evening, Danny called Ralph Ponzi.

"Sir, Danny Nowak here. Make your plans, sir. We'll be there for Christmas."

At that very moment Officer Brown was sitting in his car with Revenue Agent Burman.

Burman's face was heated. "I need them out before Christmas, Officer. You're negligent in your duties. Their home is one big violation."

"I'm not a city inspector," Brown scoffed. "Besides, I've seen the inspectors out plenty of times writing tickets."

Burman remained unconvinced.

"Look," Brown insisted, "I scared the wits out of the big guy the other day."

"Moses?"

"Yep. He's one big marshmallow. I took out my cuffs and he started crying hysterically."

"So he's the weak link?" Burman asked.

"Yeah and Nowak's soft on him. All anyone has to do is put a little pressure on the big guy and Nowak crumbles."

"You think they're homos?" Burman asked.

Brown rubbed his chin. "What's really a homo? Do they really exist? I think it's just a choice of convenience. A fat woman can't get laid so she turns. A feminine guy can't get any so he turns."

Burman stared and Brown continued. "I know Danny racks up the cokehead girls. Maybe he swings both ways." Brown looked out the passenger window as if he were thinking. After a few seconds Brown continued. "There really can't be another reason for it, they must be swapping fluids. Why else would anyone stick his neck out for a moron like that?"

Burman smiled and nodded. "He's a marshmallow, huh?"

"Soft as they get," Brown said.

"Keep the pressure on," Burman said with the air of an arrogant army general. "This will work for everyone." He nodded. "What about that house on 50th, the Jones family?"

"I called my pal at the sheriff's office. While no one was home they put the furniture on the street. The Joneses abandoned the building."

Burman smiled again. "This is going to work nicely to cushion your retirement, Brown."

Slowly the neighborhood was clearing. The city was legally confiscating dozens of homes and empty lots weekly. The pace was picking up. Rothstein was calm and the CEO of the city was confident that she'd face no serious challenge in the next election. There was peace on earth.

Danny lay awake on his cot. There was a knock at the door. Elaine and Dude began barking.

Danny opened the door. "Sully, what you got?"

"I got some copper and brass in the car."

Sully, a tall descendant of Swedes, preferred to sell the stuff to Danny and not to the scrapyards. There were twenty warrants out for Sully's arrest. He knew that he could trust Danny and he was happy to partner with such an honorable guy.

Danny lifted the box and brought it into the house. He closed the door.

"Sully?" Mountain asked.

"Yeah."

"He got more copper?"

"Yeah."

"Why does he bring it to you, Danny?"

"To stay out of trouble."

"That's all he has to do to stay out of trouble, Danny? I wish it was that easy for me."

"Mountain, in fifty, sixty days we'll be out of here. It will be easy to stay out of trouble in Greencastle."

"Indiana," Mountain added. "Danny, what would I do without you to help me stay out of trouble?" He stared into the dark and continued. "If you weren't here, I'd be in a bad way." Mountain hesitated. "Danny, seems like New City is full of trouble for me. What will I do if you ain't around and trouble finds me, Danny?"

"I told you, Mountain, if something happens, anything, go by the bush at the lagoon where we go, and wait for me. I'll find you."

"Promise, Danny?"

"Have I ever let you down?"

"Elaine!" Mountain called the old girl. "Come on over here."

Elaine walked over and Mountain rubbed her head. "Elaine likes me now, Danny."

"I imagine she loves you," Danny said.

"We're taking her and Dude to Greencastle, Indiana, right Danny?"

"Of course . . . Greencastle, Indiana," Danny muttered as he laid back down on his cot, falling into a deep sleep.

Chapter 10

Final Preparations

Prices in New City were moving up on Zillow. This was a bad sign for Rothstein. The higher they climbed, the more the deal would cost.

Rothstein and Redman were supposed to be on opposite sides of the street, almost natural enemies: people that enslaved others for greed and the people who were supposed to protect the common men from them. But things had taken a dramatic change.

In the new capitalism, Rothstein was a savior to the career politicians who needed his donations to be reelected. To the defenseless working poor, he was a vulture picking the flesh right off their bones.

Mayor Redman hadn't gotten to where she was by being anyone's fool. Rothstein pushed hard, sure in his conviction that speed protected price fluctuation and profit. Instead, the mayor wanted him to pay as much as possible, to the city for the properties and to her campaign war chest.

It was a fragile balance and the mayor had to be careful not to push the developer to desperation and the other side.

The only sure result was that, in the end, the working folks would be further in the hole, victims of the partnership between big business and the politicians they owned.

Rothstein got a foothold on the city through a business associate, Max, who was the former mayor of Chicago's brother, and incidentally a large shareholder of Lyft shares; and the rich help the rich.

Redman wanted Rothstein's clan to pay a large price for the development land. The more they paid for the city land, the easier it would be for the mayor to justify the deal, as the municipal deficit would be more positively affected. Still, Redman had some restraints. If she couldn't get the deal consummated, there was a risk of it falling apart.

Redman wanted the announcement as near the holidays as possible, preferably Christmas Day when no one pays attention. There would be no physical kickbacks, but Rothstein would owe the mayor in a big way.

This debt would lead to a huge donation to the mayor's reelection war chest, or maybe a loan which would be forgiven and forgotten. Other times, donations, which are almost always an investment to the donor, result in jobs for relatives or some other untraceable or traceable legal payment. The poor still used cash. The rich had long evolved past that.

The mayor played the game with skill, knowing that she would be criticized no matter what the deal was. Years of battling with the Chicago Police had made her a master negotiator and she would not fail, herself.

That's what it was all about. Them. I mean, why else would people spend their own resources and beg, borrow, and steal to take a job which likely meant a significant cut in pay?

Burman was feeling more confident, too. He remembered people giving him dirty looks when he first drove up in the Revenue Van; a few even yelled out obscenities. Machiavelli was right, the masses were ignorant and could be trained to support most any oppression. You had to feed it to them teaspoon by teaspoon . . . RICO, the Biden crime bill, the Patriot Act.

Burman wasn't a bad guy and he loved happy endings. His favorite film was *Cool Hand Luke*, with Paul Newman. He shivered with delight at the end when the warden told the sheriff that they'd take the mortally wounded Luke to the prison hospital which was more than an hour away. "Get out of the way," the warden said to the sheriff's objections, "he's ours."

Some of the more economically comfortable New City residents were actually warm to Burman. They respected what he represented. They knew that their property values would rise.

The rest hid or avoided contact. He basked in their terror and fear, which is a far more powerful emotion than respect.

Danny had also read Machiavelli and he saw what he believed were the first teaspoons fed to us by Ronald Reagan in 1982, when the president lowered taxes on the people who could most afford to pay them and went after the air traffic controllers' union. Since then the working class lost terrain, year after year. By Danny's calculations, the minimum wage should have been thirty dollars by 2020.

Burman only grew more and more arrogant in dealing with the freeloaders. Like Cool Hand Luke, they were his. He began yelling at them and berating them publicly. His favorite part of the day was arriving with the sheriffs to throw a deadbeat family's possessions out of their home and onto the street. There were a few stragglers who tried to rebel. For them, the sheriff employed a Taser. Burman carried one himself and was just itching to use it.

Sometimes, when at home in the evening, Burman stood in front of the mirror, pretending to confront one of the violent free-loaders. Burman stared into the mirror. "Back off, buster." Burman's face became hard and steely. "I said back off!" Burman smiled and jammed the Taser into the sink, pretending to zap the imaginary person he was speaking to in the mirror.

Burman especially disliked Danny, who had helped steal millions over the years from the gas, water, electric companies, and the city. Danny had that Cool Hand Luke way about him. He never angered and you'd never know he was much of a public enemy, but he was the worst of the worst. He was honorable. And Burman put it in his mind to get even with Danny for this.

Danny also read *Atlas Shrugged*, the novel by Ayn Rand. Today it seems to have collected an almost cult following. "Reward the gifted and scoff the nonproducers," was its message. Danny saw it more as, "punish people for their poverty."

Danny was a thinker. He laid awake late at night trying to make sense of it all. What kind of society allows families to accumulate billions when there is no health care and schools for all? What kind of society permitted 1 percent of the population to generate 80 percent of the wealth? The answer to Danny was an oppressive society, where freedom is only a government-sanctioned fantasy.

Danny reflected that after the move to Greencastle he might never see his pal Pat again. Who could say, though? If anyone would visit him, it would be Pat, driving up on a sunny day in his old Sebring convertible.

Danny might need to ask Pat for some finish-up cash. At the rate things were going, they'd get the ten thousand by Christmas, but they might be a thousand or so short for the moving expenses and utility deposits and whatnot. Danny was sure that Pat would find a way to help if the future Greencastlers needed it. He and Pat had shined shoes together when they were just tots and today they were as close as ever.

Pat made it and became famous and all, but he never became like the rest of them. Like Danny, Pat was always just a shoeshine boy and would die a shoeshine boy.

The blue summer sky had long since surrendered to the autumn gray. The daytime streets which a few months ago were filled with playing children were now filled with fall leaves. It was a more solitary time for everyone. Danny and Mountain were junking every day, and Mountain was finally convinced that they'd be going to Greencastle, Indiana.

Danny was right. *Big Clem never knew what he was talking about.* Mountain stopped quizzing Danny about whether or not they'd be going, now convinced that they would. He couldn't wait to feed the chicks. He had never hoed a vegetable garden, but he was more than willing to learn.

Mountain also noticed that Danny was upbeat. They were coming close to the legendary ten thousand. Napoleon gave his stash to Danny, making him promise to not give any of it back. If the stash was around, Napoleon would use it. Danny was a sure thing.

A few times a week, Danny would reach under Elaine's red and tattered sleeping cushion and open the envelope. The stacks had rubber bands around them. Each had two thousand dollars. Over the months, Danny walked to the currency exchange on 51st, changing singles, fives, tens, and twenties into hundreds and fifties. In the end, it would all fit in a long letter envelope.

Lippatu had never seen her father so industrious. He had finally found a goal. Greencastle, Indiana, filled the thoughts of each of the family members.

Robert E. had recently broken up with his girlfriend. This was actually a very good thing to Napoleon, as Robert E. had threatened to remain behind. Napoleon wanted the family the way he had grown up, in other times, before Facebook, iPhones, and corporate television ripped the American family to shreds . . . to make a buck.

Napoleon was confident that they'd have the ten grand by Christmas. For the first time, he believed in Greencastle, Indiana. He was already mentally preparing to roast the Christmas turkey in the oven he had never seen, in the kitchen he had never been in, in a house he had only dreamt of, and in a town which he had only heard about a few short months ago.

Lippatu was basking in the idea of living in Greencastle. The calm euphoria seemed like a health elixir to everyone, and Lippatu hadn't had a sickle cell crisis in months. Speaking of the clean, quiet town with no crime, she was also coaxing her other siblings to prepare. Life was going to change in a big way for all of them, for the better.

November shot in like a bully, puffing subfreezing temperatures and thirty-mile-an-hour winds. The city prepared for a snowfall that luckily never came.

Danny lit the stove up and threw on a few logs. He would miss his house of almost forty years. He'd miss the neighborhood, his friends, the buildings, the potholes, the sounds of the trains, the fire hydrants, the basketball court, the smell of the old stockyards on humid summer days, and especially the sprinkler in the park across the street.

Danny thought about his son, Little Danny, who had become mixed up with gangs and for the good of his father told Big Danny to forget about any contacts with him.

When Little Danny was young, Big Danny had called him a "Poliguat," half Polack and half Guatemalan. Big Danny didn't resist his son's request. He knew the deal and if Little Danny ever withdrew, he could find his father and would be welcomed with the fatted calf, like the prodigal son.

Mountain came into his own and was fine to be left home alone. This was a good thing. Danny needed more and more solitude to map out strategy and confront each possible challenge that could stand between them and Greencastle.

Each day Danny hooked up Elaine and Dude and drove his bike. Some days he was gone for hours, making it all the way to 67th Street, roaming up and down the streets of his youth, his life . . . Ada, Elizabeth, Carpenter, Bishop, Laflin, Justine, and Ashland. Danny glanced ahead at the street, avoiding the potholes and wondering where those street names ever came from.

Winding back into New City, Danny drove past 1453 West 50th Street, where he was born and where both his parents died. His stepmother was quite a woman, marrying his father, who already had eleven kids and then adding one of their own. Danny and his siblings cherished their memories of her. She was an incredible homemaker, judge, jury, and peacemaker. Maybe modern women know computer programs and how to act like men, but it would be nearly impossible for them to ever gain the love and respect Danny's mom had from the neighbors and the Nowak clan.

Danny would miss driving by the house. It was a beautiful place and though the family lived humbly, they never lacked a thing. He squinted and saw his old man in the yard lifting the body of a rusted Harley. His father smiled at Danny. Danny smiled at him and the old man disappeared in a poof.

Today, it seems we have everything, computers, HD TVs, and smartphones, but we really have nothing. We have psychiatrists and doctors dispensing dope, Ashley Madison and Tinder sex, but we really don't have now a smidgen of what we had. Danny always said that he'd pay a million to have one of his parent's hugs . . . right now $10,000 was much more than a million.

After passing his old house, Danny turned back south on Laflin Avenue. He got to 51st Street and drove west. This had been where he and Pat had shined shoes so many years ago. Most of the saloons were closed and many buildings were torn down or in a state of terminal disrepair. Still, Danny loved the street.

A drug dealer on the corner waved. "Danny!"

Danny waved back and the man raised a peace sign. Soon he would be replaced by a Walgreens pharmacy. Danny pulled his bike over on the northeast corner of 51st and Hermitage. He jumped off and petted Elaine and Dude. Elaine growled as Dude pushed his way closer to Danny.

"Leave him alone, girl. He's just like you, looking for a little affection."

Elaine sat down and placed her head on Danny's lap.

Pat and Danny were robbed a few times right there on 51st Street, but their first really big struggle had happened on this corner where 51st intersected Hermitage, many years ago. Danny reflected as he had hundreds of times about their first real battle, when boys tried to take their shoeshine boxes. Pat and Danny had handed their money over a few times, but no one was getting their shoeshine boxes. That was their livelihood.

Danny reflected about a special Saturday. The following day was Pat's sister Bernadette's first Communion. Pat's mother had borrowed a dress from a Mexican family whose daughter had made her communion the week before. Pat saw it as his place to secure a gift for his little sister. He told Danny, and they were both enthusiastic to give it all they had.

When they got to Damen, Pat walked into a small jewelry store. He spotted a women's Timex watch and was immediately convinced.

"Sir, how much for that Timex?"

"What's the occasion?"

"It's my sister's communion."

"Perfect choice," the man said. "It's a little under twelve dollars, son."

Pat looked at Danny, who nodded. "What time do you close?"

"Five."

Danny took the north and Pat took the south side of the street. When they hit Trumbull, about two miles west, they sat on the curb.

"How much?" Danny asked.

"I got almost five dollars. How 'bout you?"

"Three-eighty." Danny said solemnly. Heading back, Danny took the south and Pat the north side of the street. At twenty minutes to five, the boys were still a mile and two bucks short.

"A guy just gave me fifty cents!" Danny yelled across to Pat.

The store was in view but it was already a few minutes after five. Pat's heart pounded, they both ran. The shade on the front door had been lowered. The distressed shoeshine boys looked at each other as they walked to the front of the store. Pat pushed on the door and amazingly it opened. They were as happy as two lost puppies would be, finding their owner. They walked in.

"Hi, fellas," the owner said with a smile.

"Hello, sir," Pat said.

"Hello, sir." Danny nodded.

"Well, where we at?"

Both boys emptied the change from their pockets onto the counter. They counted twice but the second time it was still only ten dollars and eighty-three cents. The boys frowned.

"Sir," Pat asked, "could we bring the rest to you on Monday? I'll shine after my sister's first Communion tomorrow."

"Sorry, son, I don't work that way."

The boys looked at each other. Distraught, they began putting the change back into their pockets.

The man's voice broke the mournful silence. "But I do like what you're doing, so I'll put in what you're shy," the man said. "Consider the balance a gift from me to your sister."

The man packed the magical gift, magical because the boys had worked a miracle to get that much money in a day. It broke all records.

He came from around the counter, put an arm around each boys' shoulders, and walked them to the door. "Your sister is lucky to have a brother like you," he said.

Pat smiled.

"And you're lucky to have a friend like this," the merchant continued.

The man smiled at Danny and Danny choked up.

As Danny rode the bike further west with the dogs in tow, he recalled all the old taverns, their owners and bartenders. It was a great time to grow up. *Back then, kids were men a lot younger than today,* Danny thought. Somehow there wasn't all the animosity between the races. All sorts of people worked at Central Steel on 51st and California. Back then, people were just people. They may have had names for each other like Polack, spic, wop, mick, spaghetti-bender, spook, garlic-eater, nigger, Kraut, and greaseball, but few thought much of the names and even fewer thought them offensive. It depended on your intent, not on a word.

Words didn't mean anything, people did, and much of the time the words were used as an affectionate way of teasing between members of each group. That's not to say that some people didn't use them in a cruel way, but intent marked the offense, not CNN or some media loudmouth.

Danny pulled up to the fountain in Cornell Park, giving Elaine and Dude turns slurping up the water. Danny took the ropes off the dogs and they went galloping into the Cornell Park field.

It was about fifty-five degrees and sunny. The temperature suited him just fine. Danny laid down and put his hands under his head. Within a few moments he had dozed off.

Back at the house, Mountain was stripping plastic and rubber off wire. He felt a little drowsy and he walked inside the house. He didn't bother taking off his army jacket; it was chilly inside. He quickly fell asleep on his cot.

Burman walked out of his office. Things were going better, but his constant need for money and the assurance that more would arrive still kept him awake at night. His parents had been extremely well-to-do until Burman's teen years, and he yearned to return to the lifestyle of his childhood. He pulled the van out of the city lot and drove towards Nowak's home. He hated few people more than he hated the criminal enabler, Danny Nowak.

He was certain that had Nowak not existed, Burman would have achieved his goal long ago. He was convinced of nothing more, and this fact drove an uncontrollable anger in him. Burman parked his van and put the Taser into his right jacket pocket. Carrying the Taser always made him feel taller and carrying it added a bit of elaborate kink to his step. *If only Rothstein could see him now.*

The children were at school and the block was completely void of life. Burman walked up the stairs and tapped on the door. The dogs hadn't barked, which meant that no one was home. Burman pushed the door open and entered. The house smelled like a place would smell where two men who rarely bathed lived with two dogs. The walls were stripped down to the wood and light entered through tiny holes in the outside walls.

Burman walked right past the cot, not noticing Mountain sleeping. Burman looked in the bathroom. The toilet was black and dry. He walked into the kitchen and looked over the food supply: quite impressive. He spotted a dog's bed and noticed that there was a slight bulge under the red cushion and the ear of an envelope protruding.

In the other room, Mountain stirred but Burman didn't hear a thing. Burman was too busy marveling at the contents of the envelope. He tucked it in between his shirt and his jacket and turned. As he hit the partition between the kitchen and the front room, he heard a noise and stopped.

Mountain approached from Burman's right side, startling him. Burman reflectively put his hand in his pocket. He had the Taser and was secure against anyone, including this marshmallow, especially against this marshmallow.

"What are you doing here?! This place is supposed to be vacant. You and your boyfriend, whatever his name is, were supposed to be out of here!"

"Danny," Mountain said meekly. He wasn't quite sure how to react to this intrusion.

"I told you. The city told you. You need to be out of here." Burman approached the mountain of a man. "Don't you understand English?"

"I do."

As Burman rushed to be face to face with Mountain, the envelope fell out of his jacket to the floor.

Mountain immediately recognized it. "That's our Greencastle, Indiana money," the big man said.

Burman hesitated. His mind raced. He wanted to leave the house with the loot. "This is tax money! You and your boyfriend owe the taxpayers of this city lots of money."

"Danny," Mountain whispered. "Danny!" he screamed.

Burman reached down for the envelope.

"You're not stealing our Greencastle, Indiana money." Mountain stepped on the envelope just as Burman began lifting it up. Burman froze and looked up at Mountain. "You're gonna be really sorry if you don't get your foot off of city property," he said.

"It's our money. We're going to use it to buy a house in Greencastle . . . Indiana," Mountain replied.

Mountain looked down to make sure that his foot was still on the precious Greencastle, Indiana loot. It was. He smiled. Burman couldn't take the impertinence. He stood and slapped Mountain in the face. Mountain barely felt it and just stared.

"Look. It's the law, this is tax money and you need to get out of this house." Burman stared and tried to look kindly. "It's the law."

Mountain stared back, holding his foot on the stash. Burman took the Taser out of his pocket.

Mountain thought that it looked like a flashlight. Burman turned it on. "Do you see this? This is a Taser and it will knock you on your ass. Now get your foot off the loot before I use it on you."

Mountain wasn't sure what a Taser could do, but he was sure that he wasn't getting his foot off the envelope.

Burman pushed the Taser against Mountain's arm. The burning pinch didn't change Mountain's mind and Mountain grabbed Burman by the neck. "You're not taking our Greencastle, Indiana, money!"

Burman reached around trying to make better contact through Mountain's layers of clothes. He attempted to zap the big man again.

Mountain grimaced and squirmed, but he wouldn't take his foot off the envelope and grabbed Burman's arm, trying to pull the Taser away from him.

"Stop it," Mountain said.

Burman again attempted to Taser the giant.

Mountain heard Danny in his head. "Defend yourself. Punch back or you won't ever feed the chicks!"

Mountain swung his fist at Burman's head with all his might. Burman went down to the ground. Mountain stared for a few seconds. Burman didn't move.

Mountain's eyes quickly darted from side to side. He knew that Burman was in a bad way.

Mountain looked toward the front door. "Danny!" he yelled. "Danny! Why did you leave me here?"

Tears filled Mountain's eyes. There was only one thing to do.

Officer Brown drove down 50th Street and noticed the white revenue van. He also noticed that the door to Nowak's house was open. He parked the car and got out. "Anybody home?!" he yelled at the front door. "Anybody home?!" he repeated. "Burman!"

Brown took his gun out of its holster and stepped inside. He found Burman dead on the kitchen floor. Brown walked out of the house and called for backup. Within minutes there were ten squad cars in front of Danny's home.

Danny woke up from his nap in Cornell Park. The falling sun was shining and he felt good. They'd get to Greencastle soon, and life would change for the better, for everyone. "Elaine, Dude, get over here!" he yelled.

Dude sat still, but Elaine still wasn't accustomed to having a rope around her neck. "Come on, girl," Danny said, "it won't be long and we won't need to be doing this. Yous will have the run of the land and the forest behind the house." Danny patted his pant leg. "Come on, girl."

Danny rode east on 51st Street and turned north on Loomis. As soon as he turned east on 50th he saw the squad cars. He pumped the pedals to get home. When he arrived, Napoleon's kids, except for Robert E., were standing on their porch. Napoleon was talking to one of the cops.

Danny jumped off the bike. "Napoleon, what happened?"

"They say there's a dead guy in the house," Napoleon said.

Shocked, Danny asked, "In my house?"

Napoleon nodded.

"Is Mountain inside?"

Napoleon shook his head. "They say it's a white dude."

Brown walked up to Danny. "Danny, where were you at?"

"Me? I was walking the dogs. We went to Cornell Park."

"I hope you got witnesses. A city revenue agent named Burman is in your house stiffer than a two-by-four."

"What?" Danny asked. "That's impossible."

Homicide investigator Dirsten walked up to Brown and Danny. "Do you live here, sir?"

"Yes, I do," Danny answered.

"What is your name?"

"Daniel Nowak."

Dirsten pushed Danny towards the stairs and they entered the house together. Danny walked into the kitchen. Burman was, in fact, on the floor.

"Do you know this man, Mr. Nowak?"

Danny nodded. "Yeah, he's a revenue agent, Burman."

"You're going to have to come to the station and answer a few questions, Mr. Nowak."

Danny remained quiet. "Do you have any weapons in the house, Mr. Nowak?"

"Yeah, I have a gun. I took it off a kid trying to kill André Baracca."

"I'd have let him snuff him," Dirsten snapped. "Where's the gun?" Dirsten took his pistol out of his holster. "You're covered."

Danny tapped his foot on a board on the floor. "It's in there."

Dirsten opened the floor but there was nothing in the hole. "Where's the gun?"

"It's gone." Danny's mind was racing.

"I see that. Where's it at?" Dirsten asked impatiently.

"I'm not sure" Danny replied.

"Does anyone else live here?"

"Moses."

"Do you think he took the gun?"

"I guess it's possible."

Danny spent a few hours in the station. Dirsten decided that he wasn't a suspect. The department put out an all-points bulletin for Moses Moore, a murder suspect, armed and dangerous.

Chapter 11

Going Home

The doors closed on Napoleon's blue car and silence entered and accompanied him and Danny home.

Napoleon hit the wipers but they had no effect. He realized that it was his own tears blocking his view. "They're going to crucify Mountain. He won't stand a chance. Today, killing a revenue agent's like killing a cop. They're the guards of the castle."

Danny remained silent.

"Those cops are thieves, like the politicians. Either they already stole our stash or they'll steal it off of Moses when they find him." Another tear rolled down Napoleon's face. He and his family would soon be on the streets, or worse, in shelters. "We'll save up, Danny. We'll get to Greencastle." Napoleon patted Danny's leg.

Danny gave no response.

When they arrived home, Danny opened the door and stood momentarily. Danny wished he could turn the clock back twenty-four hours, just a day. He regretted going to Cornell Park.

An hour later, Danny walked out. The air was cool but not cold for this time of the year. The wind hit Danny's face in pleasant wisps. He headed down Throop. He wasn't sure what time it was, but for sure it was after midnight. The drug dealers were in their dens. The late-night users knew the addresses. The streets were empty.

Danny crossed 51st and looked at the space where Saint John the Baptist once stood. It was a Gothic church built enthusiastically by immigrants less than a hundred years ago. They could have never known the fate of their treasure, which was torn down fifteen years ago. They say that the altar and the stained-glass windows were priceless and sent out to a church in a wealthy suburb of Milwaukee. Jesus didn't go out of style, He just moved.

Danny hit the first blades of grass. They felt like a carpet under his feet. He walked solemnly. Sherman Park was closed at dusk and empty as the food kitchen on Tuesday afternoon.

Danny spotted the pier. There were no ducks, no geese; they had all left for their winter homes in milder climates.

Danny could see Mountain's head protruding from the top of the bushes where he was hiding. Danny approached slowly. Mountain felt Danny's presence, froze, and then looked mechanically towards him.

"Danny," Mountain mumbled quietly to himself.

The whisper numbed Danny's senses. He moved closer. The full moon reflected off the Sherman Park Lagoon like it was giving some sort of light show. For a moment, the moon struck Danny as behaving arrogantly, then he realized that they were both sons of the same creator. If the moon was arrogant, then so was he.

Danny approached the bushes cautiously. Mountain remained still. Danny was within ten feet and then five and then he finally was standing over his friend. They were both silent, their eyes fixed on each other. Danny smiled slowly. Mountain mimicked his mentor.

"I didn't mean to hurt no one, Danny."

Danny shook his head. "Don't worry. It will all be fine."

Danny's words created an instantaneous transition to calm on Mountain's face.

"Can I still feed the chicks?"

"Of course you can."

"Can I get up, Danny?"

"Sure."

"My legs and butt hurt." Mountain rubbed the back of his pants as he stood. With colossal effort, he smiled. "I been sitting in this position for a long time. I did just what you told me, Danny. When something happened that I couldn't handle, I came here and waited for you." He looked in Danny's eyes. "Didn't I, Danny?"

Danny nodded kindly.

Mountain stood up. "Where's Elaine and Dude?"

"They're at the house. I didn't want to wake 'em."

"But they love to go out at any time, Danny," Mountain said, scrutinizing Danny's eyes as he spoke.

Danny smiled. "I needed time to think."

Danny walked towards the lagoon. Mountain followed.

"Did you think of something, Danny?" Mountain asked.

"Sure," Danny nodded. "Everything will be fine."

Danny sat down and pulled a blade of grass. In the cooler air, the first three snapped but he managed to remove the fourth and fifth intact. He handed one to Mountain and stuck the other in his mouth. Mountain sat next to Danny and sucked on the blade of grass. "Everything's gonna be fine, Danny?"

"Just fine, big man."

"That agent tried to steal our Greencastle, Indiana, stash." Mountain stared at Danny. "I had to stop him."

"You did good, Mountain." Danny hesitated. "You did good."

"I'll hoe the garden patch, too, Danny. I don't want you to think that I'll only feed the chicks," Mountain said softly. "My Auntie Bee told me in a dream to listen to you, Danny. I will, all you need to do is tell me what to do and I swear, Danny, I'll do it."

Danny smiled and gazed into Mountain's eyes. "OK then, hush and look out at the lagoon. Imagine Greencastle, the house sitting on a plot of green, green grass, with tall trees and a little pond in the back."

A few seconds passed.

Mountain stared at the lagoon. "Danny, I see it. I see Greencastle," he turned towards Danny, "Indiana."

Danny nodded. "OK, Mountain, just keep looking at it, the ducks on the pond and the little fish jumping out of the water."

Danny reached his right hand into his pocket. Mountain turned towards him as if he noticed that Danny was reaching.

"You told me you'd listen to me," Danny said, "now just look out at the pond, look at the corn stalks and the vegetable garden."

Mountain stared into the darkness. A tear fell from his right eye. He nodded. "Everything will be fine, Danny?"

"Yes," Danny sighed, "just look at the lagoon and see our home in Greencastle."

Mountain whispered, "Indiana," and looked at the lagoon. After a few seconds, he turned to Danny. "I'm gonna feed the chicks, Danny."

Danny nodded. "That's right, Mountain, you're gonna feed the chicks."

"And Dude and Elaine won't get near them 'cause I'll give them what for."

Danny felt inside his pocket. Mountain looked back at the lagoon and concentrated. "Get out of the garden patch and leave those chicks alone, Dude, you old bandit you," Mountain said.

Danny raised the luger to the back of Mountain's head.

"You too, Elaine. Get out of the garden." Mountain moved his head slightly but his eyes remained fixed on the pond.

"I'll make you proud of me, Danny. Are you proud of me?"

"Sure I am," Danny said as he pulled the trigger.

Mountain slumped over.

Danny looked at the moon, begging for absolution. The moon responded with the favor of a lifetime. It shone down on Mountain's white-toothed smile.

Almost immediately the air filled with the sounds of sirens. The department had been concentrating on this area for the manhunt of Moses Moore, alias Mountain. Danny stood. The lights of a squad car beamed on him. Several squads rushed up and screeched to a halt.

"Put your hands up in the air!"

Danny stood still.

"Put your hands in the air, or we will shoot!"

Danny slowly raised the pistol; when it got to his waist, he pointed it at the searchlight on the front squad car and squeezed the trigger. He heard a few pops and then left to join Mountain in Greencastle, Indiana.

Lippatu walked out and cupped her hands to her mouth. "Danny! Danny! You get in here and do your homework. Those fish will be waiting for you when you're done!"

"Oh, leave that pup alone, girl," Napoleon said. Lippatu was the mistress of the house and she paid little heed to Napoleon or anyone else.

"And keep those scraggly dogs out of this house, young man. One of them swiped what was left of my cake!"

"I got that cake, girl," Napoleon confirmed. "Don't be riling up that boy."

Lippatu stared at her father and shook her head. "And what about your diabetes, Napoleon?"

Napoleon put his thumb and finger together. "It was just a small piece, honey."

Lippatu watched Danny leap over the bushes as he scrambled towards them. He certainly resembled his namesake in many ways. She shook her head at her father and walked into the house.

Napoleon continued to sway back and forth in the back porch rocking chair. It was his favorite place in the whole world.

Napoleon was graying now and didn't much care to shave. His beard wasn't full, and a bit scraggly like its patron.

Robert E., a deputy for the Greencastle's Sheriff's Department, was married and living up the road. Little Danny was Robert E. and his bride's son.

Shareece was also married and living in town. Ray Ray and Darren were still living at home with Lippatu and Napoleon.

Pat and friends found the money for Napoleon and the family to move to Greencastle, Indiana.

The family decided to sprinkle Mountain's and Danny Nowak's ashes under the large elm tree that headed up the road out the back of the house to the pond.

Every member of the family spotted Mountain, Elaine, Dude, and Danny at one time or another sitting by the pond fishing, talking about life, and suckin' on roots of grass at all hours of the night.